Praise for *I Know Who You Are*

"Feeney is quickly establishing herself as a luminary of psychological thrillers, a reputation this novel is sure to bolster. This is suspense as it was meant to be written."
—CrimeReads

"Superb no-holds-barred plotting. This story romps toward a startling and totally unexpected conclusion that will satisfy the most experienced thriller fans."
—*Daily Mail* (UK)

"A roller coaster of a ride. Alice Feeney goes where others might fear to tread. I loved it!"
—Jane Corry, *Sunday Times* bestselling author of *My Husband's Wife* and *The Dead Ex*

"Clever, compulsive . . . You will never guess the ending of this one!"
—Louise Candlish, *Sunday Times* bestselling author of *Our House*

"With twists, suspense, and a shock ending, I never knew what was coming next. Fantastic."
—*The Sun* (UK)

"A tightly woven, intricately plotted, heart-in-your-throat thriller. I couldn't put this book down! *I Know Who You Are* is expertly crafted. I never once guessed the end."
—Christina McDonald, bestselling author of *The Night Olivia Fell*

"A tightly written thriller with a stunning twist . . . There's no way you'll be able to stop reading."
—*Daily Express* (UK)

"A fiendishly well-plotted, deliciously dark, and twisting read—it kept me guessing throughout and reading way past my bedtime. Readers, you are in for a huge treat with this one!"
—Lucy Foley, author of *The Hunting Party*

"What a ride. I loved this book and the brilliant Hitchcockian twist!"
—Sarah Michelle Gellar

Praise for *Sometimes I Lie*

"Feeney weaves a murderously twisty little tale."

—*Entertainment Weekly*

"A gripping debut with a brilliant twist. I loved it!"

—B. A. Paris, bestselling author of *Behind Closed Doors*

"Satisfyingly serpentine and with a terrific double twist in the tale, it leaves you longing for more."   —*Daily Mail* (UK)

"Boldly plotted, tightly knotted—a provocative true-or-false thriller that deepens and darkens to its ink-black finale. Marvelous."

—A. J. Finn

"A spine-tingling psychological thriller."   —*People* magazine

"This brilliant psychological thriller kept me guessing until the very last page."   —Jessica Knoll

"The twists pile up. . . . Visceral and haunting."   —Oprah.com

"Faster and more twisted than a roller coaster, with an ending that'll make your stomach drop, Alice Feeney's *Sometimes I Lie* is not to be missed. I loved it!"   —Mary Kubica

"If you're looking for a *Gone Girl*–esque fix, then this is the book for you."   —*Cosmopolitan*

I Know Who
You Are

Also by Alice Feeney

Sometimes I Lie

I Know Who You Are

Alice Feeney

FLATIRON
BOOKS
NEW YORK

I KNOW WHO YOU ARE. Copyright © 2019 by Diggi Books Ltd. All rights reserved. Printed in the United States of America. For information, address Flatiron Books, 120 Broadway, New York, NY 10271.

www.flatironbooks.com

The Library of Congress has cataloged the hardcover edition as follows:

Names: Feeney, Alice, author.
Title: I know who you are : a novel / Alice Feeney.
Description: First Edition. | New York : Flatiron Books, 2019.
Identifiers: LCCN 2018037893 | ISBN 9781250147349 (hardcover) | ISBN 9781250229168 (international, sold outside the U.S., subject to rights availability) | ISBN 9781250147332 (ebook)
Subjects: | GSAFD: Suspense fiction. | Mystery fiction.
Classification: LCC PR6106.E34427 I36 2019 | DDC 823/.92—dc23
LC record available at https://lccn.loc.gov/2018037893

ISBN 978-1-250-14735-6 (trade paperback)

Our books may be purchased in bulk for promotional, educational, or business use. Please contact your local bookseller or the Macmillan Corporate and Premium Sales Department at 1-800-221-7945, extension 5442, or by email at MacmillanSpecialMarkets@macmillan.com.

First Flatiron Books Paperback Edition: April 2020

10 9 8 7 6 5 4 3 2 1

For Jonny. Agents come in all shapes and sizes. I got the best.

Not everybody wants to be somebody. Some people just want to be somebody else.

I Know Who
You Are

One

London, 2017

I'm that girl you think you know, but you can't remember where from.

Lying is what I do for a living. It's what I'm best at; becoming somebody else. The eyes are the only part of me I still recognize in the mirror, staring out beneath the made-up face of a made-up person. Another character, another story, another lie. I look away, ready to leave her behind for the night, stopping briefly to stare at what is written on the dressing room door:

AIMEE SINCLAIR

My name, not his. I never changed it.

Perhaps because, deep down, I always knew that our marriage would only last until life did us part. I remind myself that my name only defines me if I allow it to. It is merely a collection of letters, arranged in a certain order; little more than a parent's wish, a label, a lie. Sometimes I long to rearrange those letters into something else. *Someone* else. A new name for a new me. The me I became when nobody else was looking.

Knowing a person's name is not the same as knowing a person.

I think we broke us last night.

Sometimes it's the people who love us the most that hurt us the hardest; because they can.

He hurt me.

We've made a bad habit of hurting each other; things have to be broken in order to fix them.

I hurt him back.

I check that I've remembered to put my latest book in my bag, the way other people check for a purse or keys. Time is precious, never spare, and I kill mine by reading on set between filming. Ever since I was a child, I have preferred to inhabit the fictional lives of others, hiding in stories that have happier endings than my own; we are what we read. When I'm sure I haven't forgotten anything, I walk away, back to who and what and where I came from.

Something very bad happened last night.

I've tried so hard to pretend that it didn't, struggled to rearrange the memories, but I can still hear his hate-filled words, still feel his hands around my neck, and still see the expression I've never seen his face wear before.

I can still fix this. I can fix us.

The lies we tell ourselves are always the most dangerous.

It was a fight, that's all. Everybody who has ever loved has also fought.

I walk down the familiar corridors of Pinewood Studios, leaving my dressing room, but not my thoughts or fears too far behind. My steps seem slow and uncertain, as though they are deliberately delaying the act of going home; afraid of what will be waiting there.

I did love him, I still do.

I think it's important to remember that. We weren't always the version of us that we became. Life remodels relationships like the sea reshapes the sand; eroding dunes of love, building banks of hate. I told him it was over last night. I told him that I wanted a divorce, and I told him that I meant it this time.

I didn't. Mean it.

I climb into my Range Rover and drive towards the iconic studio gates, steering towards the inevitable. I fold in on myself a little, hiding the corners of me I'd rather others didn't see, bending my sharp edges out of view. The man in the booth at the exit waves, his face dressed in kindness. I force my face to smile back, before pulling away.

For me, acting has never been about attracting attention or wanting to be seen. I do what I do because I don't know how to do anything else, and because it's the only thing that makes me feel happy. The shy actress is an oxymoron in most people's dictionaries, but that is who and what I am. Not everybody wants to be somebody. Some people just want to be somebody else. Acting is easy; it's being *me* that I find difficult. I throw up before almost every interview and event. I get physically ill and am crippled with nerves when I have to meet people as myself. But when I step out onto a stage, or in front of a camera, as somebody different, it feels like I can fly.

Nobody understands who I really am, except him.

My husband fell in love with the version of me I was before. My success is relatively recent, and my dreams coming true signaled the start of his nightmares. He tried to be supportive at first, but I was never something he wanted to share. That said, each time my anxiety tore me apart, he stitched me back together again. Which was kind, if also self-serving. In order to get satisfaction from fixing something, you either have to leave it broken for a while first, or break it again yourself.

I drive slowly along the fast London streets, silently rehearsing for real life, catching unwelcome glimpses of my made-up self in the mirror. The thirty-six-year-old woman I see looks angry about being forced to wear a disguise. I am not beautiful, but I'm told I have an interesting face. My eyes are too big for the rest of my features, as though all the things they have seen made them swell out of proportion. My long dark hair has been straightened by expert fingers, not my own, and I'm thin now because the part I'm playing requires me to be so, and because I frequently forget to eat. I forget to eat because a journalist once called me "plump but pretty." I can't remember what she said about my performance.

It was a review of my first film role last year. A part that changed my life, and my husband's, forever. It certainly changed our bank balance, but our love was already overdrawn. He resented my newfound success—it took me away from him—and I think he needed to make me feel small to make himself feel big again. I'm not who he married. I'm more than her now, and I think he wanted less. He's a journalist, successful in his own right, but it's not the same. He thought he was losing me, so he started to hold on too tight, so tight that it hurt.

I think part of me liked it.

I park on the street and allow my feet to lead me up the garden path. I bought the Notting Hill town house because I thought it might fix us while we continued to remortgage our marriage. But money is a Band-Aid, not a cure for broken hearts and promises. I've never felt so trapped by my own wrong turns. I built my prison in the way that people often do, with solid walls made from bricks of guilt and obligation. Walls that seemed to have no doors, but the way out was always there. I just couldn't see it.

I let myself in, turning on the lights in each of the cold, dark, vacant rooms.

"Ben," I call, taking off my coat.

Even the sound of my voice calling his name sounds wrong, fake, foreign.

"I'm home," I say to another empty space. It feels like a lie to describe this as my home; it has never felt like one. A bird never chooses its own cage.

When I can't find my husband downstairs, I head up to our bedroom, every step heavy with dread and doubt. The memories of the night before are a little too loud now that I'm back on the set of our lives. I call his name again, but he still doesn't reply. When I've checked every room, I return to the kitchen, noticing the elaborate bouquet of flowers on the table for the first time. I read the small card attached to them; there's just one word:

Sorry.

Sorry is easier to say than it is to feel. Even easier to write.

I want to rub out what happened to us and go back to the beginning. I want to forget what he did to me and what he made me do. I want to start again, but time is something we ran out of long before we started running from each other. Perhaps if he'd let me have the children I so badly wanted to love, things might have been different.

I retrace my steps back to the lounge and stare at Ben's things on the coffee table: his wallet, keys, and phone. He never goes *anywhere* without his phone. I pick it up, carefully, as though it might either explode or disintegrate in my fingers. The screen comes to life and reveals a missed call from a number I don't recognize. I want to see more, but when I press the button the phone demands Ben's pass code. I try and fail to guess several times, until it locks me out completely.

I search the house again, but he isn't here. He isn't hiding. This isn't a game.

Back out in the hall, I notice that the coat he always wears is where he left it, and his shoes are still by the front door. I call his name one last time, so loud that the neighbors on the other side of the wall must hear me, but there's still no answer. Maybe he just popped out.

Without his wallet, phone, keys, coat, or shoes?

Denial is the most destructive form of self-harm.

A series of words whisper themselves repeatedly inside my ears:

Vanished. Fled. Departed. Left. Missing. Disappeared.

Then the carousel of words stops spinning, finally settling on the one that fits best. Short and simple, it slots into place, like a piece of a puzzle I didn't know I'd have to solve.

My husband is *gone*.

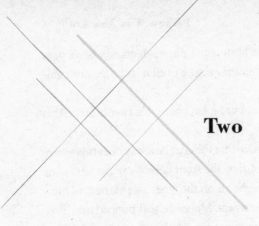

Two

I wonder where other people go when they turn off the lights at night.

Do they all drift and dream? Or are there some, like me, who wander somewhere dark and cold within themselves, digging around inside the shadows of their blackest thoughts and fears, clawing away at the dirt of memories they wish they could forget? Hoping nobody else can see the place they have sunk down into?

When the race to sleep is beaten by the sound of my alarm, I get up, get washed, get dressed. I do all the things that I would normally do, if this were a normal day. I just can't seem to do them at a normal speed. Every action, every thought, is painfully slow. As though the night were deliberately holding me back from the day to come.

I called the police before I went to bed.

I wasn't sure whether it was the right thing to do, but apparently there is no longer any need to wait twenty-four hours before notifying the police when someone disappears. The word makes it sound like a magic trick, a *disappearing* act, but I'm the actress, not my husband. The voice of the stranger on the phone was reassuring, even though the words it delivered weren't. One word in particular, which he repeatedly hissed into my ear: *missing.*

Missing person. *Missing* husband. *Missing* memories.

I can remember the exact expression my husband wore the last time I saw his face, but what happened next is a blur at best. Not because I am forgetful, or a drunk—I am neither of those things—but because of what happened afterwards. I close my eyes, but I can still see him, his features twisted with hate. I blink the image away as though it were a piece of grit, a minor irritant, obstructing the view of us I prefer.

What have we done? What did I do? Why did he make me?

The kind policeman I eventually spoke to, once I'd managed to dial the third and final number, took our details and said that someone would be in touch. Then he told me not to worry.

He may as well have told me not to breathe.

I don't know what happens next and I don't like it. I've never been a fan of improvisation; I prefer my life to be scripted, planned, and neatly plotted. Even now, I keep expecting Ben to walk through the door, deliver one of his funny and charming stories to explain it all away, kiss us better. But he doesn't do that. He doesn't do anything. He's gone.

I wish there were someone else I could call, tell, talk to, but there isn't.

My husband gradually reorganized my life when we first met, criticizing my friends and obliterating my trust in all of them, until we were all we had left. He became my moon, constantly circling, controlling my tides of self-doubt, occasionally blocking out the sun altogether, leaving me somewhere dark, where I was afraid and couldn't see what was really going on.

Or pretended not to.

The ties of a love like ours twist themselves into a complicated knot, one that is hard to unravel. People would ask why I stayed with him if they knew the truth, and I'd tell them the truth if they did: because I love us more than I hate him, and because he's the only man I've ever pictured myself having a child with. Despite everything he did to hurt me, that was still all I wanted: for us to have a baby and a chance to start again.

A brand-new version of us.

Refusing to let me become a mother was cruel. Thinking I'd just accept his choices as my own was foolish. But I'm good at pretending. I've made a living out of it. Papering over the cracks doesn't mean they're not there, but life is prettier when you do.

I don't know what to do now.

I'm trying to carry on like normal, but struggling to remember what that is.

I've been running nearly every day for almost ten years, it is something I file away in the slim folder of things I think I am good at, and I enjoy it. I run the same route every single morning; a strict creature of habit. I make myself put on my trainers; shaky fingers struggling to remember how to tie laces they've tied a thousand times before. Then I tell myself that staring at the bare walls isn't going to help anyone or bring him back.

My feet find their familiar rhythm: fast but steady, and I listen to music to disguise the sound track of the city. The adrenaline rush kicks in to dismantle the pain, and I push myself a little harder. I run past the pub on the corner where Ben and I used to go drinking on Friday nights, before we forgot who and how to be with each other. Then I run past the council tower blocks and the millionaires' playground of terraced luxury on the neighboring street; the haves and have-nots side by side, at least in proximity.

Moving to an expensive corner of West London was Ben's idea. I was away in L.A. when we bought the place; fear persuaded me it was the right thing to do. I didn't even step inside before we owned it. When I finally did, the whole house was quite transformed from the photos I had seen online. Ben renovated our new home all by himself; new fixtures and fittings for the brand-new us we thought we could and should be.

As I run around the corner of the street, my eyes find the bookshop. I try not to look, but it's like the scene of an accident and I can't help it. It's where we arranged to meet for our first date. He knew about my love of books, which is why he chose this place. I arrived a little early that night, filled with anticipation and nerves, and browsed the shelves while I waited. Fifteen minutes later, when my date still hadn't turned up, my anxiety levels were peaking.

"Excuse me, are you Aimee?" asked an elderly gentleman with a kind smile.

I felt confused, a little sick, he was *nothing* like the handsome young man in the profile picture I had seen. I considered saying no and fleeing from the shop.

"Another customer came in earlier; he bought this and asked me to give it to you. He said it was a clue." The man beamed as though this were the most fun he'd had in years. Then he held out a neatly wrapped brown-paper parcel. With the tension removed from the situation, things seemed to fall into place, and I realized this was the owner of the shop, not my date. I thanked him and took what I guessed was a book, grateful when he left me alone to unwrap it. It was one of my childhood favorites: *The Secret Garden*. It took a while for the penny to drop, but then I remembered that the florist on the corner shared the same name as the book.

The woman in the flower shop grinned as soon as I walked inside, my entrance accompanied by the tinkle of a bell on her door.

"Aimee?"

When I nodded, she presented me with a bouquet of white roses. There was a note:

> *Roses are white.*
> *So sorry I'm late.*
> *Can't wait for tonight.*
> *You're my perfect date.*

I read it three times, as though trying to translate the words, then noticed the florist still smiling in my direction. People staring at me has always made me feel uncomfortable.

"He said he'd meet you at your favorite restaurant."

I thanked her and left. We didn't have a favorite restaurant, having never eaten out together, so I walked along the high street carrying my book and flowers, enjoying the game. I replayed our email conversations in my mind, and remembered one about food. His preferences had all been so fancy; mine . . . less so. I had regretted telling him my favorite meal and blamed my upbringing.

The man behind the counter at the fish-and-chips shop smiled. I was a regular back then.

"Salt and vinegar?"

"Yes, please."

He shoveled some chips into a paper cone, then gave them to me, along with a ticket for a film screening later that night. The chips were too hot, and I was too anxious to eat them as I hurried along the road. But as soon as I saw Ben, standing outside the cinema, all my fear seemed to disappear.

I remember our first kiss.

It felt so right. We had a connection I could neither fathom nor explain, and we slotted together as though we were meant to be that way. I smile at the memory of who we were then. That version of us was good. Then I stumble on the uneven pavement outside the cinema, and it brings me back to the present. Its doors are closed. The lights are off. And Ben is gone.

I run a little faster.

I pass the charity shops, wondering if the clothes in the windows were donated in generosity or sorrow. I run past the man pushing a broom along the pavement, sweeping away the litter of other people's lives. Then I run past the Italian restaurant where the waitress recognized me the last time we ate there. I haven't been back since; it feels as if I can't.

I am paralyzed with a unique form of fear when strangers recognize me. I just smile, try to say something friendly, then retreat as fast as I can. Thankfully it doesn't happen too often. I'm not A-list. Not yet. Somewhere between B and C I suppose, a bit like my bra size. The version of myself I wear in public is far more attractive than the real me. It's been carefully tailored, a cut above my standard self; she's someone nobody should see.

I wonder when his love for me ran out.

I take a shortcut through the cemetery, and the sight of a child's grave fills me with grief, redirecting my mind from thoughts of who we were, to who we might have been, had life unfolded differently. I try to hold on to the happy memories, pretend that there were more than there were. We are all programmed to rewrite our past to protect ourselves in the present.

What am I doing?

My husband is missing. I should be at home, crying, calling hospitals, doing something.

The memory interrupts my thoughts but not my footsteps, and I carry on. I only stop when I reach the coffee shop, exhausted by my own bad habits: insomnia and running away from my problems.

It's already busy, filled with overworked and underpaid Londoners needing their morning fix, sleep and discontentment still in their eyes. When I reach the front of the queue, I ask for my normal latte and make my way to the till. I use contactless to pay and have disappeared inside myself again, until the unsmiling cashier speaks in my direction. Her blond hair hangs in uneven plaits on either side of her long face, and she wears a frown like a tattoo.

"Your card has been declined."

I don't respond.

She looks at me as though I might be dangerously stupid. "Do you have another card?" Her words are deliberately slow and delivered with increased volume, as though the situation has already exhausted her of all patience and kindness. I feel other sets of eyes in the shop joining hers, all converging on me.

"It's two pounds forty. It must be your machine, please try it again." I'm appalled by the pathetic sound impersonating my voice coming from my mouth.

She sighs, as though she is doing me an enormous favor, and making a huge personal sacrifice, before stabbing the till with her nail-bitten finger.

I hold out my bank card, fully aware that my hand is trembling and that everyone can see.

She tuts, shakes her head. "Card declined. Have you got any other way of paying or not?"

Not.

I take a step back from my untouched coffee, then turn and walk out of the shop without another word, feeling their eyes follow me, their judgment not far behind.

Ignorance isn't bliss; it's fear postponed to a later date.

I stop outside the bank and allow the cash machine to swallow my card, before entering my PIN and requesting a small amount of money. I read the unfamiliar and unexpected words on the screen twice:

SORRY.
INSUFFICIENT FUNDS AVAILABLE.

The machine spits my card back out in electronic disgust.

Sometimes we pretend not to understand things that we do.

I do what I do best instead: I run. All the way back to the house that was never a home.

As soon as I'm inside, I pull out my phone and dial the number on the back of my bank card, as though this conversation could only be had behind closed doors. Fear, not fatigue, withholds my breath, so that it escapes my mouth in a series of spontaneous bursts, disfiguring my voice. Getting through the security questions is painful, but eventually the woman in a distant call center asks the question I've been waiting to hear.

"Good morning, Mrs. Sinclair. You have now cleared security. How can I help you?"

Finally.

I listen while a stranger calmly tells me that my bank account was emptied, then closed yesterday. Over ten thousand pounds had been sitting in it; the account I reluctantly agreed to make in joint names, when Ben accused me of not trusting him. Turns out I might have been right not to. Luckily, I've squirreled most of my earnings away in accounts he can't access.

I stare down at Ben's belongings still sitting on the coffee table, then cradle my phone between my ear and shoulder to free up my hands. It feels a little intrusive to go through his wallet—I'm not that kind of wife—but I pick it up anyway. I peer inside, as though the missing ten thousand pounds might be hidden between the leather folds. It isn't. All I find is a crumpled-looking fiver, a couple of credit cards I didn't know he had, and two neatly folded receipts. The first is from the restaurant we ate at the last time I saw him, the second is from the petrol station. Nothing unusual about that. I walk to the window and peel back the edge of the curtain, just enough to see Ben's car parked in its usual spot. I let the curtain fall and put the wallet back on the table, exactly how I found it. A marriage starved of affection leaves an emaciated love behind; one that is frail, easy to bend and break. But if he was going to leave me and steal my money, then why didn't he take his things with him too? Everything he owns is still here.

It doesn't make any sense.

"Mrs. Sinclair, is there anything else I can help you with today?" The voice on the phone interrupts my confused thoughts.

"No. Actually, yes. I just wondered if you could tell me what time my husband closed our joint account?"

"The final withdrawal was made in branch at seventeen twenty-three." I try to remember yesterday, it seems so long ago. I'm fairly sure I was home from filming by five at the latest, so I would have been here when he did it. "That's strange . . ." she says.

"What is?"

She hesitates before answering. "Your husband didn't withdraw the money or close the account."

She has my full attention now. "Then who did?"

There is another long pause.

"Well, according to our records, Mrs. Sinclair, it was you."

Three

"Mrs. Sinclair?" The bank's call center sounds very far away now, even farther than before, and I can't answer. I've come undone. Time seems like something I can no longer tell, and it feels as if I'm tumbling down a hill too fast with nothing to break my fall.

I think I'd remember if I went to the bank and closed our account.

I hang up as soon as I hear the knock at the door and run to answer it, practically tripping over my feet. I'm certain that Ben and a logical explanation will be waiting behind it.

I'm wrong.

A middle-aged man and a young girl, wearing cheap suits, are standing on my doorstep. He looks like a guy with friends in low places, and she looks like lamb dressed as mutton.

"Mrs. Sinclair?" she says, coating my name in her Scottish accent.

"Yes?" I wonder if they might be selling something door-to-door, like double glazing or God, or, even worse, whether they might be journalists.

"I'm Detective Inspector Alex Croft and this is Detective Sergeant Wakely. You called about your husband," she says.

Detective? She looks like she should still be in school.

"Yes, I did, please come in," I reply, already forgetting their names and ranks. It's very loud inside my head right now, and my mind is unable to process the additional information.

"Thank you. Is there somewhere we could all sit down?" she asks, and I lead them into the lounge.

Her petite body is folded into a nondescript black trouser suit, with a white shirt tucked underneath. The ensemble is not unlike a school uniform. Her face is plain but pretty, and without a smudge of makeup. Her shoulder-length mousy hair is so straight it looks as though she might have ironed it at the same time as her shirt. Everything about her is neat and uncommonly tidy. I think she must be new at this, perhaps he is training her. I wasn't expecting detectives to appear on my doorstep; a uniformed officer perhaps, but not this. I wonder why I'm receiving special treatment and shrink away from the potential answers lining up inside my head.

"So, your husband is missing," she prompts as I sit down opposite them both.

"Yes."

She stares, as though waiting for me to say more. I look at him, then back at her, but he doesn't seem to be much of a talker, and her expression remains unchanged.

"Sorry, I'm not really sure how this works." I already feel flustered.

"How about you start by telling us when you last saw your husband?"

"Well . . ." I pause to think for a moment.

I remember the screaming argument, his hands around my throat. I remember what he said and what he did. I see them share a look and some unspoken opinions, then remember I need to answer the question.

"Sorry. I've not slept. I saw him the night before last. And there's something else I should tell you . . ."

She leans forward in her chair.

"Someone has emptied our joint account."

"Your husband?" she asks.

"No, someone . . . else."

She frowns, overworked folds appearing on her previously smooth forehead. "Was it a lot of money?"

"About ten thousand pounds."

She raises a neatly plucked eyebrow. "I'd say that was a lot."

"I also think you should know that I had a stalker a couple of years ago. It's why we moved to this house. You'll have a record of it, we reported it to the police at the time."

"Seems unlikely that this and that are related, but we'll certainly look into it." It seems odd to me that she is being so dismissive of something that might be important. She leans back in her chair again, frown still firmly in place, fast becoming a permanent feature. "When you called last night, you told the officer you spoke to that all your husband's personal belongings are still here, is that right? His phone, keys, and wallet, even his shoes?" I nod. "Mind if we take a look around?"

"Of course, whatever you need."

I follow them through the house, not sure whether I'm supposed to or not. They don't talk, at least not with words, but I pick up on the silent dialogue they exchange between glances, as they search every room. Each one is filled with memories of Ben, some of which I would rather forget.

When I try to pinpoint the exact moment we started to unfold, I realize it was long before I got my first film role and went to L.A. I'd been away filming in Liverpool for a few days, a small part in a BBC drama, nothing special. I was so tired when I got back, but Ben insisted on going out for dinner, pulled his warning face when I said I'd rather not. I dropped my earring getting ready, and the back of it disappeared beneath our bed. That tiny sliver of silver was the butterfly effect that changed the course of our marriage. I never found it. I found something else instead: a red lipstick that did not belong to me and the knowledge that my husband didn't either. I suppose I wasn't completely surprised; Ben is a good-looking man, and I've seen how other women look at him.

I never mentioned what I found that day. I didn't say a word. I didn't dare.

The female detective spends a long time looking around our bedroom, and I feel as though my privacy is being unpicked as well as invaded. I was taught as a child not to trust the police and I still don't.

"So, remind me again of the exact time you last saw your husband," she says.

When he lost his temper and turned into someone I no longer recognized.

"We were having a meal at the Indian restaurant on the high street. . . . I left a bit earlier than him. . . . I wasn't feeling well."

"You didn't see him when he got home?"

Yes.

"No, I had an early start the next day. I'd gone to bed by the time he got back." I know she knows I'm lying. I'm not even sure why I am, a mixture of shame and regret perhaps, but lies don't come with gift receipts; you can't take them back.

"You don't share a bedroom?" she asks.

I'm not sure how or why this is relevant. "Not always, we both have quite hectic work schedules, he's a journalist and I'm—"

"But you *did* hear him come home that night."

Heard him. Smelt him. Felt him.

"Yes."

She notices something behind the door and takes a pair of blue latex gloves from her pocket. "And this is the bedroom *you* sleep in?"

"It's where we both sleep most of the time, just not that night."

"Do you ever sleep in the spare room, Wakely?" she asks her silent companion.

"Used to, if we'd had a fight, when we still had enough time and energy to argue. But none of our bedrooms are spare anymore, they're all full of hormonal teenagers."

It speaks.

"Any reason why you have a bolt on the inside of your bedroom door, Mrs. Sinclair?" she asks.

At first, I don't know what to say.

"I told you, I had a stalker. It made me take home security pretty seriously."

"Any reason why the bolt is busted?" She swings the door back to reveal the broken metal shape and splintered wood on the frame.

Yes.

I feel my cheeks turn red. "It got jammed a little while ago, my husband had to force it open."

She looks back at the door and nods slowly, as though it is an effort. "Got an attic?"

"Yes."

"Basement?"

"No. Do you want to see the attic?"

"Not this time."

This time? How many times are there going to be?

I follow them back downstairs, and the tour of the house concludes in the kitchen.

"Nice flowers." She looks at the expensive bouquet on the table and reads the card. "What was he sorry for?"

"I'm not sure, I never got to ask him."

If she thinks something, her face doesn't show it. "Great garden." She stares out through the glass folding doors. The looked-after lawn is still wearing its stripes from the last time Ben mowed it, and the hardwood decking practically sparkles in the early-morning sun.

"Thank you."

"It's a nice place, like a show home or something you'd see in a magazine. What's the word I'm looking for . . . ? *Minimalist*. That's it. No family photos, books, clutter . . ."

"We haven't unpacked everything yet."

"Just moved in?"

"About a year ago." They both look up then. "I'm away a lot for work. I'm an actress."

"Oh, don't worry, Mrs. Sinclair. I know who you are. I saw you in that TV show last year, the one where you played a female police officer. I . . . enjoyed it."

Her lopsided smile fades, making me think that she didn't. I stare back, feeling even more uncomfortable than before, and completely clueless about how to reply.

"Do you have a recent photograph of your husband that we can take with us?" she asks.

"Yes, of course." I walk through to the mantelpiece in the lounge, but there is nothing there. I look around the room at the bare walls, and sparse shelves, and realize that there is not a single photo of him, or me, or us. There used to be a framed picture of our wedding day in here, I don't know where it has gone. Our big day was rather small; just the two of us. It led to even smaller days, until we struggled to find each other in them. "I might have something on my phone. Could I email it to you or do you need a hard copy?"

"Email is fine." That unnatural smile spreads across her face again, like a rash.

I pick up my mobile and start to scroll through the photos. There are plenty of the cast and crew working on the film, lots of Jack, my co-star, a few of me, but none of Ben. I notice my hands are trembling, and when I look up, I see that she has noticed too.

"Does your husband have a passport?"

Of course he has a passport. Everyone has a passport.

I hurry to the sideboard where we keep them, but it isn't there. Neither is mine. I start to pull things out of the drawer, but she interrupts my search.

"Don't worry, I doubt your husband has left the country. Based on what we know so far, I don't expect he is too far away."

"What makes you say that?"

She doesn't respond.

"Detective Croft has solved every case she's been assigned since joining the force," says the male detective, like a proud father. "You're in safe hands."

I don't feel safe, I feel scared.

"Mind if we take these?" She slips Ben's phone and wallet inside a clear plastic bag without waiting for an answer. "Don't worry about the photo for now, we can collect it next time." She removes her blue plastic gloves and heads out into the hall.

"Next time?"

She ignores me again and they let themselves out. "We'll be in touch," he says, before walking away.

I sink down onto the floor once I've closed the door behind them. I felt as if they were silently accusing me of something the whole time they were here, but I don't know what. Do they think I murdered my husband and buried him beneath the floorboards? I have an urge to open the door, call them back, and defend myself, tell them that I haven't killed anyone.

But I don't do that.

Because it isn't true.

I have.

Four

Galway, 1987

I was lost before I was even born.

My mummy died that day and he never forgave me.

It was my fault; I was late and then I turned the wrong way. I'm still not very good at looking where I am going.

When I was stuck inside her belly, not wanting to come out for some reason that I do not remember, the doctor told my daddy he'd have to choose between us, said he couldn't save us both. Daddy chose her, but he didn't get what he wanted. He got me instead, and that made him sad and angry for a very long time.

My brother told me the story of what happened. Over and over.

He's much older than me, so he knows things that I don't.

He says I killed her.

I've tried awful hard not to kill things since then. I step over ants, pretend not to see spiders, and when my brother takes me fishing, I empty the net back into the sea. He says our daddy was a kind man before I broke his heart.

I hear them, down in the shed together.

I know I'm not allowed, but I want to know what they are doing.

They do lots of things without me. Sometimes I watch.

I stand on the old tree stump we use for chopping wood, and peek through the tiny hole in the shed wall. My right eye finds the chicken first, the white one we call Diana. There is a princess with that name in England, we named the chicken after her. Daddy's giant fist is wrapped around its throat, and its feet are tied together with a piece of black string. He turns the bird upside down and it hangs still, except for its little black eyes. They seem to look in my direction, and I think that chicken knows I'm watching something I shouldn't.

My brother is holding an ax.

He's crying.

I've never seen him cry before. I've heard him through my bedroom wall, when Daddy uses his belt, but this is the first time I've seen his tears. His fifteen-year-old face is red and blotchy and his hands are shaking.

The first swing of the ax doesn't do it.

The chicken flaps its wings, thrashing like a banshee, blood spurting from its neck. Daddy clouts my brother around the head, makes him swing the ax again. The noise of the chicken screaming and my big brother crying start to sound the same in my ears. He swings and misses, Daddy hits him again, so hard he falls down on his knees, the chicken's blood spraying all over their dirty white shirts. My brother swings a third time and the bird's head falls to the floor, its wings still flapping. Red feathers that used to be white.

When Daddy has gone, I creep into the shed and sit down next to my brother. He's still crying and I don't know what to say, so I slip my hand into his. I look at the shape our fingers make when joined together, like pieces of a puzzle that shouldn't fit, but do; my hands are small and pink and soft, his hands are big and rough and dirty.

"What do you want?" He snatches his hand away and uses it to wipe his face, leaving a streak of blood on his cheek.

I only want to be with him, but he is waiting for an answer, so I make one up. I already know it is the wrong one.

"I thought you could walk me to town, so I could show you the red shoes I wanted for my birthday again." I'll be six next week. Daddy said I could have a present this year, if I was good. I haven't been bad, and I think that's the same thing.

My brother laughs, not his real laugh, the unkind one. "Don't you get it? We can't afford red shoes, we can barely afford to eat!" He grabs me by the shoulders, shakes me a little, the way that Daddy shakes him when Daddy is cross. "People like us don't get to wear red bloody shoes, people like us are born in the dirt and die in the dirt. Now fuck off and leave me alone!"

I don't know what to do. I feel strange and my mouth forgets how to make words.

My brother has never spoken to me like this before. I can feel the tears trying to leak out of my eyes, but I won't let them. I try to put my hand in his again, I just want him to hold it. He shoves me, so hard that I fall backwards and hit my head on the chopping block, chicken blood and guts sticking to my long black curly hair.

"I said fuck off, or I'll chop your bloody head off too," he says, waving the ax.

I run and I run and I run.

Five

London, 2017

I run from the car park to the main building at Pinewood. I'm never late for anything, but the unscheduled police visit this morning has thrown me off-balance in more ways than one.

My husband has disappeared and so has ten thousand pounds of my money.

I can't solve the puzzle because no matter how I slot the pieces together, too many are still missing to complete the picture. I remind myself that I have to keep it together for just a little while longer. The film is almost finished, just three more scenes to shoot. I bury my personal problems somewhere out of reach as I hurry along corridors towards my dressing room. As I turn the final corner, still distracted, I walk straight into Jack, my co-star in the film.

"Where have you been? Everyone is looking for you," he says.

I glance down at his hand gripping the sleeve of my jacket and he removes it. His dark eyes see straight through me and I wish they didn't, it makes it almost impossible to lie to him, and I can't always speak the truth; my inability to trust people won't allow it. Sometimes, when you spend this long working with someone, when you get this close, it's hard to hide the real you from them completely.

Jack Anderson is consciously handsome. His face has earned him a small fortune, and more justifiably than his intermittent acting skills. His uniform of chinos and slim-fitted shirts are cut to flatter and hint at the muscular shape of him underneath. He wears his smile like a prize and his stubble like a mask. He's a bit older than me, but the gray flecks in his brown hair only seem to make him more attractive.

I am aware that we have a connection. And I am aware that he is aware of that too.

"Sorry," I say.

"Tell it to the crew, not me. Just because you're beautiful doesn't mean the world will wait for you to catch up with it."

"Don't say that." I look over my shoulder.

"What, beautiful? Why? It's true, you're the only one who can't see it, which just makes you even more enchanting." He takes a step closer. Too close.

I take a tiny step back. "Ben didn't come home last night," I whisper.

"So?"

I frown and his features readjust themselves, to reflect the caution and concern most people would display in these circumstances. He lowers his voice. "Does he know about us?"

I stare at his face, so serious all of a sudden. Then the creases fold and fan around the corners of his mischievous eyes, and he laughs at me. "There's a journalist waiting in your dressing room, too, by the way."

"What?" He may as well have said *assassin*.

"Apparently your agent arranged the interview, and they only want to speak to you, not me. Not that I'm jealous . . ."

"I don't know anything about—"

"Yeah, yeah. Don't worry, my bruised ego will regenerate itself, always does. She's been in there for twenty minutes, I don't want her writing something shit about the film because you can't set an alarm, so you might want to be a little more *tout suite* about it." He often adds a random French word to his sentences, I've never understood why. He isn't French.

Jack walks off down the corridor without another word, in either language, and I question what it is about him that I find so attractive. Sometimes I wonder if I only ever want things I think I can't have.

I don't know anything about any interview, and I would never have agreed to do one today if I had. I hate interviews. I hate journalists; they're all the same—trying to uncover secrets that aren't theirs to share. Including my husband. Ben works behind the scenes as a news producer at TBN. I know he spent time in war zones before we met; his name was mentioned in online articles by some of the correspondents he worked with. I've no idea what he is working on now, he never seems to want to talk about it.

I found him romantic and charming at first. His Irish accent reminded me of my childhood and bred a familiarity I wanted to climb inside and hide in. Whenever I think it might be the end, I remember the beginning. We married too fast and loved too slowly, but we were happy for a while, and I thought we wanted the same thing. Sometimes I wonder whether the horrors of the world he saw because of his job changed him; Ben is nothing like the other journalists I meet for work.

I know a lot of the showbiz and entertainment reporters now; the same familiar faces turn up at junkets, premieres, and parties. I wonder if it might be one of the ones I like, someone who has been kind about my work before, someone I've met. That might be okay. If it's someone I haven't met before, my hands will shake, I'll start to sweat, my knees will wobble, and then, when my unknown adversary picks up on my absolute terror, I'll lose the ability to form coherent sentences. If my agent had any understanding of what these situations do to me, he wouldn't keep landing me in them. It's like a parent dropping a child who is scared of water into the deep end, presuming that the child will swim, not sink. One of these days I know I'm going to drown.

I text my agent; it's unlike Tony to set something up and not tell me. Other actresses might throw their toys out of their prams when things don't go according to plan—I've seen them do it—but I'm not like that, and hope I won't ever be; I know how lucky I am. At least a thousand other people wish they could walk in my shoes, and they are more deserving than I am to wear them. I'm still fairly new to this level of this game, and I've got too much to lose. I can't go back to the start, not now, I worked too hard and it took so long to get here.

I check my phone. There's no response from Tony, but I can't keep the journalist waiting any longer. I paint the smile I have perfected for others on my face before opening the door with my name on, and finding someone else sitting in my chair, as though she belongs there. She doesn't.

"I'm so sorry to have kept you waiting, great to see you," I lie, holding out my hand, trying to keep it steady.

Jennifer Jones smiles up at me as though we are old friends. We are not. She's a journalist I despise, who has been horribly unkind about me in the past, for reasons I'll never understand. She's the bitch who called me "plump but pretty" when my first film came out last year. I call her Beak Face in return, but only in the privacy of my own thoughts. Everything about her is too small, especially her mind. She leaps up from the chair, flutters around me like a sparrow on speed, then grips my fingers in her tiny, cold, clawlike hand, giving my own an over enthusiastic shake. Last time we met, I'm not convinced she had seen one frame of the film I was there to talk about. She's one of those journalists who thinks that because she interviews celebrities, she is one too. She isn't.

Beak Face is middle-aged and dresses as her daughter would, had she been willing to pause her career long enough to have one. Her neat brown hair is cut into a style that was almost fashionable a decade ago, her cheeks are too pink, and her teeth are unnaturally white. She's a person whose story has already been written, and she'll never change her own ending, no matter how hard she tries. From what I've read about her online, she wanted to be an actress herself when she was younger. Perhaps that's why she hates me so much. I watch her tiny mouth twitch and spit as she squawks fake praise in my direction, my mind already racing ahead, trying to anticipate the verbal grenades she plans to throw at me.

"My agent didn't mention anything about an interview . . ."

"Oh, right. Well, if you'd rather not? It's just for the TBN website, no cameras, just little old me. So you don't need to worry about your hair or how you look at the moment . . ."

Bitch.

She winks and her face looks as if it has suffered a temporary stroke.

". . . I can come back another time if—"

I force another smile in reply and sit down opposite her, my hands knotted together in my lap to stop them from shaking. My agent wouldn't have agreed to this unless he thought it was a good idea. "Fire away," I say, feeling as if I really am about to get shot.

She takes an old-fashioned notebook from what looks like a school satchel she probably stole from a child on the street. I'm surprised; most journalists I meet nowadays record their interviews on their phones. I guess her methods, like her hair, are stuck in the past.

"Your acting career started when you got a scholarship to RADA when you were eighteen, is that correct?"

No, I started acting long before that, when I was much, much younger.

"Yes, that's right." I remind myself to smile. Sometimes I forget.

"Your parents must have been very proud."

I don't answer personal questions about my family, so I just nod.

"Did you always want to act?"

This one is easy, I get asked this all the time, and the answer always seems to go down well. "I think so, but I was extremely shy when I was a child . . ."

I still am.

"There were auditions for my school's production of *The Wizard of Oz* when I was fifteen, but I was too scared to go along. The drama teacher put a list of who got what part on a notice board afterwards, I didn't even read it. Someone else told me that I got the part of Dorothy and I thought they were joking, but when I checked, my name really was there, right at the top of the list—*Dorothy: Aimee Sinclair.* I thought it was a mistake, but the drama teacher said it wasn't. He said he believed in me because he knew I couldn't. Nobody had ever believed in me before. I learned my lines and I practiced the songs and I did my very best for him, not for me, because I didn't want to let him down. I was surprised when people thought I was good, and

I loved being on that stage. From that moment on, acting was all I ever wanted to do."

She smiles and stops scribbling. "You've played a lot of different roles in the last couple of years. . . ."

I'm waiting for the question, but realize there isn't one. "Yes. I have."

"What's that been like?"

"Well, as an actor, I really enjoy the challenge of becoming different people and portraying different characters. It's a lot of fun and I relish the variety."

Why did I use the word relish? *We're not talking about condiments.*

"So, you like pretending to be someone you're not?"

I hesitate without meaning to, still recoiling from my previous answer. "I guess you could put it that way, yes. But then I think we're all guilty of that from time to time, aren't we?"

"I imagine it must be hard sometimes, to remember who you really are when the cameras aren't on you."

I sit on my hands to stop myself from fidgeting. "Not really, no, it's just a job. A job that I love and I'm very grateful for."

"I'm sure you are. With this latest movie your star really is rising. How did you feel when you got the part in *Sometimes I Kill*?"

"I was thrilled." I realize I don't sound it.

"This role has you playing a married woman who pretends to be nice, but in reality has done some pretty horrific things. Was it a challenge to take on the part of someone so . . . damaged? Were you worried that the audience wouldn't like her once they knew what she'd done?"

"I'm not sure we want to give away the twist in any preview pieces."

"Of course, my apologies. You mentioned your husband earlier . . ."
I'm pretty sure I didn't.

"How does he feel about this role? Has he started sleeping in the spare room in case you come home still in character?"

I laugh, hoping it sounds genuine. I start to wonder if Ben and Jennifer Jones might know each other. They both work for TBN, but in very different departments. It's one of the world's biggest media companies, so it has never occurred to me that their paths might have crossed. Besides, Ben knows how much I hate this woman, he would have mentioned it if he knew her.

"I don't tend to answer personal questions, but I don't think my husband would mind me saying he's really looking forward to this film."

"He sounds like the perfect partner."

I worry about what my face might be doing now and focus all of my attention on reminding it to smile. What if she *does* know him? What if he told her that I'd asked for a divorce? What if that's why she's really here? What if they are working together to hurt me? I'm being paranoid. It will be over soon. Just smile and nod. *Smile and nod.*

"You're not like her then, the main character in *Sometimes I Kill*?" she asks, raising an overplucked eyebrow in my direction and peering at me over her notepad.

"Me? Oh, no. I don't even kill spiders."

Her smile looks as if it might break her face. "The character you're playing tends to run away from reality. Was that something you found easy to relate to?"

Yes. I've spent a lifetime running away.

A knock at the door saves me. I'm needed on set.

"I'm so sorry, I think that might be all we have time for, but it's been lovely to see you," I lie. My phone vibrates with a text as she packs up her things and leaves my dressing room. I take it out as soon as I'm alone again and read the message.

Tony: We need to talk, call me when you can. And no, I didn't arrange or agree to any interviews, so tell them to bugger off. Don't speak to any journalists before speaking to me for the time being, no matter what they say.

I feel as if I might cry.

Six

Galway, 1987

"There now, why are you spoiling that pretty face with all those ugly tears?"

I look up to see a woman smiling down at me outside the closed shop. I ran all the way here after my brother shouted at me. All I wanted was to look at the red shoes I thought someone might buy me for my birthday this year, but they're gone from the window. Some other little girl is wearing them, a little girl with a proper family and pretty shoes.

"Have you lost your mummy?" the woman asks.

I start to cry all over again. She takes a crumpled tissue from the sleeve of her white knitted cardigan, and I wipe my eyes. She's very pretty. She has long dark curly hair, a bit like mine, and big green eyes that forget to blink. She's a bit older than my brother, but much younger than my daddy. Her dress is covered in pink and white flowers, as if she were wearing a meadow, and she is the spit of how I imagine my mummy would have looked. If I hadn't killed her with a wrong turn. I blow my nose and hand back the snotty rag.

"Well now, don't you be worrying yourself, worrying never solved anything. I'm sure we can find your mummy." I don't know how to tell her that we can't. She holds out her hand, and I see that her nails are the same color red as the shoes I wish were mine. She waits for me to hold it, and when I don't, she bends down, until her face is level with my own.

"Now, I know you've probably been told not to talk to strangers, and that there are some bad people in the world, and that's good if you have, because it's true. But that's also why I can't leave you here on your own. It's getting late, the shops are closed, the streets are empty, and if something were to happen to you, well, I'd never forgive myself. My name is Maggie, what's yours?"

"Ciara."

"Hello, Ciara. It's nice to meet you." She shakes my hand. "There, now we're not strangers anymore." I smile; she's funny and I like her. "So, why don't you come with me, and if we can't find your mummy, we can call the police and they can take you home. Does that sound all right with you?" I think about it. It's an awful long walk back home, and it is getting dark already. I take the nice lady's hand and walk beside her, even though I know home is back the other way.

Seven

London, 2017

Jack takes my hand in his. He stares at me across the hotel restaurant table, and it feels as though everyone in the room is watching us. It's impossible not to form a relationship offscreen when you spend this many months filming together. I know he's enjoying this moment, and his touch feels more intimate than it should. I'm scared of what is about to happen, but it's far too late for that now, too late to pretend we both don't know what happens next. I can see people staring in our direction, people who know who we are, and I think he senses my apprehension, gently squeezing my fingers in silent reassurance. There's really no need. When I make my mind up about something, it's almost impossible for anyone to change it, including me.

He pays the bill with cash, then stands, leaving the table without another word. I wipe my mouth with the napkin from my lap, even though I've hardly eaten a thing. I think about Ben for the briefest of moments, instantly wishing that I hadn't, because the thought of him is hard to extinguish once inside my head. I can't remember the last time Ben took me for a romantic meal or made me feel attractive. But then, the present is always a superior time; looking down its nose at the past, turning away from the temptations of the future. I ignore the fear trying to hold me back and follow Jack. Despite my hesitation, I always knew that I would when the time came.

He gets into the hotel lift up ahead of me. The doors start to close but I don't run to catch up, I don't need to. The metal jaws slide open again, right on time, to swallow me whole as I step inside. We don't speak in the lift, just stand side by side. We've evolved as a species to hide our lust, like a dirty secret, even though finding other people attractive is exactly what we were designed to do. Still, I've never done anything like this before.

I'm aware of other people in the lift around us, aware of being watched. With each floor we pass I feel more anxious about our final destination. I always knew this was going to happen, even the first time we met. My heart changes speed inside my ears, I'm breathing too fast and I worry that he can tell how scared I am of what we're about to do. His hand brushes mine as we step out onto the seventh floor, by accident I think. I wonder if he might hold it, but he doesn't. He is not here to offer romance. That isn't what this is and we both know that.

He slots the key card into the door, and for a moment I think it won't work. Then I hope it won't, something to buy me just a little bit more time. I don't want to do this, which makes me wonder why I am. I seem to have spent my life doing things I don't want to.

Inside the room, he takes off his jacket, flinging it onto the bed, as though he is angry with me, as though I have done something wrong. His handsome face turns to look in my direction, his features twisted into something resembling hate and disgust, as though he is mirroring my own thoughts about myself in this moment, in this room.

"I think we need to have a talk, don't you? I'm married." His final two words are like an accusation.

"I know," I whisper.

He takes a step closer. "And I love my wife."

"I know." I'm not here for his love, she can keep that. I look away, but he takes my face in his hands and kisses me. I stand perfectly still, as though I don't know what to do, and for a moment I worry that I can't remember how. He is so gentle at first, careful, as though worried he might break me. I close my eyes—it's easier to do this with them closed—and I kiss him back. He changes gear faster than I was anticipating, his hands sliding down from my cheeks, to my neck, to the dress covering my breasts, his fingertips tracing the outline of my bra beneath the thin cotton.

He stops and pulls away. "Fuck. What the fuck am I doing?"

I try to remember how to breathe. "I know, I'm sorry," I reply, as though this were all my fault.

"It's like you're inside my head—"

"I'm sorry," I say, again. "I think about you all the time. I know I shouldn't, and I promise I've tried so hard not to, but I can't help it—" My eyes fill with tears. He's at least ten years older than me, and I feel like an inexperienced child.

"It's okay. This, whatever this is, is not your fault. I think about you too."

I stop crying when he says that, as though the latest sentence to have spilled from his mouth changes everything. He lifts my chin, turning my face to look up at his own, which my eyes search, trying to determine whether there is any truth in his words. Then I reach up to kiss him, my eyes offering an unspoken invitation, and this time he doesn't hesitate. This time, our lives outside of this moment are buried and forgotten.

Jack's hands move down to the front of my dress, expert fingers removing me from it, revealing the black lace of my bra underneath. He lifts me onto the desk, knocking the room-service menu and hotel phone to the floor. Before I know what is happening, he's on top of me, pinning my arms down, forcing his body between my legs.

"And, cut," says the director. "Thanks, guys, I think we got it."

Eight

Galway, 1987

Maggie held my hand all the way back to the cottage on the seafront. She held it so tight, it hurt a little bit some of the time. I think she was just afraid I might run away again, and that a bad person might find me like she said. But the only running I did was to keep up with her walking. She's a fast walker and I'm tired now. She kept looking around the whole time, as though she was scared, but we didn't pass any other people at all along the back streets, good or bad.

The cottage is very pretty, just like Maggie. It has a smart blue door and white bricks; it's nothing like our house at home. She doesn't have much stuff, and when I ask why not, she says this is just a holiday cottage. I've never been on holiday, so that's why I didn't know about things like that. She's busy putting clothes in a suitcase now, and just when I think she might call the police, she decides to make us some tea and a snack instead, which is nice. On the walk here I told her all about how my brother said we can't afford to eat, so she probably thinks I'm hungry.

"Would you like a slice of gingerbread cake?" she asks from the little kitchen. I'm sitting in the biggest armchair I've ever seen. I had to climb it just to sit on it, like a mountain made of cushions.

"Yes," I say, feeling pleased with myself, sitting in the nice chair about to eat cake with the nice lady.

She appears in the doorway. The smile that was always on her face before has vanished. "Yes, what?"

I don't know what she means at first, but then have an idea. "Yes, please?"

Her smile comes back and I am glad.

She puts the cake down in front of me, along with a glass of milk, then puts on the television for me to watch while she goes to use the phone in the other room. I thought she had forgotten about calling the police, and now I feel sad. I like it here, and I want to stay a bit longer. I can't hear what she is saying over the noise of Zig and Zag on the TV, she's turned the volume up very loud. When I've finished the cake, I lick my fingers, then I drink the milk. It tastes chalky, but I'm thirsty, so I finish the whole glass anyway.

I feel sleepy when she comes back in the room.

"Now then, I've spoken to your daddy, and I'm afraid he says that what your brother told you is true; there isn't enough food for you at home anymore. I don't want you to start your worrying again, so I've said to your daddy that you can stay here with me for a few days, and then I'll take you back home once he's sorted himself out. Does that sound grand?"

I think about the TV, and the cake, and the comfy chair. I think it might be nice to stay here for a little while, even though I will miss my brother a lot and my daddy a bit.

"Yes," I say.

"Yes, what?"

"Yes . . . please . . . and thank you."

Only when she leaves the room again do I wonder how she spoke to my daddy when we don't have a phone at home.

Nine

London, 2017

I check my phone again before getting out of the car. I've tried to call my agent three times now, but it just keeps going to voice mail. I even called the office, but his assistant said Tony was unavailable, and she used that tone people reserve for when they know something you don't. Or perhaps I'm just being paranoid. With everything else that is happening, I suppose that's possible. I'll try again tomorrow.

The house is in complete darkness as I trudge up the path. I keep thinking about Jack and the way he kissed me on set. It felt so . . . real. I wear the idea of him like a blanket, and it makes me feel safe and warm, the cloak of fantasy always more reliable than cold reality. But lust is only ever a temporary cure for loneliness. I close the front door behind me, leaving longing back in the shadows, out on the street. I switch on the lights of real life, finding them a little bright; they permit me to see more than I want to. The house is too quiet and too empty, like a discarded shell.

My husband is still gone.

I'm instantly dragged back in time, reliving the precise moment when his jealousy climaxed and my patience expired, generating the perfect marital storm.

I remember what he did to me. I remember everything that happened that night.

It's a strange feeling when buried memories float to the surface without warning. Like having all the air sucked out of your lungs, then being dropped from a great height; the perpetual sense of falling combined with the unavoidable knowledge that you're going to hit something hard.

I feel colder than I did a moment ago.

The silence seems to have grown louder, and I look around, my eyes frantically searching the empty space.

I feel like I'm being watched.

The sensation you get when someone is staring at you is inexplicable, but also very real. I feel frozen to the spot at first, trying, but failing, to reassure myself that it's just my overactive imagination, understandably in overdrive after the last few days. Then adrenaline ignites my fight-or-flight response, and I hurry around the house, pulling all the curtains and blinds, as though they are fabric shields. Better safe than spied on.

The stalker first entered my life a couple of years ago, not long after Ben and I got together. It started with emails, but then she appeared outside our old house a few times, and delivered a series of handwritten cards when she thought nobody was home. Someone broke in when I was away in L.A., and Ben was convinced it was her. It was one of the main reasons I agreed to move here, to a house I hadn't even seen, except online. Ben took care of everything, so that we could get away from her. What if she found me? Found us?

The stalker always wrote the same thing:

I know who you are.

I always pretended not to know what that meant.

I feel lost. I don't know what to do, how to feel, or how to *act*.

Should I call the police again? Ask for an update and tell them the things I didn't last time, or just sit here and wait? You can never predict how you will behave when life goes nonlinear; you don't know until it happens to you. People are capable of all kinds of surprising things. I'm dealing with the situation as best I can, without letting others down any more than I already have. I know I must be missing something, not just my husband, but I don't know what. What I *do* know is that the only person I can rely on to get me through this is me. I don't have anyone left to hold my hand. The thought triggers a memory, and my mind rewinds to when I was a little girl; someone always liked to hold my hand back then.

Something very bad happened when I was a child.

I've never spoken about it with anyone, even after all these years; some secrets should never be shared. The series of childhood doctors I was made to see afterwards said that I had something called transient global amnesia. They explained that my brain had blocked out certain memories because it deemed them too stressful or upsetting to remember, and that the condition would most likely stay with me for life. I was just a child, and I didn't take their diagnosis too seriously back then. I knew that I had only been pretending not to remember what happened. I haven't given it too much thought in recent years. Until now.

I think I would remember if I had emptied and closed our bank account. I think a lot of things; the problem is that I don't *know*.

I keep thinking about the stalker.

I can't seem to stop my mind replaying the first time I saw her with my own eyes, standing outside our old home. I heard the letter box rattle and thought it was the postman. It wasn't. A lonely-looking vintage postcard was facedown on the doormat. There was no stamp. It had been hand-delivered, and I remember picking it up, my hands trembling as I read the then-familiar spidery black handwriting scrawled across the back.

I know who you are.

I opened the door and she was right there, standing across the street, looking back at me. I thought I was going to throw up. I'd never seen her before. Ben had, but until that moment she was still little more than a phantom to me. A ghost I didn't believe in. The previous emails, and then postcards, hadn't scared me too much. But seeing her in the flesh was terrifying because I thought I recognized her. She was some distance away, her face mostly covered with a scarf and sunglasses, but she was dressed just like *me,* and in that moment, I thought it was *her.* It wasn't. It can't have been.

She ran away when she saw me. Ben came home early and we called the police.

I should be more worried than I am about my husband.

What is wrong with me? Am I losing my mind?

It feels as if something very bad is happening again, something a lot worse than before.

Ten

Galway, 1987

I feel lost when I wake up. I don't know where I am.

It's dark and cold. I have a tummyache and feel a bit sick, just like I do when my brother takes me out on Daddy's fishing boat. I reach out into the darkness, my fingers expecting to meet my bedroom wall, or the little side table made out of driftwood from the bay, but my fingers don't feel that. Instead they touch something cold, like metal, all around me. I start to panic, but I'm very tired, so tired I realize that I must be dreaming. I close my eyes and decide that if I still don't know where I am when I've counted to fifty inside my head, then I'll let myself cry. The last number I remember counting is forty-eight.

The next time I open my eyes, I'm in the back of a car. It's not my father's car, I know that without having to think about it too much because we don't have one anymore. He sold it to pay the electricity bill when the lights went out. The seats of the car I'm in are made of red-colored leather, and my face and arms seem to be stuck to it when I first wake up—I have to peel them off.

I stare at the back of the head of the person driving, before remembering the nice lady called Maggie. Then I sit up properly and look out the window, but I still don't know where I am.

"Where are we going?" I rub the sleep from my eyes, gifts the sandman left behind scratching my cheeks.

"Just a little drive," says Maggie, smiling at me in the small mirror, which shows a rectangle of her face, even though she is facing the other way.

"Are you taking me back to my daddy's house?"

"You're staying with me for a wee while, do you remember? There isn't enough food for you at your house just now."

I do remember her saying that; I'm just so tired I forgot.

"Why don't you have another little sleep, not far to go now. I'll wake you when we get where we're going. I have a lovely surprise for you when we get there."

I lie back down on the red leather seat and close my eyes, but I don't sleep. Even though I do like surprises, I'm scared and excited all at once. Maggie seems nice, but everything I just saw out the window looked so strange: the houses, the walls, even the signs on the side of the road.

I might be wrong, but it feels like I am a long way from home.

Eleven

London, 2017

I think homes might be a little bit like children; maybe you need to establish a bond as soon as possible to achieve a lasting emotional attachment. Long days on set have meant that this house has been little more than somewhere to sleep at night. I've spent the evening searching it for a picture of the man I have been married to for almost two years. I should have been learning my lines for tomorrow, but how can I when everything feels so wrong? I'm left with more questions than concern, unanswered mainly because I daren't ask them.

I stare down at the only photo of Ben I've managed to find: a framed black-and-white picture taken when he was a child. I hate it, I always have; it gives me the creeps. Five-year-old Ben is dressed in a formal suit that looks strange on a boy so young, but it isn't that. The thing that upsets me is the haunting look on his face, the way his smiling eyes stare out of the picture as though they are following you around the room. The child in the photo doesn't just look naughty or devious, he looks evil.

I asked him to put the picture in his study so I wouldn't have to look at it, and I remember him laughing at the time. Not because he thought I was being ridiculous, but as though the photo were part of a joke that I wasn't in on. I haven't seen or thought about it since, but staring down at the black-and-white image now stirs such a peculiar feeling inside me, something that is equal in dread and disgust. My husband and I don't have any family left on either side, we are both adult orphans. We used to say that it was just me and him against the world, before it changed to me and him against each other. We never said the latter, we just felt it.

Wandering around the house tonight, I notice how horribly big it is for just two people; there's not enough life to fill up the empty spaces. Ben made it very clear—*after* we got married—that he never wanted us to have children together. I felt tricked and cheated. He should have told me before that, he knew what I wanted. Even then, I thought I could change his mind, but I couldn't. Ben said he felt too old to become a dad in his mid-forties. Whenever I tried to revisit the conversation, he'd say the same thing, every time:

"We have each other. We don't need anything or anyone else."

It's as though we had formed an exclusive club with just two members, and he liked it that way. But I didn't. I wanted to have a child with him so badly, it was *all* I wanted, and he wouldn't give it to me: a chance to clone ourselves and start again. Isn't that what everybody wants? I knew that his reluctance had something to do with his past and his family, but he never spoke about them, he always said that some pasts deserved to be left behind, and I can understand that. It isn't as though I ever shared the truth with him about my own. We exchange the currency of our dreams for a reality funded by acceptance as we get older.

I remind myself that it cannot be this hard to find a single recent photo of Ben. At one time we had albums full of them, but then I stopped making them. Not because the memories didn't mean anything, but because I always thought we'd create more. I know other people like to share every moment of their private lives by posting pictures on social media, but I've never liked that sort of thing, and neither did he; it was something else we had in common. I've fought too hard to protect my privacy to just casually give it away.

I pull down the attic ladder and climb up the steps, telling myself I'm still looking for photos. There is nowhere else I haven't already looked. Ben was supposed to take care of the move and all the unpacking. I'm guessing there must be a box full of old photo albums up here, along with all our other belongings that I can't see downstairs: books, ornaments, and the general shared detritus and dust of lives that have been lived together.

I turn on the attic light and I'm baffled by what I see.

There is nothing here.

Literally nothing. It's as though most of the life I remember has disappeared, and there is very little left of us. I don't understand. It's as though we didn't really live here.

My eyes continue to scan the dusty floorboards and cobwebs, illuminated by a single, flickering bulb. Then I see it: an old shoebox in the far corner.

The ceiling is low, and I crawl on my hands and knees, trying to protect my face from the dirt and spiders lurking in the gloom. It's cold up here, and my hands are shaking when I remove the lid from the box. When I see what is inside, I feel physically sick.

I climb back down the attic steps, with the shoebox tucked under my arm, then turn off the light. A cocktail of fear and relief stirs inside me; I'm afraid of what this could mean, but also relieved that the police didn't find it. I put the box in the bottom of the wardrobe, sliding it next to others that contain things they should, instead of things they shouldn't. Then I practically fall into bed without getting undressed. I just need to lie down for a little while, or I'll never get through a day of filming tomorrow. I close my eyes and I see Ben's face; I don't need a photo for that. It feels as if the us I thought we were is being demolished, lie by lie, leaving little more than the rubble of a marriage behind.

I'm starting to think I didn't know my husband at all.

Twelve

Essex, 1987

"Time to wake up now," says Maggie.

I wasn't sleeping.

The sky outside the car window has turned from blue to black.

"Come on, don't dawdle, out you get." She folds down the front seat so that I can climb out. Her hand scrunches itself into a cross shape, just like my daddy's hands do.

I stand on the side of the street, blinking into the darkness, looking up at the strange-looking line of shops I've never seen before. Then Maggie takes my hand and pulls me towards a large black door. I have to run to keep up. She walks just as fast at night as she did during the day.

"Where are—"

"Shh!" She flattens out the hand that was scrunched up and covers my mouth with it. Her fingers smell of bubble bath. "It's late and we don't want to be waking the neighbors. No more talking until we're inside." Her hand is covering my nose as well as my mouth and it is hard to breathe, but she doesn't take it away until I nod to show that I understand. "Fingers on lips," she whispers, and so I do what she says, copying the way she holds her finger to her own lips, doing my best to look just like her.

She takes a giant set of keys out of her bag; there must be at least a hundred of them, or maybe just ten. They are all different shapes and sizes, jingling and jangling and making far more noise than I did when I opened my mouth just now. She slots a key into the lock and opens the door.

I'm not sure what I was expecting to see, but it wasn't this.

It's just a staircase. A really long one. It goes so high that I can't even see what is at the top, as though the stairs might lead right up to the moon and the stars in the sky. I want to ask Maggie whether I could catch a star if I climb all the steps, but my finger is still on my lips, so I can't. The stairs are made of wood, which has been painted white along the side bits, but left bare in the middle. Just inside the door we've walked through is another door on the left. It's made of metal and Maggie sees me looking at it.

"You don't *ever* go through this door unless I say it is okay. Do you understand?" I nod, suddenly desperate to see what is on the other side. "Go on then, up you go." She pushes me in front of her and closes the outside door behind us.

I start to climb. The steps are quite big for my little legs so it takes me a while, but when I slow down, she pokes her fingers in my back to tell me to hurry up. Adults are always doing that, saying things with their hands or eyes instead of their mouths. There is no rail, so I put my hand on the wall. It's covered in tiles that look and feel the same as the corks that come out of my daddy's wine. My brother used to thread them with cotton to make me cork crowns and necklaces, and I would pretend to be a princess.

I'm busy looking down at my feet to make sure I don't fall, but something like a shadow high above makes me look up. It isn't a cloud or the moon or the stars though. Instead, a tall, skinny man at the top of the stairs is smiling down at me. He's funny-looking. He has three bushy black eyebrows, the third resting on top of his lip, his skin is white like a ghost, and when he smiles, I can see that one of his crooked front teeth is made of gold. I scream. I didn't mean to. I remember that I was supposed to be quiet, but I'm so scared the scream comes out all by itself. I try to turn back down the stairs, but Maggie is in the way and won't let me pass.

"Stop that noise at once," she says, twisting her hand around my arm so tight it feels like a burn. I don't want to go any farther up, but she won't let me go back down, so I'm left feeling a little bit stuck. I don't want to be here, wherever this is. I'm tired and I want to go home.

I look back at the man standing at the top of the stairs. He's still smiling, that gold tooth of his twinkling in the darkness like a rotten star.

"Well, hello there, little lady. I'm your new dad, but for now, you can just call me John."

Thirteen

London, 2017

"You can just call me Alex," she says with a childish grin.

"Thanks, but I'd rather stick with Detective Croft, if that's okay," I reply.

She's waiting for me outside my front door when I get back from my morning run. They both are. Her middle-aged sidekick says very little as usual, making the kind of mental notes that are so loud they can almost be heard. It isn't even seven o'clock.

"I have a lot to do today," I say, fumbling for my keys and opening the front door, trying to hide us all inside as soon as possible. I don't know my neighbors, I couldn't tell you any of their names, but I'm of the belief that while the opinions of strangers shouldn't matter, they often do.

"We just wanted to update you, but we can come back another time—"

"No, sorry, now is fine. I have to be at Pinewood in an hour, that's all. It's the last day of filming, I can't let them down."

"I understand." Her tone makes it clear that she doesn't. "Did you run far this morning?"

"Not really, 5K."

"Impressive."

"It's not very far—"

"No, I meant it's impressive the way you're just carrying on like normal: running, working, *acting.*" She smiles.

What the fuck does that mean?

I hold her stare for as long as I'm able, then my eyes retreat to the face of her silent partner. He towers over her, must be twice her age if not more, but never says a damn thing. I wonder if all her bravado is just her way of trying to impress this man, her superior.

"Are you just going to stand there and let her speak to me like this?" I ask him.

"Afraid so, she's my boss," he replies with an apologetic shrug.

I look back at Detective Croft in disbelief and notice that her smile has disappeared.

"Have you ever hit your husband, Mrs. Sinclair?" she asks.

The hallway feels smaller, seems to turn a little, catches me off-balance.

"Of course not! I've never hit anyone. I'm very close to making a formal complaint—"

"I'll get you a form from the car before I go. We went to the Indian restaurant you said you visited with your husband the last time you saw him . . ." She reaches inside her bag and takes out what looks like an iPad. "The place has security cameras." She taps on the screen a couple of times, before holding it up. "Is this you?"

I look at the frozen black-and-white image of us, surprisingly clear and crisp. "Yes."

"Thought so. Did you have a nice time?" She taps the screen again.

"How is this relevant—"

"I was just wondering why you hit him?" She turns the iPad around again, her childlike finger swiping and scrolling through a series of images. They show me slapping Ben across the face before leaving the restaurant.

Because he accused me of something I didn't do and I was drunk.

I feel my cheeks burn. "We had a silly row, we'd been drinking. It was just a slap." I'm mortified by the sound of my own words as they leave my mouth.

"Do you *slap* him often?"

"No, I've never done that before, I was upset."

"Did he say something to offend you?"

"Successful actresses are either beautiful or good at acting. Seeing

as you are neither of those things, I keep wondering who you fucked this time to get the part."

Ben's words that night have haunted me, I doubt I'll ever forget them.

"I don't remember," I lie, too ashamed to tell the truth. For the last few months Ben and I lived permanently in the shadows of suspicion, a mountain of mistrust caused by a molehill of misunderstanding. He thought I was having an affair.

Alex Croft looks at her sidekick, then back at me. "Did you know that a third of the phone calls we receive about domestic violence in this city are made by male victims?"

How dare she?

"I'm late."

She ignores me and takes a pair of blue plastic gloves from her pocket. "There was a receipt in your husband's wallet for the petrol station on the night you last saw him. We'd like to take a look at his car, if that's okay?"

"If you think it will help."

She appears to be waiting. I'm not sure what for. "Do you have his keys?"

They follow me into the living room. "Have you looked into the stalker yet?" I take Ben's car key from a drawer and form a protective fist around it. I'm not sure why.

She stares at me hard, skips more than just a beat before answering. "You still think a stalker might have had something to do with your husband's disappearance?"

"I don't see how you can rule it out—"

"Is that your laptop?" She points at the small desk in the corner of the room. I nod. "Mind if we take a look?" My turn to hesitate now. "You said it started with emails? We might be able to trace who sent them. Bag it up, Wakely," she says to the other detective. He obediently puts on his own set of gloves, removes a clear plastic bag from his inside pocket, and takes my laptop.

"Mrs. Sinclair?"

I stare at her small outstretched hand. "Yes?"

"Your husband's car key. Please."

My fingers reluctantly uncurl themselves, and Detective Croft takes the key. It leaves an imprint on the palm of my hand, where I'd been holding on too tightly. Before I get a chance to say anything, she's walking back out to the street, and it's all I can do to keep up with her.

She unlocks Ben's red sports car and opens the driver's door, looking inside. I remember the day I bought it for him: a peace offering when home-front hostilities were last at their worst. We took a spontaneous trip to the Cotswolds, driving with the roof down and my skirt up, his hand maneuvering between my legs and the gearstick, before pulling over at the first B&B with a vacancy sign. I remember laughing and making love in front of an open fire, eating bad pizza, and drinking a bottle of good port. I loved how desperate he was to touch me, hold me, fuck me, back then. But all my talk of having children changed that. He did love me. He just didn't want to share.

I miss that version of us.

Then I remember finding another woman's lipstick beneath our bed.

"I appreciate what a distressing time this is . . ." says Detective Croft, bringing me back to the present. She leans in a little farther and slots the key into the ignition. The dashboard lights up and the radio softly serenades us with a popular song about love and lies. Then Croft walks around to the passenger side of the car and opens the glove compartment. I only realize I've been holding my breath when I can see for myself that it is empty. She feels under the seats but doesn't appear to find anything. "A loved one going missing is always hardest on the spouse," she says, looking at me. Then she closes the door and moves to the rear of the car, staring down at the boot. I find myself staring at it too. We all are. "You must be worried now," she says, then opens it. All three of us peer inside.

It's empty.

I remember how to breathe again. I'm not exactly sure what I thought she might find in there, but I'm glad that it's nothing. My shoulders loosen and I start to relax a little.

"I think I must be missing something," she says, closing the boot. Her words intrude on my relief. She returns to the front of the car and retrieves the key. The music from the radio stops, and the silence feels as if it might swallow me. I watch as she removes the gloves from her tiny hands, then I try to speak, but my mouth can't seem to form the right words. I feel like I'm stuck inside my own bespoke nightmare.

"What do you think you are missing?" I ask eventually.

"Well, it's just that if the last place your husband went before he disappeared was the petrol station, then doesn't it seem a little strange to you that the tank is almost empty?"

Fourteen

Essex, 1987

I'm stuck halfway up the longest staircase in the world, and I'm crying because I think my daddy is dead. I don't know why else a strange man in a strange place would say he was my new dad. He keeps talking, but I can't hear him anymore, I'm crying too loud. He doesn't sound Irish like Maggie and me, his voice sounds strange, and I don't like it at all.

"Get out of the way, John, give the child some space," she says when we reach the top of the stairs. I can see four wooden doors. None of them are painted and all of them are closed. Maggie takes my hand and pulls me towards the door that is farthest away. I'm scared to see what is behind it, so I close my eyes, but this makes me trip and stumble a little. Maggie holds on to my hand so tight that my feet just have to catch up.

When I open my eyes again, I can see that I am in a little girl's bedroom. It isn't like my bedroom at home, with the patchy brown carpet and gray curtains that used to be white. This room is like something I've only seen on TV. The bed, table, and wardrobe are all painted white. The carpet is pink, and the curtains, wallpaper, and bedspread are all covered in pictures of a little red-haired girl and rainbows.

"This is your new room. Do you like it?" Maggie asks.

I do like it, so I'm not sure why I wet myself.

I haven't had an accident in my pants for a really long time. I think maybe the walls made of corks, the tall stairs, and the man with the gold tooth might have frightened the pee right out of me. I feel a hot trickle of it run down the inside of my leg, and I can't seem to make it stop. I hope Maggie won't notice, but when I look at the pink carpet, there is a dark patch between my shoes. She sees it then, and her smiley round face changes into something cross and pointy.

"Only babies wet themselves." She hits me hard across the face. I've seen Daddy hit my brother like that, but nobody has ever done it to me before. My cheek hurts and I start to cry again. "Grow up, it was just a slap." Maggie picks me up, holding me as far away from her as she can with straight arms. She marches back out into the hall and through the door nearest the top of the stairs. It's a small kitchen. The floor is covered in lines of strange, squishy green carpet, with words written on it, and the cupboards are all different shapes and sizes and made from different-colored wood. Another door at the end of the kitchen leads to a bathroom. Everything in it is green; the toilet, the sink, the bath, the carpet, and the tiles on the wall. I think Maggie must really like the color. She puts me down inside the bath and leaves the room, then comes straight back, with a big black bin bag. I worry that she wants to throw me away with the rubbish.

"Take your clothes off," she says.

I don't want to.

"I said take your clothes off!"

I still don't move.

"Now." It sounds as if the word got stuck behind her teeth. She seems awful cross, so I do as she says.

When all my clothes, including my wet pants, are in the bin bag, she picks up a little white plastic hose that is attached to the tap in the bath. "The boiler is on the blink, so you'll have to make do." She hoses me down. The water is freezing and it makes me gasp for my breath, like when I fell out of the fishing boat once at home and the cold black sea tried to swallow me. Maggie squirts shampoo on my head and roughly rubs it into my hair. The yellow bottle says No More Tears, but I'm crying. When I am covered in soap from my head to my feet, she sprays me all over with cold water again. I try to keep still the way she tells me to, but my body shivers and my teeth chatter like they do in winter.

When she is finished, she dries me with a stiff green towel, then she marches me back to my new bedroom and sits me down on the bed covered in rainbows. I don't have any clothes and I'm cold. She leaves the room for a moment, and I hear her talking to the man who said he was my new dad, even though I've never seen him before.

"She looks just like her," he says, before Maggie comes back in with a glass of milk.

"Drink it."

I hold the glass in both hands and take a couple of sips. It tastes chalky and strange, just like the milk she gave me in the house that was for holidays.

"All of it," she says.

When the glass is empty, I see that she is wearing her smiley round face again, and I am glad. I don't like her other one, it scares me. She opens a drawer and pulls out a pair of pink pajamas. She helps me to put them on, then makes me stand in front of the mirror.

The first thing I notice is my hair. It's much shorter than it was the last time I saw myself and stops at my chin.

"Where has my hair gone?" I start to cry, but Maggie raises her hand so I stop.

"It was too long and needed cutting. It will grow back."

I stare at at the little girl in the mirror. Her pink pajama top has a word written on it made of five letters: AIMEE. I don't know what it means.

"Do you want a bedtime story?"

I nod that I would.

"Has the cat got your tongue?"

I haven't seen a cat and I think my tongue is still inside my mouth, I wiggle it behind my lips to be sure.

She walks over to a shelf stacked with colorful magazines and takes the top one off the pile. "Can you read?"

"Yes." I stick my chin out a little without knowing why. "My brother taught me."

"Well, wasn't that nice of him. You can read this to yourself then. There's a whole pile of *Story Teller* magazines here, and cassette tapes, too, so you just go ahead whenever you want to. *Gobbolino* is your favorite." She throws the magazine onto the bed. "The witch's cat," she adds, when I don't say anything. I don't even like cats so I wish she'd stop talking about them. "If you can read, then tell me what it says on your top."

I stare at it, but the letters are upside down.

"It says Aimee. That's your new name from now on. It means 'loved.' You do want people to love you, don't you?"

"But I'm called Ciara." I look up at her.

"Not anymore you're not, and if you ever use that name under this roof again, you'll find yourself in very big trouble."

Fifteen

London, 2017

I'm in trouble.

The detective has clearly already made up her mind about me, but she's wrong. The only thing I'm guilty of is fraud, the relationship variety. We all sometimes pretend to love something or someone we don't: an unwanted gift, a friend's new haircut, a husband. We've evolved to be so good at it, we can even fool ourselves. It's more laziness than deceit; to acknowledge when the love has run out would mean having to do something about it. Relationship fraud is endemic nowadays.

As soon as the detectives leave, I lock the door behind them, desperate to shut the whole world out. I guess I can now add the police to the list of people who think they know me. They're in good company, with the press, the fans, and my so-called friends. But they *don't* know me. Only the version of myself I let them see. The wheels of my mind continue to drive in the wrong direction, stuck in reverse, and I relive that night, remembering things I'd rather not. We did argue in the restaurant. Detective Croft is right about that. Ben accused me of having an affair, again. I tried so hard to reassure him, but he just got more and more angry.

"Successful actresses are either beautiful or they're good at acting . . ."

The more he drank, the worse it got.

"You are neither of those things."

It was as though he wanted to hurt me, provoke a reaction.

"I keep wondering who you fucked this time to get the part."

He succeeded.

I didn't mean to slap him, I know I shouldn't have done that, and I'm deeply ashamed of myself. But I've spent a lifetime thinking that I wasn't good enough, and his cruel words echoed my own insecurities so loud and clear, something inside me just snapped. I've never felt that I'm good enough at anything; no matter how hard I try, I just don't fit. If my husband can see it, then surely it's only a matter of time until everyone else sees it too.

My response wasn't just physical. I told him I wanted a divorce, because I wanted to hurt him back. If he had let me have the child I wanted, I would have given up the career he said had come between us, but the answer was always the same: no. He didn't trust me in more ways than one. We were going weeks, sometimes months, without a shred of intimacy, as though touching me might accidentally get me pregnant. I'm so lonely now it physically hurts.

I'll never forget what he said as I walked out of the restaurant, or the expression on his face when I turned back to look at him. I don't think it was just the drink talking, he looked as if he meant it.

"I'll ruin you if you leave me."

I head upstairs, pull off my running clothes, and take a shower. The water is too hot, but I don't bother to adjust the temperature. I let it scald my skin, as though I think I deserve the pain. Then I head into the bedroom to get dressed for work. I open the wardrobe slowly, as though something terrible might be hiding inside. It is. I bend down and remove the shoebox I found in the attic, then sit on the bed before lifting the lid. I stare at the contents for a while, as though touching them might burn my fingers. Then I remove the stack of plain vintage postcards and spread them out over the duvet. There must be more than fifty. The white cotton provides a lackluster camouflage for the yellowing rectangles of card, so that my eyes are even more drawn to the spidery black ink decorating each one. They are all identical: the same words, written in the same feminine scrawl, by the same hand.

I know who you are.

I thought we had thrown all of these away. I don't know why Ben would have kept them. For evidence I suppose . . . in case the stalker ever returned.

I put the cards back in the box and slide it under the bed. Hiding the truth from ourselves is a similar game to hiding it from others, it just comes with a stricter set of rules.

Once dressed, I head back downstairs and stare at the huge bunch of flowers on the kitchen table, accompanied by the tiny card reading, *Sorry.* I pick them up, needing both hands to do so. My foot connects with the large stainless-steel pedal bin and the lid opens obediently, ready to swallow my rubbish, but also revealing its own. My hands hover above the trash while my eyes try to translate what they are seeing: two empty black plastic bottles that I've never seen before. I pick one up to read the label. Lighter gel? We don't even have a barbecue. I put the empty bottle back and push the flowers down on top of them inside the bin, a mess of petals and thorns hiding everything that lies beneath.

Sixteen

Essex, 1987

I wake up in the pink-and-white bedroom with a terrible tummyache. I can see daylight behind the curtains covered in rainbows, but when I pull them back, there are bars on the windows and a big gray sky. I'm hungry and I can smell toast, so I creep over to the door and listen. My fingers reach up for the handle; it's higher than the ones at home. As I slowly open the door, it makes a *shh* sound on the carpet, so I try extra hard to be quiet.

The walls in the hallway all look as if they have peeled, and it's cold. Something bites my feet when I take a step forward, and it hurts. When I look down, I see that the floor out here is also covered in the green spongy stuff I saw in the kitchen last night. Thin orange strips of wood are all around the edges, with little silver spikes sticking out of them. When I bend down to touch one, a bubble of blood grows on my finger, so I put it in my mouth and suck it until the pain goes away.

I follow the smell of toast, careful not to tread on any more little spikes, and stop when I reach the first door. It's locked, so I carry on. The next door is slightly open and I can hear a television behind it. I try to peek through the crack, but the door tells on me by squeaking.

"Is that you, Aimee?" asks Maggie.

My name is Ciara, so I don't know what to say.

"Come on in, no need to be shy, this is your home now."

I push the door a little harder and see Maggie sitting in bed next to the man with the gold tooth. His smile has holes in, as though he has worn it too often, and he has little bits of white toast stuck in the black hair on his face. I see the television reflected in his glasses, and when I turn to look at the screen, it says *TV-am,* before changing to a picture of a man and a woman sitting on a sofa. The walls in this room are like the walls in the hall, all patchy and bare, and there is no carpet in here either, just more of the springy green stuff.

"Come and get in with us, it's cold. Move over, John," says Maggie, and he smiles, patting a space on the bed between them. I'm shivering, but I don't want to get into their bed.

"Come on," she says when I don't move.

"Hop in," he says, pulling back the covers.

Bunny rabbits hop. I am not a bunny rabbit.

I can see that Maggie is wearing a nightie, her skinny legs sticking out from beneath the sheets. Her long black curly hair is hanging down over her shoulders, and I wish mine was still as long as that. I climb in next to Maggie, but only because her happy face looks as if it might change into her cross one if I don't.

Maggie's bedroom is a mess, which seems strange to me, because she looks like such a neat and tidy person. Dirty cups and plates are everywhere, piles of newspapers and magazines lean up against the walls, and clothes are thrown all over the floor. The duvet smells, I'm not sure what of, but it isn't nice. We all sit and stare at the TV, then my tummy rumbles so loud I'm sure everyone hears it.

"Do you want some breakfast?" Maggie asks when the adverts come on.

"Yes." Her face changes and I add, "Please," before it is too late.

"What do you fancy? You can have anything you want."

I look over at one of the dirty plates with crusts on. "Toast?"

She pulls a pretend sad face, like a clown. "I'm afraid your dad ate the last of the bread."

I'm confused at first, then remember that she means the man with the gold tooth.

"Don't worry that pretty little head of yours. I'm going to make your favorite, back in a jiffy."

I don't know what a jiffy is.

Maggie leaves the room and I'm glad she doesn't close the door. I don't want to be on my own with John. He looks as if he is wearing a rug on his chest, but up close I can see it's just more hair. He seems to have an awful lot of it. He reaches past me, and I lean out of his way. Then I watch while he picks up a packet of cigarettes and lights one, tapping the ash into an empty cup while he laughs at something on TV.

Maggie comes back with a plate, which is strange because she said she was going to make my favorite breakfast, which is porridge and honey. My brother used to make it for me at home, and I always ate it in my favorite blue bowl, even though it was chipped. My brother said it could still be my favorite bowl even when it wasn't perfect anymore. He said things that are a little bit broken can still be beautiful.

"There now, get that down you," says Maggie. Her cold, bare legs touch my feet as she climbs back under the covers.

I look down at the plate. "What is it?"

"It's your favorite, silly! Biscuits with butter. Make sure you eat them all, we need to fatten you up a bit, you've gotten far too skinny."

I think I look the same as yesterday and the day before that.

I look from Maggie to the plate and back again, unsure what to do. Then I pick up one of the round shapes and can see that it has its own name written underneath it, just like my new name is written on my pajama top. I whisper the letters inside my head: $DIGESTIVE$.

"Go on, take a bite," Maggie says.

I don't want to.

"Eat. It."

I take a small bite, chewing slowly. All I can taste is the butter, and it makes me feel a bit sick.

"What do you say?"

"Thank you?"

"Thank you, what?"

"Thank you, Maggie?"

"No, not Maggie. From now on, you call me Mum."

Seventeen

London, 2017

Today feels like a day of lasts.

My last day driving through the Pinewood Studios gates.

My last time playing this particular character.

My last chance.

I sit in front of the dressing room mirror while other people tame my hair and disguise the imperfections on my face. I'm not feeling myself today, I'm not sure I can even remember who that is. I always experience a period of grief when I stop filming; all those months of hard work and then it's over, but the finality of this day feels far more ominous than it should. Keeping everything that is happening to myself is taking its toll, but there's only one more day to get through, and I know I'm not alone. We all make daily decisions about which secrets to decant, and which to keep for a later date, when they might taste better on our tongues.

When I am all alone again, staring into the mirror, not sure who I see, I notice something that isn't mine. Nina, the wonderful woman who magically transforms my hair, has left her magazine behind. I flick through the pages, more out of boredom than curiosity, and stop when I see a double-page profile piece about Alicia White.

The woman grinning in the enormous, Photoshopped picture went to the same senior school and drama school as me. She was in the year above, but somehow looks a decade younger. Alicia White is an actress too. A bad one. We share an agent now and she always likes to remind me that he signed her first. He's all she ever talks about, as though we are participants in some kind of unspoken competition. She feels the need to put me down every time we meet, as though she wants to make sure I know my place. There's really no need; I've never had a high opinion of myself.

The sight of her face reminds me of Tony. He asked me to call, but I still haven't managed to get hold of him. My fingers search for my mobile inside my bag, and I try again. Straight to voice mail. I call the office, which I hate doing, and his assistant picks up on the second ring.

"Sure thing, he's free now," she says in a chirpy voice, and pops me on hold.

I listen to tinny classical music, which makes me feel even more stressed than before, and I feel a wave of relief when it stops and he answers. Except it isn't him.

"I'm sorry, my mistake," his assistant whispers. "He's in a meeting, but he'll call you back."

She hangs up before I get a chance to ask when.

I return my attention to the magazine, desperate for any form of distraction from the ever-growing list of anxieties lining up inside my mind. Things must be pretty bad if I'm resorting to reading about Alicia White.

I haven't always had an agent. Until eighteen months ago, nobody wanted to represent me. I belonged to an agency instead, which did little more than send my headshot off for various jobs and take 15 percent when I got one. I always had work, just not always the kind I really wanted. When Ben and I got married, I was the understudy in a play on Shaftesbury Avenue. The lead was sick one night, and I got to perform in her place. My agent's wife was sitting in the audience, and she told him about me. I owe her a debt that I can never repay, and within weeks of having an agent I landed my first film role.

Sometimes it only takes one person to believe in you to change your life forever. Sometimes it only takes one person not believing in you to destroy it. Humans are a highly sensitive species.

I rest my tired eyes for just a moment, then stare down at the photo of Alicia again. I drop the magazine onto my lap when her face becomes three-dimensional and starts talking at me. A catalog of catty comments she's said in the past spill from her red paper mouth in the present.

"Tony took *me* for a fancy lunch when he signed me, but then *I* was so in demand, *everyone* wanted to represent *me*, not like *you*," says magazine Alicia, before flicking her long blond hair. The highlighted strands unravel like paper streamers, out of the page and onto my lap.

"I was *so* surprised when he took *you* on, everybody was!" she continues, then wrinkles her perfect paper nose in my direction. "It was good of him to give you a chance, but then he's always been a charitable man." She takes a fifty-pound note from her purse, rolls it up, and lights the end. Then she starts to inhale it like a cigarette, before blowing a cloud of smoke in my face. It stings my eyes and I tell myself that's the reason they are filling with tears.

"It isn't as though your face fits with his other clients; it isn't as though *your face* fits at all." She's right about that part; I don't fit anywhere, I never have.

"You know he's going to dump you one day, don't you? Quite soon I'd imagine. And then you'll *never find work again!*" She tilts her head back and laughs like a comedy villain, tiny black-and-white paper words spewing from her mouth, while the page folds into creases around her eyes.

The sound of someone laughing outside my dressing room wakes me, and I realize I've dozed off in my chair, I've been dreaming. I've barely slept for three nights in a row; I'm so exhausted that I fear I might be losing my mind. I tear Alicia out of the magazine, screw up her face, and throw her in the bin, instantly feeling a little calmer now that she's gone.

Alicia White hates me, but can't seem to leave me alone. Over the last few months, she has copied my haircut (although I admit it does look better on her, everything does). She's copied my clothes, she's even used some of the same answers I give in interviews, literally copied them *word for word*. Apart from her peroxide-induced hair color, it's as though she wants to *be* me. People say that imitation is the sincerest form of flattery, but I don't feel flattered, I just feel freaked out.

Other than the agent, and the job, we have absolutely nothing in common. For starters, she is beautiful, at least on the outside. The inside is a different story, and one she should learn to hide better. Being a bitch might work out well in some industries, but not this one. Everyone talks, and the talk about Alicia White is rarely good. It makes me realize that I could never be an agent: I'd only want to represent nice people.

Something niggles me, and I feel the need to rewind, not just reset myself. I reach down into the bin and retrieve the ball of crumpled print, flattening the image of Alicia with my palm. I stare at her face, her eyes, her bright red lips. Then I read the final question and answer in the piece and feel physically sick.

What three items of makeup can you not leave the house without?
That's easy! Mascara, eyeliner, and my Chanel Rouge Allure lipstick.

The name of the lipstick is not new to me. It's branded in my brain, written in indelible ink inside my mind; it's the lipstick I found under my marital bed when I got back from filming last year.

Did Alicia White sleep with my husband?

The first assistant director summons me with a knock on the door, I screw Alicia's face into an even tighter ball and throw her back in the bin before following him outside. We make polite small talk as the golf buggy trundles around the lot. He's still young and worries about things he won't when he is older, the way we all did before we knew what life really had in store. I listen to his tales of woe, interjecting the occasional sympathetic word, as we drive along at less than twenty miles an hour. I enjoy the light breeze in my face, and the smell of paint and sawdust that lingers in the air around every film set. It makes me feel at home.

The designers spend months building whole new worlds, then tear them down as though they never were when filming is over. Just like a breakup, only more physical and less damaging. Sometimes it's hard saying goodbye to the characters I become. I spend so long with them that they start to feel like family, perhaps because I don't have a real one. My anxiety levels are at an all-time high by the time the buggy turns the final corner. I haven't rehearsed for today the way I normally would, there just wasn't time. The traffic of worrying thoughts has come to a standstill in my mind, as though it were rush hour up there, and I'm stuck somewhere I don't want to be.

We stop outside our final destination: an enormous warehouse that contains most of the interior film sets for *Sometimes I Kill*. I hesitate before going inside. My mind is so full of everything that is happening in my private life that for a moment I can't even remember what scene we are shooting.

"Good, you're here. I need you to deliver something special today, Aimee," barks the director as soon as he sees me. "We need to believe that the character is capable of killing her husband."

I feel a little bit sick. It's as though I'm trapped inside a life-size joke.

I stand on the set of my fictional kitchen, waiting for my fictional husband to come home, and I see Jack smile at me before our first take.

Nobody is smiling by the twentieth.

I keep forgetting my lines, which never happens to me. I'm sure the rest of the cast and crew must hate me for it. I get to go home after this scene, but they don't. The clapboard sounds, the director says, "Action," again, and I do my best to get it right this time.

I pour myself a drink I'll never swallow, then pretend to be surprised when Jack comes up behind me, slipping his arms around my waist.

"It's done," I say, turning to look up at him.

His face changes, in exactly the same way it did nineteen times before. "What do you mean?"

"You know what I mean. It's done. It's taken care of." I raise the glass to my lips.

He takes a step back. "I didn't think you were actually going to do it."

"He wouldn't give me what I wanted, but I know that you will. I love you. I want to be with you, nobody else is going to get in the way of that."

The word "Cut" echoes in my ears, and I can tell from the look on the director's face that I've nailed it this time. As soon as he's watched the scene back, I'll be free to go.

I'm chatting to Jack outside in the sunshine when the golf buggy reappears in the distance on the lot. I don't think anything of it at first, just carry on talking about the time frame for postproduction. But then my eyes find something familiar about the shape of the woman being driven towards us.

This cannot be happening.

Detective Alex Croft is wearing a smile wider than I thought her tiny face could support. The vehicle comes to a halt right in front of us and she climbs out, beaming. Her unsmiling sidekick jumps off the backward-facing rear seat, smoothing down his trousers as though sitting down has caused an upsetting crease.

"Thank you," Detective Croft says to the driver, "and thank *you*," she adds, in my direction.

"What for?" I ask.

"I have always, always wanted to drive around a film studio on a buggy, and now I have! All thanks to you! Is there somewhere we can talk?"

"This is a closed set," says the director, joining us just when I didn't think things could get any worse. "I don't know who you are, but you can't be here."

She smiles. "This is my badge and it means that I can. So sorry, I forgot to introduce myself with all the excitement and stardust. My name is Detective—"

I read the questions on Jack's face without his having to say a word.

"I'm sorry, they're here because of a personal matter. I'll deal with it," I interrupt, and wait for the others to walk away, out of earshot. Jack keeps throwing concerned glances over his shoulder, and I smile to try to reassure him that everything is okay.

"Did you have to come here?" I ask when I think nobody can hear.

"Is there some reason why you didn't want us to?"

"You could have called."

"I could have, but then I wouldn't have got to see all this. You're probably used to it, but for me, well, this is like a trip to Disneyland. Not that I've been."

"What do you want?"

"I think the first question most people in your situation might ask would be 'Have you found my husband?'"

"*Have* you found my husband?"

"Sadly no, we have not, but I need your help with something. Is there somewhere a little more private where we can talk?"

Her face lights up like a Christmas tree when we step inside my dressing room.

"There really are lights around your mirror and everything," she says, beaming.

"There really are, yes. You said you needed my help."

"I did. I think we might have got ourselves in a muddle when you gave us your statement, for which I can only apologize. We work crazy long hours, and sometimes we make mistakes." She takes her iPad from the inside pocket of her jacket. "I had down that after leaving the restaurant, you came straight home, went to bed, and went to work the following morning, presuming your husband had spent the night sleeping in a spare bedroom."

"That's right."

"Except that we didn't have a note of you going for a drive in your husband's car."

"You don't have a note of me doing that because I didn't."

"Really? Sure looks like you . . ." She turns the screen to face me, before using a small, skinny index finger, with a short, neat nail, to swipe between images. "I mean, I appreciate that the image is a little grainy, compared with what we got from the restaurant, but that looks like you parking his car at the petrol station, and that looks like you paying at the till. See, we only had the credit-card receipt, and I think most people would assume someone was buying petrol. I know I sure did, and this is why I need your help because, according to the records, this woman—the one driving your husband's car and using his card, the woman who looks a lot like you—well, *she* wasn't buying petrol. *She* was buying several bottles of lighter gel, like the stuff you squirt on a barbecue if you have an impatient personality. So . . . are you certain that isn't you? On the screen I mean, I don't need to know whether you're impatient."

I stare at the woman in the photo wearing a coat that looks just like mine, with dark curly hair resting on her shoulders, and over-sized sunglasses on her face. "No, it's not me."

"It does look like you. Don't you think it looks like Mrs. Sinclair, Wakely?"

"I thought so."

"Have you looked into the woman who was stalking me? The one I told you about?" I ask.

"Why? Does she look like you?"

"Yes. I've never seen her close up, but she used to dress like me and stand outside our old home."

"Do you know her name?"

"I already told you, no. At least not her real name."

"What name did she use?"

I hesitate, not really wanting to say it out loud, but realize that I have to now. "She called herself Maggie. Maggie O'Neil, but that isn't her real name."

"How do you know that isn't her real name?"

"Because Maggie O'Neil is dead."

Eighteen

Essex, 1987

"Look alive, you need to get up, get dressed, and come downstairs today. I don't have time to keep checking on you," says Maggie, bursting into the room in her nightie. She pulls back the curtains, revealing another rainy day behind the bars on the window. She tugs the duvet off my bed and I shiver. I am still wearing pajamas that say AIMEE on the front to remind me of my new name. I've been wearing them ever since I arrived here, which I think is three days ago now.

"Why are there bars on the window?"

"To keep the bad men out. There are bad people who try to take things that don't belong to them, and the bars help keep us safe."

I don't feel safe when she tells me this, I feel scared. Then I think about how I don't belong to Maggie, but she took me.

She opens the white wardrobe and I can see that it is full of clothes. Someone else's. Maggie takes out a purple top and a pair of trousers, then lays them on the bed, along with some underwear and socks. "Put those on," she says before leaving the room.

When she comes back, she is dressed and her face is covered in color. Orange on her cheeks, brown on her eyes, red on her lips. She's wearing a short skirt and long boots. She looks at me in my trousers, which keep falling down, then shakes her head and tuts. She tuts a lot.

"You're still too skinny, you need to eat more. Take them off."

I do as she says while she opens the wardrobe again, her hand scraping the hangers along the pole as though she is cross with everything she sees.

"Try these." She scrunches up some dark blue material, making me put one leg inside, then the other. I've never seen anything like it.

"What are they?"

"They're called dungarees," she replies, strapping me inside them. I repeat the name without making any sound, enjoying the silent shape the new word forces my tongue to make inside my mouth. "Come on then, I've got work to do. Hurry up and get downstairs."

I've never been back down the stairs since I arrived.

I'm not allowed.

There's even a white gate across the top to remind me.

When Maggie opens the gate and pushes me down the first step, I get scared. I'd forgotten how many steps there were, and I get a pain in my tummy looking down at them all. We didn't have any steps at all at home, we lived in something called a bungalow, and I think I preferred living down on the ground.

"What are these?" I ask, stepping over one of the orange strips of wood on the floor, careful not to hurt my feet on the metal spikes.

"They are carpet grippers, and the green stuff is carpet liner. Hurry up."

"Where's the carpet?" I walk my fingers along the cork wall.

"Carpet costs money, and money doesn't grow on trees. You have a nice carpet in your bedroom, that's all you need to worry about. You have the nicest room in the flat, so try to be grateful, Baby Girl." That is what she likes to call me now: Baby Girl. It is another new name, just like Aimee.

At the bottom of the stairs I think we might be going outside, and I'm worried because I'm not wearing a coat or shoes. But we are not going outside. Instead, Maggie takes out her giant set of keys and starts unlocking the metal door I saw the first night I arrived here. Then she slides the bolts at the top, middle, and bottom. When she opens the door, I can't see anything, only black, but then she flicks a switch and lights come on all over the ceiling above me. It's as though we have stepped inside a spaceship.

"This is *the shop*," she says.

It doesn't look like a shop. There are lots of TV screens everywhere, and I wonder how anyone could watch more than one television program at a time. Bits of newspapers are taped to the white walls, next to posters covered with numbers and pictures of horses. There are black leather stools that are taller than I am, and ashtrays everywhere. In the corner of the room is a counter that looks a bit like the ones you see in a bank. It has a glass panel with just a few holes for speaking through.

"You are never to come into *the shop* when we have customers. You are to stay in the *back room*." She unlocks the door that leads behind the counter, where I can see two shopping tills and lots of little bits of paper.

"What does the shop sell?"

"We're bookmakers."

I think about that for a little while. "Then where are all the books?"

She laughs. "We don't sell books, Baby Girl."

"Then what do you sell?"

She thinks for a moment, then smiles at me. "Dreams."

I don't understand.

We walk through another room where there are telephones, a big scary-looking machine, and a dirty-looking sink. Then we're inside a smaller room, with just a dusty desk, a chair, a tiny TV, and another door with locks that looks as if it might lead outside. She pushes me down onto the chair, and her hand hurts my shoulder.

"Will I be allowed to go home in time for my birthday next week? I'm going to be six on the sixteenth of September."

"This is your home now, and it is not your birthday next week. Your birthday is in April, and you're going to be seven next year."

I don't know what to say about that. She is wrong. I know how old I am, and I know when my birthday is.

"Do you know what a bet is?" she asks.

"Yes."

"Tell me."

"It's like I bet you one conker that it will rain today."

She laughs and I remember how pretty she looks when she smiles. "Yes, clever girl, that's exactly what it is. The shop is somewhere people come to place bets, but not about the weather; they mostly bet on horses and sometimes dogs."

"Horses and dogs? How can you bet on a horse?"

"Well, the horses race, and the people place bets on which one will come first. But they don't do it for conkers, they do it for money."

I try to make sense of it all. "What if they lose?"

"Good question. If they lose, we keep their money and buy more carpets for upstairs. Do you understand?"

I shake my head no, and she starts to look cross again.

"If it's a shop, then don't you have to sell something?"

"We do, I told you already. We sell dreams, Baby Girl. Dreams that will never come true."

Nineteen

London, 2017

"I'm afraid I still don't follow," I say.

Detective Alex Croft and her sidekick have been in my dressing room for some time now, and it's starting to feel as if there isn't enough oxygen in here for the three of us. I keep staring at the door, like an emergency exit I'd like to escape through, but she just keeps staring at me, then expels another sigh before speaking.

"I'm asking you, again, what happened when you got back from the petrol station?"

"And I've told you, several times now, that I was never *at* the petrol station. I left the restaurant and went home to bed, alone."

She shakes her head. "Did you ever wonder why two detectives were sent to your house when you reported Ben missing?"

"Well, I—"

"It's not standard procedure, but your husband was deemed to be high risk. Do you want to know why?"

I stare back at her, not sure that I do.

"Because earlier that day he visited the local police station and reported you for assault and battery. Either you really are a great actress, or I'm guessing you didn't know."

It feels like I'm falling, so I sit down. It's as though I've slipped into a messed-up parallel universe in the last couple of days, one where I'm still myself, but everything and everyone around me has twisted all out of shape. When I don't say anything, she just carries right on.

"Your husband mentioned that you had been diagnosed with some form of amnesia when you were a child. That the condition meant you sometimes forgot traumatic events, blanked them out of your memory completely, without even knowing that you had. He suggested that your symptoms were ongoing, but that you were in denial about that. So that you *think* you have a perfect memory but that in reality, you might have forgotten some of the things that you did when you were upset. Does any of this ring true?"

"No. I mean, yes, I was diagnosed with a condition when I was a child, but it was a misdiagnosis. I haven't forgotten anything since."

I didn't forget anything that happened then either, I just pretended to. I carry my memories of my life before in an old trunk inside my head. It's been locked for a long time.

"And you're sure about that? That you're not still experiencing some form of memory loss? It was one of the reasons your husband decided not to press charges."

"Press charges for what?"

"Do you drink, Mrs. Sinclair?"

"Everybody drinks."

"Do you think it's possible that you were too drunk to remember what happened between you and your husband that night?"

No. I remember everything. I'm just selfish with most of my memories; I choose not to share them.

"Do I need a lawyer?"

"I don't know, *do* you? You said it was, and I quote, *just a slap*?" She waits for me to respond, but I don't. I'm starting to think it might be best to say as little as possible. "Where is your husband, Mrs. Sinclair?"

Something inside me snaps. "I. Don't. Know! That's why I called you people!"

The volume of my voice surprises me, but she doesn't flinch. "Did you manage to find a recent photo of Ben to help with our investigation?"

"No."

"Not to worry, I have one here." She reaches inside her pocket, then produces a photo of Ben's face, bloodied and bruised, one eye almost completely swollen shut. I have never, ever, seen him look like this. He's almost unrecognizable. "This is what your husband looked like when he came to the police station, on the day *you* say he went missing. His nose was broken in two places. I'm not a medical professional, but I'd guess these injuries were caused by more than *just a slap*. The only reason we didn't bring you in then was because he refused to press charges in the end. I think he was afraid of you."

I accept that my mind might have a hairline fracture, but my memory works just fine.

I'm not crazy.

"This is insane! I've never seen him looking like that—"

"In his statement, your husband said he had confronted you about an affair he believed you were having with Jack Anderson, your co-star in this movie. Any truth in that?"

"That's none of your business!"

"Anything that helps me find your husband and ensure his safety is my business. A few hours after he left the police station, you reported him missing. Where is he now, Mrs. Sinclair?"

Everything is too loud, I just want her to stop talking, or for someone to explain what is happening in a way that makes a shred of sense. "I told you, I don't know. If I knew where he was, or if I had hurt him myself, why would I call the police?"

She shakes her head. "One last question. Can you remind me what time you said you came home the night you realized he was ... missing?"

"About five p.m. I guess, I'm not sure exactly." I notice Wakely scribble something down.

"See, now that's interesting, because it means you were home when your husband made his final call from the phone you said was his, the one that was left on the coffee table. He has been seeing a domestic abuse counselor for a little while now. He said this wasn't the first time you attacked him, and he left a message on his counselor's phone. Want to know what Ben said?"

Not really.

She hits a button on her iPad, and Ben's hushed voice fills my dressing room. It's like hearing a ghost.

"I'm sorry to call, but you said that I could if I ever felt in danger again, and I think she's going to kill me."

Twenty

Essex, 1987

"You'll get square eyes," Maggie says, getting out of bed and turning off the TV. I've been living here for a long time now and she's always saying that, so I check my eyes as often as I can in the mirror to make sure they are still round. I carry on staring at the screen anyway, even though the picture has gone. I can see a girl in it, like a little gray ghost of me. She smiles when I smile, and stands when I stand, and looks sad when I look sad. I don't see what she does when I turn and walk away, but sometimes I imagine she stays right where she is inside that screen. Watching me.

"Do you know the best thing about Christmas?" Maggie asks.

I'd forgotten that she said it was Christmas today and don't answer.

"Surprises!" She ties one of her bras around my head, like a blindfold. I don't always like Maggie's surprises. She pulls me up and leads me to the door in the flat I've never been through before. It's locked and I'm afraid of what might be behind it. I hear her take out the giant set of keys, then she opens the door, and we shuffle inside. It's dark, but I can feel soft carpet beneath my toes, just like in my bedroom. She takes the bra off my face, which I'm glad about, but I still can't really see until she opens the heavy-looking curtains.

The room is beautiful, like the grotto in Dunnes Stores in Galway at Christmas. A pretty pattern of red and white flowers is all over the walls, and there is red carpet on the floor. I see a big red sofa, with lots of cushions, and the fireplace is a bit like the one at home. Paper chains are hanging down from the swirly white ceiling, and in the corner of the room there is a giant green tree, covered in tinsel, with a big silver star on top. Best of all, there are presents underneath, more presents than I've ever seen before.

"Well, go on then, see if there's anything there for you," says Maggie. Her yellow T-shirt with a smiley face comes down to her knees, but her teeth are chattering, which seems to make mine do the same. It's as though the cold in the room is like the colds that make you cough and sneeze—something you can catch. She turns on a switch next to the fireplace, and I see that the fire is not real, only pretend with blue flames. Then she flicks another switch, and little colored lights appear all over the tree. It's beautiful. But then the lights on the tree and the fire go off, and Maggie's face turns from happy to cross awful fast.

"Damn it, John, this was meant to be perfect." She looks behind me. I turn and see John in the doorway. I didn't even know he was there, he always seems to be hiding in the shadows.

"Hold your horses." He reaches inside the pocket of his jeans and disappears down the hall. It's a silly thing to say because Maggie doesn't have any horses to hold.

A thing called a meter lives inside the big cupboard at the top of the stairs. It's where the ironing board and Hoover live, too, not that we ever use those. If we don't put enough fifty-pence coins inside the meter's mouth, the power goes off. It needs feeding all the time, the way I think a pet dragon might. John must have fed it, because the lights and the fire come back on.

Maggie is wearing her happy face again, just like the one on her T-shirt. "Well, go on."

I walk a little closer to the tree, and when I bend down, I can see that all the presents have little name tags tied on with ribbon. I turn one over and it says AIMEE. I look at another and it says the same thing. But they are all covered in dust, as though they have been sitting under the tree for a very long time. I look around the room and see that everything else in here is covered in dust too.

"Aren't you going to open something?" asks John, lighting a cigarette and sitting down on the sofa. "I don't see nobody else called Aimee around here, do you?"

Just as he says it, I do see another little girl in the room, or at least a picture of her in a frame on the mantelpiece. She looks a bit like me, but older, with exactly the same length hair. Maggie sees me looking at it and lays the frame down flat.

"Open your presents," she says, folding her arms.

I pick up the one nearest to me, getting dust on my fingers and pajamas. I open it slowly, peeling back each piece of Sellotape, trying not to tear the pretty paper. I see what looks like orange wool inside and pull it out. John takes a picture of me with his Polaroid camera; he likes doing that. He takes pictures of me everywhere all the time— in the shop, in my bedroom, in the bath. I don't think the photos he takes of me in the bath or in bed at night can be very good; he never shows them to me or Maggie afterwards.

"It's Rainbow Brite, your absolute favorite! Do you like her?" asks Maggie. I nod, not sure who Rainbow Brite is, but remembering her from the duvet and wallpaper in my bedroom. "Well, go on, open another."

This time it is a red machine.

"It's a brand-new Fisher-Price cassette player, so you can play all those Story Teller tapes you like so much. Just try not to break this one."

I didn't break anything.

"Now, what do you say before you open the next one?"

I think hard before answering. Maggie gets awful cross when I get things wrong. When I think I know the answer, I turn and look at her. "Thank you, Mum."

I pick up another present, hoping I'm still allowed to open it.

She smiles at me. "You're welcome, Baby Girl."

Twenty-one

London, 2017

"Are you okay?" asks Jack.

No.

My husband is trying to frame me.

The only person who ever really knew me, who I thought loved me, is coming after me in a majorly messed-up way. I feel terrified and broken and so fucking angry all at once.

Jack knocked on my dressing room door less than a minute after the police left. I thought they had come back, so seeing him standing there instead brings nothing but relief.

"I'm fine," I say, as he steps inside uninvited and I close the door behind him.

"You're a great actress, but you're a terrible liar. Tell me to mind my own business if you like, but I thought you might need to talk, and I wondered if you fancied getting a quick drink in the bar. That was our final scene together after all, and I think I'm going to miss your face."

I would love a drink right now. It isn't as though I have anything to look forward to at home. Ben has clearly decided to punish me in the most elaborate and inventive way. I find it hard to believe he came up with something like this all by himself. Now that I know he went to the police and told them some story about me attacking him, any concern I felt has unraveled into hate, but he surely can't plan on keeping this up forever. Faced with the facts that have stacked themselves higher than misremembered truths, and although I'm sure it's the wrong decision, I *do* want a drink.

"Yes, that sounds nice, I'll just grab my bag."

"Great, you might want to change first, too, *mon amie*."

I follow Jack's gaze down my body and realize I'm still wearing the silk nightie that wardrobe dressed me in earlier. I can't believe I spoke to the police looking like this. Everything is covered up, but I'm completely naked underneath. I can see the outline of my nipples through the thin pink material.

"Are you sure you're okay? You know you can trust me, don't you?" The kindness in his voice pierces my emotional armor and my eyes fill with tears. "Shit, I'm sorry, I didn't mean to make you cry." He wraps one arm around my waist and pulls me close. I just stand there, not knowing what to do at first without a script and stage directions. He wipes my tears away, then kisses my forehead. It feels a little fake, but that's the problem with actors, they never know when to stop. I do start to relax, though, resting my head on his shoulder and closing my eyes, while he strokes my hair. I breathe in the smell of him, and when he pulls me closer still, I don't resist. I enjoy the feel of his body next to mine, picture his chest beneath his shirt, imagine taking it off. I can hear his heart beating almost as fast as my own.

"If you want to wear a sexy see-through nightie to the bar, then you go ahead, there's really no need to cry about it, I won't try to stop you."

I laugh. Jack is one of those men who thinks you can heal any hurt with humor.

"Or I can help you slip out of it?"

I presume he is still joking, so I step behind the screen to change into something a little less revealing. Then I quickly wipe all the tearstained makeup from my face, while Jack plays with his phone. He's concentrating so hard I wonder what on earth he can be doing; checking his Twitter account no doubt.

We walk along the corridor to the Club Bar at Pinewood, attracting stares from everyone we pass along the way. The bar is sometimes used as a set, but the rest of the time anyone can drink here, a good example of life imitating art and making a healthy profit. The place is busy, but the manager asks two other people to move, freeing a table for us to sit down at. It's the sort of thing that I hate, but I'm too tired to stand so I go along with the suggestion. Besides, it's Jack they are being asked to move for, not me. He is most definitely A-list, *everyone* says hello to him and smiles in his direction. It's like walking into a bar with a tall Tom Cruise, and I'm only too happy to hide in his shadow.

"You don't have to talk about it with me if you don't want to, but I'm here for you if you do," he says once we've chosen a bottle of wine. Everyone else has to order at the bar, but not Jack.

"Ben is still missing."

He frowns at me. "So why are the police coming here and not out looking for him?"

"Because they think I had something to do with it."

It feels good to say it out loud. Less terrifying somehow.

He stares at me for a little while, then tilts his head right back and laughs. His face turns red and he holds his chest as though the laughter is causing him too much pain.

"Shh, it's not funny," I whisper. But his reaction has made me smile for the first time in days.

"I'm sorry, I can't help it. I know you play a proper badass onscreen, but anyone who knows you in real life knows that you could never hurt anyone."

I guess I must be a better actress than I give myself credit for.

"I'm sure it's all just a misunderstanding, he'll turn up tomorrow. I frequently didn't come home without telling my wife where I was; perhaps that's why I'm no longer married. Besides, he's a journalist isn't he, your chap? He's probably pissed in a bar somewhere, isn't that what they do?"

"Yes, maybe you're right," I say, knowing he's wrong.

"Bien sûr, je suis très intelligent!"

"What's with all the random French?"

"I'm trying to impress a certain little lady I know. Do you think I'm getting any better?" I shake my head. *"Merde."*

Jack excuses himself and disappears to the men's room, leaving me sitting alone with my thoughts and fears. It's clear to me now that

Ben has set me up, to punish me for something I didn't even do. That's what this is: revenge. Ben is just smarter than I am. He's read more and seen more. He understands the world in a way I never will, but I'm a better judge of character. That's something he always struggled with. I understand people and why they do the things they do. And I understand him. He's trying to hurt me by damaging the career he says destroyed our marriage.

I'm not going to let that happen.

Jack returns and promptly pours two more glasses of red wine. I notice that he fills mine considerably more than his own.

I take a sip. "Thank you for this. I'm sure you're right, everything will be okay."

"Course I'm right," he says. "You wouldn't hurt a fly."

Twenty-two

I swat the fly on the TV screen with the rolled-up newspaper, just like Maggie taught me, pleased with myself that I got it first time.

I've got used to the little back room where I sit when the betting shop is open. I know all the cracks in the walls, and the marks on the desk, and I know to remember to wear a coat every morning, even though I sit inside all day, because the radiator is broken and it is cold. It's someone else's coat that I wear; it has her name sewn inside in case I forget. But it's mine now. My name, my coat.

I spend my time reading, watching TV, or listening to the Story Teller tapes on my Fisher-Price cassette player. When I run out of other people's stories to read, watch, or listen to, I make up my own about a little girl who lived in Ireland. I tell myself the story of me so that I don't forget. I whisper it so that nobody else can hear, and enjoy seeing little puffs of my own breath when the words sneak out of my mouth. Sometimes I pretend that I am a baby dragon, and that one day I'll learn how to fly away home and burn down anyone who was ever mean to me.

The shop is noisy and loud. I hear the sound of the horse races all day long, and the men who watch them shout things like, "Go on!" really loudly at the TV screens out there, as though the horses can hear them, which is silly because they can't. Sometimes I look through the stripy plastic curtain that hangs between the shop counter and the phone room, and I see them, the customers. They all look sort of the same to me, wearing blue jeans and mean faces, from what I can see through the fog of their cigarette smoke.

I know when the shop has closed because the noise stops and everything is quiet again, except for the sound of John's adding machine going clickety-click. I think he must like maths because he uses it a lot. He comes into the little back room, pretends to like a picture I have drawn, then opens the back door.

"See you later, alligator," he says, his gold tooth shining at me.

"In a while, crocodile," I reply, because he likes it when I say that. I've seen pictures of alligators and crocodiles and they look awfully alike. I don't understand why people are always pretending that things are different when they are the same. A name doesn't change what a thing is, it's just a name.

"I think it's about time you started earning your keep, Baby Girl, come with me," says Maggie, locking the door behind John and walking back out to the shop. I'm guessing it's just me and her tonight. John goes out sometimes and doesn't come home. I'm not sure where he goes, but it makes Maggie sad and cross at the same time. She calls it his "disappearing act," and for a while I wondered if John might be a secret magician.

The shop is a mess. The big black leather stools are all over the place, and there are betting slips and cigarette butts and chocolate-bar wrappers all over the floor.

There is also a broom.

"I want you to sweep all this up, put the stools back against the walls, then, when you're done, come and get me," Maggie says, and walks through the open metal door that leads upstairs to the flat. I hear the television turn on up there, then the sound of the TV show she likes so much where they all speak like John: *EastEnders*.

I start with the stools; they are taller than me and very heavy. I push them back against the walls where they are supposed to be, and they make a horrid scraping sound against the tiles. When that's done, I pick up the broom, pretend to fly around the shop on it like a witch, then start to make little piles of rubbish. I don't know how to make the piles go inside the black bin bag Maggie left behind, so I use my hands. When I am finished, they are dirty and sticky. I stand at the bottom of the big stairs and call her name several times.

"Maggie!" I yell on the third try, but she still doesn't reply. I'm tired and hungry. I think we're having spaghetti hoops on toast tonight; we normally have something on toast for dinner. It can be beans or cheese or eggs, but whatever it is, we eat it on toast. Maggie says toast goes with everything. I think of something and try calling her again. "Mum!"

"Yes, Baby Girl?" She appears at the top of the stairs as if by magic.

"I've finished sweeping."

She comes down and looks around at the shop floor, nodding. "You did good. Are you hungry?" I nod. "Would you like McDonald's?" I nod again, twice as fast. McDonald's is what she buys me when her face is happy. McDonald's is way better than anything on toast. It comes in a box with a toy and I like it a lot.

"Well then, just you wait there." She walks to the back of the shop, through the door that leads behind the glass counter, and out back behind the phone room where I can't see. I hear the sound of water, then she comes back with a mop and bucket; it's steaming and has bubbles like a minibath. "I want you to mop this whole floor, including the customer toilet, and I'm going to go and get you a Happy Meal. You just do it like this." She drops the mop into the bucket, then lifts and twists it, squeezing out almost all of the water, before sliding it backwards and forwards across the floor. She puts the mop in my hand and walks to the front of the shop. Then she takes out the enormous set of keys that she carries everywhere, unlocks the door, and slams it shut behind her. I have never been through that door, I don't even know what's out there. I haven't been outside at all since I first arrived. I wait for a little while after Maggie has left before looking through the letter box. I can see a row of houses, a road, an old man with white hair walking his dog, and a bus stop. I wonder if I caught a bus from there whether it might take me all the way home.

I start to mop the floor. It's pretty big and dirty so it takes a long time, and the bucket is too heavy for me to lift, so I have to keep stopping to push it around with both hands. I have never been inside the customer toilet before. It smells bad, so I stay standing in the doorway. The toilet seat is up, there are lots of yellow and brown stains on the inside of the white bowl, and little puddles on the floor. I don't want to go in there wearing my favorite socks, so I just mop everywhere else instead.

I hear the door at the front of the shop and think Maggie has come back with the McDonald's. But it isn't Maggie.

"Hello, little girl, what's your name then?" says the old man. He's the one I saw when I peeked out the letter box earlier. He has a white beard like Father Christmas and a dog, so I think he must be nice.

"Ciara." It sounds strange to hear the sound of my real name inside my ears again. I bend down to stroke the ball of fur next to him. It's a little brown-and-white thing, with big eyes and a waggy tail. I think he looks like Toto from *The Wizard of Oz*.

"You'll have to speak up, child. My ears aren't what they used to be."

"My name is Ciara," I say a little louder, distracted with rubbing the dog's tummy. I think he likes it.

"That's a very pretty name."

"We're closed," says Maggie.

I look up and see her standing right behind the old man. She is holding the McDonald's Happy Meal, but she does not look happy.

"Oh, I'm sorry, my mistake." He shuffles back out of the shop, as though his feet are very heavy.

Maggie closes the door behind him, locks it, then turns and hits me hard across the face.

"Your. Name. Is. Aimee." She looks around at the shop floor. It's all wet, I haven't missed any. She walks towards the back of the shop, her shoes leaving a line of dirty footprints behind her, then she stops outside the customer toilet, looking inside. I know I'm going to be in even more trouble, I'm just not sure how much. She comes out of there so fast, it's as though she is flying. With my Happy Meal in one hand, she pinches the top of my arm with her other, then drags me across the wet floor, my socks slipping and sliding all over the place.

"I told you that your name is Aimee, and I told you to mop this floor. Did you mop this floor, Baby Girl?" She points inside the customer toilet.

I look at the sticky yellow puddles. "Yes," I lie, already wishing that I hadn't.

"You did? Oh, well, that's all right then. It really looked like you didn't, but you wouldn't lie to me, would you? Not after everything I've done for you, putting food in your belly and clothes on your back when your daddy didn't want you anymore?"

I wish she'd stop saying that about my daddy.

"No," I whisper, and shake my head, thinking maybe she doesn't know that I lied and can't see the puddles and dirt.

She tips my Happy Meal all over the floor of the customer toilet, then mushes it and slides it around with the heel of her shoe, until all the french fries are flat and all the chicken nuggets are broken.

"Eat it."

I don't move.

"Eat. It," she says again, louder this time.

I pick up half a chip, the one farthest from the toilet, and put it in my mouth.

"All of it." She folds her arms. "There are only three rules we follow under this roof. I keep telling you what they are, but seems to me you keep forgetting. What is rule number one?"

I make myself swallow the chip. "We work hard."

"Keep eating. Why do we work hard, Aimee?"

I feel scared and sick, but I pick up a tiny corner of a mushed chicken nugget. "Because life doesn't owe us anything."

"That's right. Rule number two?"

"We don't trust other people."

"Correct. Because other people can't be trusted, no matter how *nice* they might pretend to be. Rule number three?"

"We don't lie to each other."

"How many of the three rules did you break tonight?"

"All of them," I mumble.

"I can't hear you."

"All of them."

"Yes, you did. I need you to learn a lesson, and it has to be a hard one, Baby Girl, because I need you to remember, and I need you to grow up. So, you're going to eat all of your dinner off of this floor, no matter how long it takes, and then I hope you'll never lie to me again."

Twenty-three

London, 2017

"I really should eat something if we're going to have another bottle," I say. Jack appears to have ordered a second while I was in the bathroom.

"Nonsense, that will only make it more difficult for me to get you drunk and have my wicked way with you. It's what I do with all my leading ladies on the last day of the shoot, haven't you heard? It's probably written in your contract somewhere, you really should read those things." He tops up my glass.

There is a reason why Jack drinks. He hides it well, but I know his divorce earlier this year hurt him far more than he lets on. I never ask about it because I know he's like me: he's careful about which version of himself he lets others see. Some people don't believe they deserve to be happy. We are only and always what we ourselves believe.

I give up resisting temptation and take another sip from my glass, glancing around the bar. It's even busier now, standing room only, with more and more people coming here to relax and unwind after a long day of filming. Some faces I recognize, most I don't, and when I see all the eyes staring in our direction, my shyness stings a little.

"You were great today," Jack says. "The way you just turned on the tears was amazing, no eye drops or anything . . . how do you do that?"

I just think of something really sad.

I listen to Jack as he moves on to his favorite subject: himself, and continue to scan the bar from time to time while he talks. That's when I see Alicia White. She glides in like a robotic swan, her long pale neck twisting out of a tight-fitting red dress in search of prey. I watch, transfixed, as she moves back and forth like a powerful Hoover, sucking up all the attention and any crumbs of praise in her path. I remember the lipstick, but dismiss the idea of her being involved with my husband, she's out of his league. I almost didn't recognize her; she's dyed her blond hair dark brown, so that she looks a lot like me, albeit a much prettier version. I look away too late, she's already spotted us.

"Jack, darling," she purrs, interrupting him mid-monologue.

He leaps to his feet and embraces her, kissing both her cheeks and staring down at her cleavage briefly before making eye contact. "Alicia, how gorgeous to see you, *tu es très jolie ce soir*." He allows himself another virtual drink of her body. My secondary-school French translates the compliment, but she looks a tad confused. "Let me introduce you to Aimee. We've been working on a film together, and she's the next big thing, you heard it here first."

Her face falters for just a second; she didn't like hearing that. I wonder if Jack is learning French to try to impress Alicia somehow, and the idea of it hurts me a little.

"We know each other actually," she says. The words are neatly unpacked, cool and crisp. "Aimee is like my little shadow. She followed me from senior school to drama school, and then a few years later got the same agent. You know Tony, don't you, Jack?"

"Best agent in town."

"Exactly, so imagine my surprise when little Aimee Sinclair's name popped up right next to mine on his client list? Some might say she's stalking me!"

Alicia throws her head back and they both laugh. I don't, but I do manage a small smile. It hurts my face.

"What was the part you've just finished playing?" she asks me, as though she doesn't already know. Her hair and makeup are perfect, as usual, and I now regret coming to the bar without any armor. Her bright red lips form a well-practiced pout in anticipation.

"It was the lead in a film called *Sometimes I Kill*, we finished filming today." I notice the way her mouth twitches when I say the word *lead*.

"*Sometimes I Kill,*" she says, lifting her manicured fingers to her perfect chin in an exaggerated thinking pose.

Did I mention she can't act for shit?

"*Sometimes I Kill,*" she repeats. "Oh, yes, I do remember now. Tony sent me that script, he said that I was the director's first choice, but I turned it down. It wasn't the right role for *me,* but I'm sure it was just perfect for *you.* At this early and *uncertain* stage in your career, I imagine you can't be too picky. In fact, I suppose it's rather lucky for you that I did say no—that meant dearest Tony could send them your headshot instead."

"I suppose I should be thanking you?"

"I suppose you should!" She beams at me, either not understanding irony or choosing to ignore it. Then her face exchanges the smile for a frown, and she puts her icy-cold hand on mine. "I'm sure you've heard the rumors about Tony slimming down his client list?" My eyes must answer for me, because she can tell from my face that I haven't and looks delighted. "I just hope, for your sake, he doesn't adopt a 'last in, first out' policy. It would be dreadful for your career if he dropped you now." I zone out for a moment, remembering that Tony said we needed to talk, but hasn't returned any of my calls since. I keep my concerns to myself.

Alicia joins us and I drink more wine than I should. I listen to the two of them gossip about directors, producers, and fellow actors, while silently worrying that my agent is about to dump me. Jack's eyes are smiling and wide open, but he can't seem to see her for who and what she is. Alicia isn't just two-faced, it's more complicated than that; she has several sides, all equally self-beneficial. She's like a loaded dice, but most people don't know when they're being played. She spends the whole time constantly looking over Jack's shoulder, to see if someone more famous is in the room for her to pounce on. Last I heard she was taking a break from acting for a little while, so it seems odd to find her here at Pinewood.

I admire her false eyelashes, which flutter with every false word, and stare in amazement as each tiny synthetic hair transforms into the shape of a letter. A paper chain of miniature black words start to stream from her eyes, her nose, the corners of her mouth, until her whole face is covered in a tattoo of little black lies. I know I am imagining this, and I consider the possibility I might have had too much to drink. She smiles and I notice a tiny bit of red lipstick has made itself at home on her white teeth; the sight of it brings me untold happiness, so I take another big sip of my wine in celebration.

When the bottle is empty, I order another, topping up my glass as soon as it arrives. I look at the way Jack is staring at Alicia and wish she would just *go away*, I want him to look at me like that. Only me. The thought generates a moment of guilt; I am still married, but then I remember what Ben is doing to me now, and what he has done to me in the past. The lipstick under our bed didn't get there by itself, and he couldn't have come up with a plan this elaborate on his own either.

Who is she? Who is helping my husband try to destroy me? When I find out, I'll destroy them both.

I am most definitely drunk.

Alicia stands to leave and I can smell her perfume as she kisses the air on either side of my cheeks. Her scent is too strong, overpowering and sickly, just like the woman wearing it. I slur my words when I try to say goodbye. It's just Jack and me now, he's finally looking back in my direction, and ready or not I know what I want.

Twenty-four

Essex, 1988

"I still don't know if she's ready for this," says Maggie.

"She's ready," John replies. "All she's got to do is walk and hold my hand, it ain't difficult."

I think maybe they are going to have a fight. They fight a lot, and it makes me wonder if my real mummy and daddy fought a lot, too, before she died. Maybe that's just what grown-ups do: shout loud words at each other that have nothing to do with what they are really cross about.

"Would you rather something happened to *me*?" asks John. "I'm starting to wonder who you care more about? Me, or a child who isn't even really ours?"

I hear the sound Maggie's hand makes when it hits a cheek. I know the sound because sometimes it's my cheek that it's hitting. Then I hear the sound of John's big leather boots coming towards my bedroom and the door bursts open. He grabs my wrist and pulls me into the hall. I only see Maggie for a second as we fly past their bedroom; I've never seen her cry before.

I trip on the stairs a couple of times on the way down, but John holds me up by one arm until my feet make contact with the wood again. When we get to the bottom, I think we are going to turn right through the metal door that leads into the betting shop, but we don't do that. John bends down until his face is right in front of mine. His breath smells strange, and when he speaks, little bits of his spit land on my nose and cheeks.

"You stay with me the whole time. You hold my hand. You don't do anything or say anything to anyone, or I'll whip your arse so good you won't be able to sit down for a week. Anyone says anything to you, you just smile. I'm your dad, and you and me are just going for a walk. You understand?"

I don't understand most of what he just said, but I forget to answer because I'm watching him chew. He's been chewing gum instead of smoking cigarettes, and I think maybe he should just smoke because chewing gum makes him cranky.

"Hello, is anybody home?" He knocks on my head as though it were a door. It hurts when he does this, and I wish that he wouldn't. "Put your shoes on."

I haven't worn them since I first arrived, and it takes me a little while to remember what to do. I think my feet must have grown too, because my shoes are awfully tight now. John shakes his head as though I've done something else wrong, but then he opens the big front door that I came through the night I arrived, and I realize that we are going *outside*.

There are houses and trees and grass and sunshine, there is so much to see, but we are walking so fast along the road that everything rushes by in a blur, like a painting. John walks so quickly I have to run to keep up. He's holding me tight with one hand, and holding a black-and-red bag with the word HEAD written on it in the other.

He only lets go of my hand when we are inside the bank. I know it's a bank because it looks like one, and because it said so on the sign out front. I spend so much time reading now that I think I'm pretty good at it. The counter is almost exactly like the one in the betting shop, with glass between us and the woman behind it. I'm not tall enough to see her, but I can hear her voice through the holes in the screen. I decide that she sounds pretty and wonder if she is.

John unzips the bag and starts taking out bundles of money, then he puts it on the counter. The woman I can't see slides a drawer so that she can empty it, then she slides it back and they do it all over again. There is a lot of money, so it takes a long time. First there are bundles of notes tied with thick rubber bands, then he takes out lots of different-colored mini plastic bags with coins. The green ones have ten-pence and twenty-pence coins inside, yellow is for fifty-pence, and pink is for pounds. There are a lot of pink bags. When the big bag that says HEAD is empty, John thanks the woman behind the counter and asks if he can take her for a drink sometime. I guess she must look thirsty.

He holds my hand less tight on the way back to the betting shop. I walk as slowly as I can because I like being outside. I like seeing the sky and the trees again, and feeling the sun on my cheeks. I like the sound of the man standing outside the fruit-and-vegetable shop saying, "Ten plums for a pound," and the way the little green man made of light, inside a black box, tells you when it is safe to cross the road. John says we don't have time to wait for him on the way back, so we cross even though it is the red man's turn to shine.

"You've been a good girl and I think you deserve a treat," says John when we are almost back where we started. I don't reply because he says the word *treat* just like Maggie says the word *surprise,* so I think it might not be a good thing after all.

John calls the little row of shops where we live a "parade." I'm not sure why. A parade at home is colorful and loud with lots of people in costumes marching down the main road. A parade here seems very quiet. There are five shops in a row: a greengrocer (which is a person who sells fruit and vegetables, he is not actually green), a video shop, our betting shop, a place where people wash their clothes, and then a little shop on the corner, I'm not sure what it sells. From what I can see in the window, it looks like it might sell everything.

A bell rings when the door opens, and I see a woman with dark skin sitting behind a till. I have only ever seen people with dark skin on the television. She has a red dot on her forehead, and I think she is the most beautiful person I have ever seen.

"Close your mouth, Aimee, we are not a codfish," says John, and I laugh because it's something Mary Poppins says and it is like a little joke between him and me. *Mary Poppins* is a film that John recorded for me onto something called a VHS at Christmas. I like to watch it over and over again. "Hurry up and choose something, before I change my mind."

I stand and stare at rows and rows of sweets and crisps. I've never seen so many and I've only had Tayto's before. I don't know what any of these are, so I don't know what to pick.

"How about some Monster Munch? Maybe some Hula Hoops for Maggie, and a big bar of Dairy Milk for us all to share?" he says when I can't decide.

We walk to the till and John takes some money out of his pocket to pay the beautiful lady. She gives him his change and he gives me a ten-pence coin.

"She'll have the ten-p mix please," he says, and lifts me up so that I can see behind the counter. There are jars and jars full of sweets in every color and shape you can imagine. "You just point to a jar, sweetheart, and the nice lady will put one of the sweets in a paper bag for you. Choose ten."

I do as he says, pointing at the jars that look the prettiest, and when the pink-and-white-striped bag is full, she gives it to me. I want to touch her skin to see if it feels the same as mine, but she thinks I want to shake her hand, so we do that instead.

"It's good to meet you. What's your name?" Her voice sounds like a song, and her hand feels soft and warm.

"My name is Aimee."

"Good girl," says John, and I can tell that he means it, and that I said the right name.

We are happy when we leave the shop. John smiles at me and I smile too, even though I can see his gold tooth. We are almost back at the flat and I don't want to go inside again.

"John?"

"Dad."

"Dad, what happened to the little girl in the picture in the front room?" I don't know what made me think of her. I guess I wondered whether John bought her sweets too.

"She disappeared." He walks a little faster, so that I have to run again to keep up.

"Disappeared?"

"That's right, Pipsqueak. She disappeared, but now she's come back and she's you."

I'm not sure what he means. Surely only I can be me.

The high street was full of people and noise, but it's quiet here on the parade, as though John and I are the only people out for a walk. We're just a few steps from the betting shop when there is a loud screeching sound in the road, and a car, and lots of shouting. Everything happens too quickly, like when we press fast-forward on the VHS machine. Three men, all dressed in black, are all wearing scary-looking woolly masks that cover their whole faces, like giant black socks with holes for eyes.

"Give me the bag," the tallest one says. I think he means my bag of sweets, so I drop it on the pavement. But he isn't talking to me, he's talking to John and he is pointing something at him. It looks like the gun the hunter has in *Bugs Bunny*, but shorter, like someone has cut the end off.

"I don't have any money, I'm on the way *back* from the bank, you fuckin' idiots."

One of the other men punches John in the stomach and he bends over and coughs.

"Last. Fuckin'. Chance," says the man with the gun.

I run, I want Maggie.

"Stay where you are, you little runt," says the third man, grabbing my hair and pulling me backwards.

"Don't hurt the girl! The bag is empty, take it, see for yourself."

The man with the gun hits John hard in the face with it, so that he falls down onto the pavement.

Then I hear a loud bang.

When I open my eyes, I can see that it wasn't the man with the gun who made the sound, it was Maggie. She is standing outside the betting shop with a gun of her own, and she's got her angry face on. She looks madder than I have ever seen her.

"Let the girl go, get back in your car, and drive away now. Or I will end you all."

The man holding me smirks, and she shoots the gun in our direction. I fall on the pavement and feel strange. Maggie is right there in front of me, I can see that her lips are moving, but at first I can't hear what they are saying. It's as if someone is ringing a bell inside my head. She's looking at something behind me, and I turn to see what it is. The three bad men are back in their car, and we watch as they drive away. I don't think she shot the one who was holding me. I think maybe she missed on purpose. She strokes my hair, and my right ear decides to start hearing things again.

"You're okay now, Baby Girl, you're safe." She holds me and I hold her back for the first time, because even though she hurts me, I know she won't let anyone else. She picks me up. I wrap my arms around her neck, and my legs around her waist, and I only start to cry when I see that all the sweets that were in my ten-p paper bag have fallen out onto the pavement.

Twenty-five

London, 2017

I wake up to the sound of someone trying to get into my bedroom.

The room is pitch-black when I open my eyes, and at first the sound is so faint that I think maybe I'm imagining it. But as I blink and adjust to the least dark shadows masquerading as light, I start to see things, things I don't want to. My ears pinpoint the sound and my eyes focus all of their attention on the handle of my bedroom door. As it slowly starts to turn, I already know that something very bad is behind it.

My heart is thudding inside my ears as well as my chest, I want to scream, but I can't seem to move or make a sound, my body rendered stationary with fear and dread.

The handle twists all the way, but the door won't open. The bolts I had fitted on the inside see to that, and I experience a brief remission of relief before the terror returns, spreading even faster than before through my rigid body. The sound of someone repeatedly kicking the door reverberates around the room. It shudders several times, then flies open, rebounding against the wall. Before I have time to reach for something to protect myself with, he's on me.

It's dark, but I can see who it is.

I can't move, I don't even try to.

His hands are around my neck, he's squeezing, too tight.

"They'll see the bruises," I try to whisper. My croaky words are heard and acknowledged. He loosens his grip, then he starts to hurt me on the inside instead, where the bruises can't be seen.

I let him do what he wants to me. I don't react, I don't make a sound. I've tried to fight him off before, and it never ends well. This is not the first time, but it's already the worst. I know he planned it; he's only this hard and it only lasts this long when he takes a little blue pill. He stops. I hear him remove his condom and drop it to the floor; he doesn't need it for what comes next; nobody ever got pregnant from doing it that way.

He flips me over, as though I were a doll, so that I am facedown. I close my eyes, vacate my body, and wonder whether the rest of the world would still call it rape if they knew it was my husband who did it to me.

He's always sorry afterwards.

I know why he hurts me like this, but I don't know how to make him stop. He thinks I don't love him anymore, but I do. It's as though he is trying to prove that he still owns me. But he doesn't. He never did. Only I own me.

He climbs off. I hear him walk to the bathroom and flush the used condom down the toilet. I think it is over, but then I hear him come back to the bed, take the belt from his discarded trousers, and I understand that it is going to be one of those nights. I lie perfectly still, facedown, exactly how he left me, used and discarded. He starts to hit me with the belt, in the places he knows that nobody else will see. My husband has always insisted on reading my scripts, not because he cares, but because with each new role I play, he wants to know which pieces of me the world will get to see, and which parts of me will stay only his. He hits me again and I try not to give him the satisfaction of crying, no matter how much it hurts.

Twenty-six

London, 2017

I'm woken by a sound I can't translate.

I sit up in the bed, coated in my own sweat. I'm panting and shaking and crying because I know that what I have just experienced was a dream of a memory, rather than a memory of a dream. I remember how badly Ben hurt me the last time I saw him. I remember how he followed me back from the restaurant after I said I wanted a divorce, kicked the bedroom door open, and did what he did.

I didn't even ask him to stop.

I think on some level, I thought I deserved it.

We marry our own reflections; someone who is the opposite of ourselves, but who we see as the same. If he is a monster, then what does that make me?

It wasn't the first time, but I promised myself that night that it would be the last, and that I would never let him hurt me like that again. I always keep my promises, especially the ones I make to myself.

What if I did do something to him that I can't remember?

I didn't. I'm sure of it. Almost completely.

An uncharted corner of my consciousness uncurls like a treasure map, and I start to think there might be buried memories inside my head after all. Maybe when you've seen men do things they shouldn't as a child, it can be harder as an adult to fully comprehend how wrong those things are. We are all conditioned and fine-tuned to our own unique brand of normal; we wear it like a fingerprint. We're taught to fit in with others and learn what is expected of us from the moment we are born. Everything we ever do is an act.

I was foolish to marry someone so quickly, without really knowing who he was. I thought I knew, but I was wrong. I was seduced by our whirlwind romance, and I thought I might lose him if I said no. I thought we were the same. I thought he was my mirror, until I looked properly and realized too late that I needed to run from what I saw. I spent month after month dipping into my savings of happier memories, until the account was empty. I thought I could change him. If we had had a child, I think things might have been different, but he wouldn't give me what I wanted, so in revenge I took away what he desired most: me. I withheld my affection, my love, my body, thinking he would change his mind. I didn't realize he was the sort of man who would take what he wanted anyway, regardless of whether it was given to him.

I hear something again, footsteps in the distance, the sound pulling me back into the present. I try to sit up, but the pain in my head disables me. I open my eyes a fraction, just enough to establish where and when I am, but the light is too bright, so I close them again.

I do not feel good.

I remember being in the bar at Pinewood with Jack. I remember Alicia White joining us. I vaguely remember a third bottle of wine and then my memory of the evening stops.

Where am I?

I force my eyes to open and relax a little when I see the familiar sight of my own bedroom. So, I made it home, that's something at least. My throat hurts and I notice the foul taste inside my mouth; I've been sick. I'm such an idiot, I know I can't drink that much on an empty stomach. I don't know what I was thinking. I guess I wasn't. I hope I didn't embarrass myself before I left, and I hope I got a taxi, there's no way I would have been able to drive.

I can't remember what happened.

I try so hard to fill in the gaps, but there's nothing there. The detective's suggestion—that I have a condition which makes me forget traumatic experiences—comes back to haunt me. If I can't remember last night, what if I can't remember what really happened to Ben too? But I dismiss that thought; this has nothing to do with amnesia, just alcohol.

How did I get home?

I hear something again, and this time I pay attention.

There is someone downstairs.

My first instinct is that it must be Ben, but then the rest of my memories start to slot into place and I remember what has happened. I remember the photo Detective Croft showed me yesterday of Ben's face bloodied and bruised, and I remember that she accused me of being responsible.

I hear another sound down below. Quiet footsteps.

Either my missing husband has returned, or someone else is creeping around downstairs, someone who shouldn't be.

The penny doesn't just drop, it nose-dives, and I'm convinced it's *her,* the stalker.

Having a stalker is neither glamorous nor exciting; it can be horrific.

When the postcards started being hand-delivered to our home, that fear became a living thing that followed me around during the day, and when Ben said he started seeing a woman hanging around outside the house, I stopped being able to sleep during the night. When I saw her myself, I thought I'd seen a ghost.

I know who you are.

The message was always the same, and so was the signature: *Maggie.*

Ben and I hadn't been together long when it started. A few profile pieces about me had appeared in the papers for the first time, with my picture, and previews about the film I had been cast in, so I guess you could describe her as a fan. Nothing like that had ever happened to me before. The police didn't take it seriously, but I did. When Ben called me in L.A. to say someone had broken into our old home, I knew it was her and decided to do something about it.

I agreed to move to a house I had never seen, and I bought a gun.

Guns don't frighten me, people do.

I didn't tell Ben about it because I know his opinions on firearms, but Ben and I had very different lives growing up. He thinks he knows the world, but he hasn't seen what I've seen. I know what bad people are capable of. Besides, I'm good at shooting, I *enjoy* it, it's something I've done for years to help me relax. I was still a child when I held my first gun. There's nothing illegal about it: I have a license and I belong to a club in the countryside. Not that I get much time to practice now.

I feel beneath the bed, where I normally keep it.

It isn't there.

The thoughts and fears colliding inside my throbbing head stop when I hear the sound of footsteps coming up the stairs towards the bedroom. I reach down again, my fingers desperately feeling beneath the wooden bed frame for my gun, but it's gone.

Someone is right outside the door.

I try to scream, but when I open my mouth, no sound comes out.

I see the door handle start to slowly twist and experience a sickening sense of déjà vu.

I could hide, but I'm too scared to move.

The door opens and I'm completely shocked by what I see.

Twenty-seven

Essex, 1988

I've tried to go to sleep, like Maggie told me to, but every time I close my eyes I can see the three bad men with woolly masks and shouty voices outside the shop.

I didn't know Maggie had a gun.

I thought only bad people had things like that.

My ears still feel funny, as though tiny bell ringers have moved inside my head. I've thought about it, a lot, and I'm sure she missed the bad man on purpose, that she just wanted to warn him or something. I pull the duvet up over my head; it feels safer under here. It's warm too, but I still can't stop shivering.

Maggie and John have been arguing a lot tonight, even more than normal. They are still at it now, but they're doing the quiet kind of shouting that they think I can't hear, their words hissing like snakes. I need the toilet, but I'm too scared to walk past their bedroom to get there. I'm also scared of wetting the bed if I don't go. I get up and creep over to my bedroom door, the pink carpet soft beneath my toes. I put my ear right up against the bare wood, to see if I can hear what they are saying.

"I told you we should have found a shop further out," Maggie says.

"And I told you it wouldn't have made no difference. What kind of men pull a stunt like that in front of a child anyway?" says John.

"Exactly the kind of men we're dealing with. I asked you not to take Aimee, you put her in danger."

"Well, I didn't take *Aimee*, did I? How could I have? *Aimee* is dead."

I hear something smash.

I'm not dead.

I climb back into the bed and hide under the duvet again. Seconds later my bedroom door opens and I hold my breath. In my head this makes me invisible.

Invisible, but not dead.

I hear someone walk closer to the bed and I hope that it is Maggie, not John. He comes into my room sometimes at night. I think he must be worried about me being too hot or something because he always takes the duvet off the bed. He does it slowly and quietly, as though he is trying not to wake me, so I pretend to still be asleep, even when I'm not. Sometimes I hear his Polaroid camera and wonder what he is taking pictures of in the dark. Sometimes I hear other things.

Somebody pulls the covers back, then gets in beside me. She puts her arm around my tummy and kisses my head; I know that it is Maggie because I can smell her perfume. She calls it "number five" and it smells nice, but I always wonder what the other numbers smell like. Maggie is squeezing me awful tight, so that it hurts a little bit, but I don't say anything. She is crying, and the back of my neck is soon wet with her tears.

"Don't you worry, Baby Girl. Nobody is ever going to hurt you, not while I'm alive."

I think she says this to make me feel better, but it makes me feel worse. My first mummy died the day I was born. Maggie could die anytime and then I'd be all alone. She stops crying after a while and goes to sleep, but I don't. I can't. I know she is sleeping because small snoring sounds come out of her mouth and into my ears, playing a little tune with the tiny bells that are still ringing. I try to sleep too, but all I can think about is Maggie dying, those three bad men coming back to the shop, and nobody being here to save me.

Twenty-eight

London, 2017

"Don't worry, this will save you." Jack walks into my bedroom with two steaming mugs of what looks like coffee.

"What are you doing here?" I pull the duvet up around me.

"Well, that's gratitude for you! I was just going to put you in a taxi last night, but I wasn't sure you'd make it, and I was right. You puked on the journey home. Twice. And that was just the beginning. I thought you said you could drink? I stayed the night to make sure you didn't choke on your own vomit. I think the words you are probably looking for right now are *thank you*."

"Thank you," I say after a little while, processing everything he has just said, unsure whether his words fit the gaps that the holes in my memory have left behind. I take the coffee, it's too hot, but it's strong and I gulp it down. I look at the pajamas I'm wearing, wondering how I got into them if I was as out of it as he's suggesting. It's as though he reads my mind.

"I helped get you out of your dress, mainly because you'd been sick all down the front of it just after you got out of the cab. I cleaned you up a bit and you got changed yourself. I didn't see anything I hadn't already seen on set, and I slept on the floor."

I look at where he is pointing and see a pillow and a blanket on the carpet. My cheeks are so hot I'm certain my face must have turned purple with embarrassment. I can't seem to find the right words to say, so I stick with the two that seem most appropriate given the circumstances.

"I'm sorry." As soon as the whisper of an apology escapes my lips, my eyes fill with tears. I just keep making endless mistakes and messing everything up, I don't know what's wrong with me.

"Hey, it's okay." Jack puts down his empty coffee mug and sits on the bed. "You're obviously going through a difficult time in your personal life right now after everything you said last night."

What on earth did I tell him?

"We've all been there, believe me. You'll be all right, I promise. It's lucky I knew where you lived. You were adamant about not telling the taxi driver or anyone else your address."

Having a stalker will do that to you.

My mind rewinds Jack's words and plays them again.

"How *did* you know where I live?"

His cheeks take their turn to redden, and I'm surprised to discover that Jack Anderson is capable of blushing.

"I live a couple of streets away from here, just a house I'm renting while we're filming at Pinewood. I've seen you running in the mornings. I've even said hi a couple of times, but it's like you're in your own little world, then you jog on past like we've never met."

I don't know what to say. I do tend to zone out, not even noticing the other runners that I pass, all chasing dreams they'll never catch. It seems a little strange that he would live so close and never mention it before now, but I remind myself that my husband is the bad guy in all this, not Jack and not me. I mustn't start getting paranoid.

I hear my mobile vibrate with a text. It's charging on Ben's side of the bed for some reason. I pick it up, reading the message before Jack reaches over, looking a little flustered and taking the phone from my hand.

"That's mine," he says. "Sorry, I was almost out of battery, so I borrowed your charger . . . I wasn't planning to spend the night."

That's the trouble with iPhones, they all look the same. I decide not to mention what I just read.

Call me later, Alicia xx

I had no idea that Jack and Alicia were close enough to be exchanging text messages. I tell myself that it's none of my business. I don't want to sound like some kind of jealous schoolgirl.

"Do you know where *my* phone is?" I ask.

"I'm not sure. You dropped your bag downstairs, you sort of collapsed when we got through the door. I had to carry you up to the bathroom . . ."

I stand up and everything hurts. I think I might be sick again.

"Whoa! Maybe you just stay where you are, I'll go get it," he says, and I notice that he takes his own phone with him, as though he doesn't trust me enough to leave it behind.

When he returns with my handbag, I'm relieved to find both my mobile and wallet inside; I was worried I might have lost them in that state. I turn on my phone and the screen lights up, a display of double-digit notifications on almost every app.

"That's weird—"

"Shit." Jack stares down at his own phone again.

"What is it?"

The wrinkles that fan his eyes disappear with his smile and seem to resurface on his now-furrowed brow. When he doesn't answer, I open Twitter. It's a fairly new account and I've never had so many notifications or DMs. To be fair, I don't engage with social media too often, but this is insane. I click on a link and it takes me to an article on the TBN website, written by Jennifer Jones. Beak Face.

LOVE ON AND OFF SET AT PINEWOOD STUDIOS

My eyes are drawn to the pictures before the words written beneath them, because they are of me. There's one of Jack and me in the bar last night. Another of us taken on set, simulating sex on a hotel desk. It looks real. The final one is of us in my dressing room. I'm wearing the silk nightdress from yesterday's shoot, which leaves absolutely nothing to the imagination, and Jack appears to be holding me tenderly and kissing the top of my head. I don't understand how someone could have taken this photo; we were the only two people in the room.

The words are even worse:

Jack Anderson left his wife soon after the filming of
Sometimes I Kill began. Aimee Sinclair is still married, but
didn't want to talk about her husband during the interview.
Now we know why.

I check my emails; there are hundreds. A lot of them from all
those people who used to be my friends. I scan through them without reading, stopping when I see my agent's name in among them.
The message is short, even by Tony's standards.

Aimee,
I think you should come in for a chat. Sooner the better.
Tony
x

I read the message twice. Due to the brevity, it doesn't take long.
It all makes sense now: his text the other day, the unreturned calls.
I digest his words, and having forced myself to swallow them down,
I am satisfied I have understood them correctly: my agent is going to
dump me and I am finished.

Twenty-nine

Essex, 1988

Today is Sunday.

It's the only day of the week when the betting shop isn't open, so we all stay in bed until lunchtime. We do this every Sunday, and I didn't used to like it, but I do now.

John takes me to the video shop next door on Friday afternoons, and we choose two films to rent all weekend. We always watch the first one together on Saturday night, in the front room. The Christmas tree is still up in the corner, even though it is February now. I thought that maybe it was bad luck, but Maggie says it is fine, so long as we don't turn the twinkly lights on. I think I believe her, because Maggie doesn't lie.

We eat curry on Saturday nights too, and I like eating something that isn't on toast. I'd never had curry before I lived here. It tastes wonderful and you don't even have to cook it yourself, somebody else does. The food comes all the way from India, which is a faraway place where everything is hot, including the food. It's still hot when John brings it home in a brown paper bag. It's called a takeaway because you take the food away and eat it at home.

We always watch the second VHS on Sunday mornings, in John and Maggie's bed with bacon sandwiches. Maggie calls them something else, which sounds like bacon buddies, but when I called them that for the first time, they both laughed. We all call them bacon buddies now, even though I know it is wrong.

John chooses one of the videos every week, and I choose the other. I don't think Maggie cares much; she reads newspapers and magazines most of the time while the films are on, and covers my eyes and ears for some bits when John chooses a film that says eighteen on the front. Sometimes she forgets and I see bad things, but I know they aren't real, so I don't get scared. Today we are eating bacon buddies and watching a film called *The NeverEnding Story*. It's the best film ever! We watched it last weekend too. I think we should watch it every Sunday, but Maggie said this might have to be the last time for a little while, which means a long while. For some reason, I start to think about what my Sundays were like before I came here. They were not like this.

"Why don't we go to church on Sundays?" I ask, still watching the film.

"Because God doesn't answer prayers from people like us," says John, lighting a cigarette. He's started smoking again since the bad men came. I'm a bit glad about that because it means he and Maggie argue a bit less.

"Shut up, John. Don't listen to him. Do you want to go to church, Baby Girl?"

I think about it before I answer. Sometimes her questions are tricks. "No, I don't think so." I'm still staring at the screen. It's nearly my favorite bit in the film, with a flying dog that is really a dragon. John seems bored, maybe because we've watched it before. I pretend not to see, but he keeps trying to touch and tickle Maggie. She tuts and slaps his hand away each time because I don't think she likes it when he does that. I know I don't like it when he does it to me.

When the film ends, I feel sad. Sometimes I wish I could stay inside the stories in films and books and live there instead. Maggie tells me to go to my room, close the door, and listen to one of my story cassette tapes, but I'm not ready to go from one story to the next yet. She thinks I don't hear the noises they make, but I do. It always sounds as if he is hurting her, and I don't like it. I hear Maggie use the bathroom afterwards and then she comes into my room and I hit Play on the tape machine, so that she thinks I was listening to it and not them the whole time. Her hair is sticking out all over the place and her cheeks are red.

"Put some proper clothes on, we're all going out," she says, then turns to leave.

"Out?"

"Yes, out. It's the opposite of in. Hurry up."

We leave a little while later through the back door. I have never been out the back door before, and when I step through it, I see lots of gray concrete, and fences that are too high to look over. There is a red car too, which I think I have seen before. Maggie pushes the front seat forward so that I can climb in the back, and when I do, it smells like a memory.

I'm not sure how long we drive; I can't stop staring out the windows. I think I had forgotten that there was more than just the shop and the parade. There are so many roads and houses and people, and the world seems very big all of a sudden. We stop at a pub, which is a place where people go when they are thirsty but don't want to drink at home. I know this because my real daddy liked to do that a lot.

Inside, Maggie and I sit down at a table, while John gets some drinks: a pint of Guinness for him, a Coke for her, and a lemonade for me. We drink in silence, and Maggie's face looks strange. I'm not sure what we are doing here, we have fizzy drinks at home. John says maybe we should go, but then two men come over and everyone except me hugs or shakes hands. One of the men rubs me on the head, messing up my hair, which had just been brushed.

"Remember me?" he says, with a smile that doesn't fit his face.

I do not remember him because we have never met, but he does remind me of someone.

"I'm your uncle Michael, and last time I saw you, you were just a baby girl."

"She's still my Baby Girl, aren't you, Aimee?" Maggie gives me that look that says, *Be quiet,* without her actually having to say the words.

His hair is orange, just like Rainbow Brite's, and he has small hands for a man. He is not my uncle, but then Maggie is not really my mum, and John is not really my dad. People here seem to like pretending to be someone they are not. The two men sound like Maggie, not John, and the way they speak reminds me of before, when my home was in Ireland. I think Michael must be Maggie's brother; they do look a lot alike with the same sort of lips and eyes.

They talk for a long time and I start to feel sleepy. Maggie tells me to stop fidgeting, but I can't help it. I'm bored, and I would have brought one of my *Story Teller* magazines if I'd known I would just have to sit still all afternoon.

"I'm telling you, the last three shops they went after all had Irish links. The feckin' eejits think we're IRA just because we speak with an accent," says Maggie.

"Keep your voice down." John sees me staring. "What you gawping at, Pipsqueak? Why don't you go play over there." I look where he is pointing and see three colorful tall machines standing in the corner, all with flashing lights and buttons. John puts his hand in the pocket of his jeans and gives me some coins, but I don't know what to do with them.

"She's too little, John. She doesn't understand." Maggie sucks through the straw in her empty glass, making a funny noise. She tells me off when I do that.

"Nonsense! She's bright as a button! Always got her head in a book, this one. Here, let me show you." John lifts me up. He carries me to the first machine, then drags a chair from an empty table and stands me on top of it, so that I can reach. He lifts my hand in his to push a button, which plays a tune. "This is Pac-Man and I think you're going to love it."

"She's turned into a proper little daddy's girl," says the man who says he is my uncle.

Everyone smiles, except Maggie.

Thirty

London, 2017

I shower and put on some clean clothes. I've taken a couple of paracetamol and I should be starting to feel better, but I don't. My agent is going to dump me. He didn't even reply to the email I sent, his assistant did, and only to say that Tony could squeeze me in an hour from now, giving me almost no time at all to get ready. This latest invasion of reality into the fictitious happy life I had curated for myself was unexpected. I don't have sufficient defenses left to stop, or even subdue, the attack of anxiety that follows. I've only just got the life I thought I wanted; I can't possibly lose it now.

"Your agent probably just wants to have a chat, like his email says. I think you're reading far too much into it," says Jack, as I attempt to apply some makeup.

I don't normally bother with the whole face-paint routine when I'm not working; I'm not good at that sort of thing. My fingers find the shape of a lipstick inside my bag. I try to steady them enough to put it on, then realize too late that the bright red lipstick isn't mine. It's *hers*. The woman who left it here when I wasn't. Only my lower lip is red, and for a moment I'm so tired and confused I consider leaving it that way.

"It's just one stupid article, everyone will have forgotten about it by tomorrow, and I'm sure your agent doesn't care whether you are having an affair," Jack adds.

I turn to face him. "But we're *not* having an affair."

"You don't have to tell me." He's sitting on Ben's side of the bed with his feet up. I don't know why I feel so guilty when I haven't done anything wrong.

"I still don't understand how Jennifer Jones got those pictures." I apply the color to my upper lip and look at my reflection. For a moment, it's Alicia's face that I see. The idea that she is having an affair with my husband, and that the two of them are trying to frame me, still seems ridiculous, but stranger things have happened. Maybe I was too quick to dismiss it. Ben is handsome and charming, witty and fun. At least that's the version of himself he presents to the rest of the world. Nobody would believe who Ben is behind closed doors. Just the idea of the two of them together feeds the hate that has been growing inside me all these years. Alicia has been a bitch to me ever since school.

"How well do you know Alicia?"

"Not so well." Jack laughs. "But I don't think she's been taking secret pictures of us on her iPhone and selling them to the press, if that's what you mean."

"I wasn't suggesting that." I think, however, I might have been. I try to think about it logically. "It was a closed set, only a member of the crew could have taken a photo of our sex scene. I suppose there are lots of people who could have taken a photo of us in the bar last night, but the picture in my dressing room?"

"Jennifer Jones was waiting in your dressing room for you on the morning you did the interview."

"So?"

"So, she must have planted a small camera before you arrived."

"Really? That sounds highly unlikely. She's a showbiz journalist, not James Bond. Is that even legal?"

"I think you'll find people will do almost anything for a story nowadays, regardless of whether it is ethical or true."

We head downstairs, and I pause in the kitchen to drink some water. Going into town to see my agent with a hangover is not ideal, but I'm keen to get this, whatever it is, over. I catch sight of the bin in the corner of the room and remember what is inside it: the empty bottles of lighter gel that the police think I bought. I feel sick all over again.

"I'm just going to put the rubbish out, I think it's starting to smell."

Jack comes towards me. "I can do that for you—"

"No, really I'm fine. Why don't you wait in the lounge, it will only take a minute."

Jack is staring at something in his hand when I come back inside a short time later.

"Who's this scary-looking chap?" He holds up the framed black-and-white photo of my husband as a child.

"Ben when he was a boy. It's the only photo I could find of him."

"Strange."

"I know. I looked everywhere, there used to be lots—"

"No, I meant strange as in it looks nothing like him."

I had forgotten that Jack and my husband met at a party a few months ago. Ben invited himself along in a fit of jealousy and para-noia, and I was furious. I found it flattering when we first got together, the way he wanted me all to himself. But as time went on, the flattery faded into an afterglow of resentment. I've made a bad habit out of loving people who put me down, hoping they'll pull me up. They never do. I just fall further, harder, faster.

I remember seeing Jack and Ben talking together in the corner at the party that night, as though they were thick as thieves, and find-ing it strange. The memory unsettles me, as though I preferred the two of them being separate entities in my life, the fact that they've met somehow contaminating my future with my past. A mental note scratches itself onto my subconscious; like a sharpened pencil it leaves a mark, but will be easy to erase.

Jack puts the creepy picture back down, follows me out of the lounge and into the hallway. I open the front door, not expecting to find someone standing on the other side about to ring the bell.

"Well, well. Fancy finding the two of you together this morning," says Detective Croft with a wide smile. Wakely stands by her side, and I can see two large police vans parked on the street behind them.

"I might head off." Jack looks almost disappointed, as though he was expecting there to be someone else outside. "I'll see you later." I frown, not sure why he is saying that, especially in front of the detective. "At the wrap party," he explains, seeing the confusion on my face. I had forgotten that was tonight.

"The wrap party! How exciting, what a thrilling life you superstars lead. Can we come in?" Croft is already stepping towards the door.

I block her path. "No, I'm sorry. I'm on my way out."

"It won't take long. I wanted to update you about the stalker you mentioned."

She has my attention now, but I still can't be late to meet my agent, not today. "So, update me." I keep the front door half-closed.

She smiles again. "All right. First, I just wanted to show you some more footage we've obtained. It's from the day you reported Ben missing." She takes out her trusty iPad and gives it a swipe. "Here is some CCTV footage of the bank, at the exact time your account was emptied and closed."

I stare at the screen and see the back of a woman who looks just like me walk up to a counter. "I told you, she dresses like me—"

"*She* had your passport as a form of ID."

I hesitate. "Well, then it must have been fake, I—"

"We checked the emails that you claimed were sent to you by someone calling themselves Maggie O'Neil. We traced the IP address and discovered that you had sent them to yourself. From your own laptop."

I can't speak at first. The suggestion is ludicrous, I haven't been sending myself emails, why would I? "You're mistaken," I say, hearing my voice crack a little as I do.

"We traced the IP address. There's no mistake."

"I don't understand."

"Is your passport missing?"

I think for a moment, then remember that it wasn't just Ben's passport that had disappeared from the drawer where we keep them. "Yes, it is!"

She sighs. "Does anyone else have access to your home?"

"No. Wait. Yes, we used to have a cleaner."

"Used to?"

"She returned her key, but she could have made a copy."

"Why did you fire her?"

"I didn't fire her . . . we just stopped using her."

Because I'm a private person and didn't like the idea of someone snooping around my home, touching my things.

Croft stares at me long enough for my cheeks to flush with color, but I've learned not to say more than I need to.

"Do you think your ex-cleaner is your stalker?"

It seems unlikely, but I still consider the possibility. Maria was a little older than me, but about the same height. She changed her hair color more often than most people change their sheets, but she had access to my clothes and my passport. I suppose we might look the same from the back. But it can't be her, she always seemed so . . . nice.

"We also checked the search history on your laptop," Croft continues without waiting for my conclusions. "Someone, presumably you, was looking up divorce lawyers . . . or do you think that might have been your former cleaner too? Perhaps she doesn't have internet at home."

That was me. But I didn't call any of them. I was just upset. How dare Croft invade my privacy in this way. I let them take my laptop in good faith, and once again she's using everything against me.

"Do you own a gun, Mrs. Sinclair?"

I don't answer.

"According to our records, you do. Do you think that the amnesia your husband mentioned might have made you forget that too?"

No. I remember everything. I always have.

"It's not a crime to own a legally registered gun."

"That's right, it's not. Can I see it?"

I hold her stare. "If you had anything real on me, you would have arrested me by now."

She smiles, takes a step closer. "You're right, I would."

"Have you even heard of innocent until proven guilty?"

"Yep, sure have. I've heard of God and Father Christmas too. I don't believe in them either. We'd like to search the property again, if it's convenient." She looks over her shoulder at the two police vans. The side doors are open and I can see several officers inside each one.

"It isn't convenient, and don't you need a warrant to search my home?"

"Only if you refuse to give us permission."

"Then I suggest you get one."

Thirty-one

Essex, 1988

"I've got you some new tapes," says Maggie, walking into my bedroom. She smells of hairspray and her number five perfume all at once. She's wearing a yellow suit today, and for some reason the shoulders are padded to make them look bigger than they are. I'm pleased about the new tapes. I've listened to all the old ones over and over, and I know all the stories by heart.

"Now, these tapes are very special." She slides one of them into my Fisher-Price cassette player and presses Play. A strange voice comes out of the machine.

"Today, children, we are going to learn about vowel sounds. Repeat after me: 'How now brown cow.'"

Maggie hits the Pause button. "Well, go on then, do what she says."

This story tape doesn't sound fun at all. I open my mouth, but I've already forgotten what I am supposed to say. Maggie tuts. She hits another button, and when the sound of the tape rewinding stops, she presses Play again. I try hard to remember this time.

"Today, children, we are going to learn about vowel sounds. Repeat after me: 'How now brown cow.'"

Maggie hits Pause and I repeat the words. "How now brown cow." I think she will be pleased, but she isn't.

"Not like that! You have to say it the way *she* says it. No more Irish, you need to start sounding more like her, like *them*. You need to fit in."

"Why can't I speak like you?"

"Because people judge you for what's on the outside, for how you look and sound, nobody cares what's on the inside. I want you to think of it like acting, that's all it is, and there is nothing wrong with that. Some people make a pretty good living from it."

"I don't want to act."

"Sure you do. That film you love so much, what's it called? *The NeverEnding* bloody *Story*, that's just actors acting, it's not real." She's making me want to cry, but I know she'll slap me if I do, so I blink the tears away. "Acting is super fun, and if you can learn to speak like them, then you'll be able to have all kinds of amazing adventures when you're older, just like the little boy in the film."

"Can I fly a dragon dog one day?"

"Probably not, but you can do other things if you work hard and learn to speak nicely."

"If I need to learn things, then why don't I go to school?"

Maggie's face starts to change. "Because you're not old enough yet."

I am.

"Then why is there a school uniform in my wardrobe?"

Maggie's face twists and I think it might turn into her angry one, but it doesn't do that, it does something different, something I don't remember seeing before. She walks over to the wardrobe and opens the doors, slowly, as though she might be scared of what is inside. Her hand moves along all the little hangers, until her fingers find the one right at the end. She lifts it out. The price tags are still attached to the blue jacket, shirt, and stripy tie.

"You mean this?" she asks, so quietly I almost don't hear her. I nod. "Well, this was meant to be a surprise, and I think the pinafore might still be a little too big for *you*, but by September, I reckon it will fit just right."

"You mean I'm going to school in September?"

"Yes," she says after a little while, and I stand up and jump on the bed. "If . . ." I sit back down. "If you learn to speak like them. You just need to listen to all these elocution tapes and do what the lady says. You'll soon get the hang of it."

"But why do I have to? Why can't I just sound like me?"

"People judge your dad and me because of how we speak, and I don't want that for you, Baby Girl. I want you to grow up to be anyone you want to be. It's just an act, that's all. We all have to learn to act, Aimee. It's never, ever, a good idea to let strangers see the real you. So long as you never forget who you really are, acting will save you."

Thirty-two

London, 2017

I'm pretty good at acting as if I'm okay, even when I'm not. I've had a lot of practice. But the face I'm wearing today doesn't feel like my own, and piece by piece, it feels like my life is falling apart. There seems to be nothing I can do to keep what remains of it together. And my agent thinks *now* is a good time to drop me, which will be career-ending.

Tony's office is right in the middle of town. It's a sunny day, so I walk some of the way, avoiding the tube and the army of people who crowd onto it. Just because I've chosen a life on-screen, it shouldn't mean that I am no longer entitled to a life of my own, a life that is private. Despite today's online attack, I'm not too worried about people recognizing me; people tend to see what they want nowadays rather than what is actually there. I've seen other actresses go out in hats and sunglasses, but that just draws attention. Leaving my hair curly, not wearing too much makeup, and dressing just like everyone else is a much better disguise. Sometimes people stare in my direction for a fraction longer than average, you can see it in their eyes, that moment of recognition. But they can't place me, can't remember where they've seen my face before.

And I like that.

I'm early, so I wander around Waterstones in Piccadilly. For the first time in days I lose myself just a little, and it is a nice place to get lost; there are so many books all under one roof. I come here quite often and love that nobody ever knows who I am. Sometimes I wish I could hide in here and only come out when everyone else has gone, and the staff have locked up and left for the day. I'd spend the night reading something old, and at dawn I'd read something new. You can't allow the past to steal your present, but if you siphon off just the right amount, it can help fuel your future.

I've always felt safe in bookshops. It's as though the stories inside them can rescue me from myself and the rest of the world. A literary sanctuary filled with shelves of paper-shaped parachutes, which will save you when you fall. Some people manage to blow their own child-like bubbles, to hide inside to protect themselves from the truth of the world. But even if you float through life, safe inside your own bubble, you can still see what's going on all around you. You can't shut the horror out completely, unless you close your eyes.

I buy a book. Surrounded by so many, it would seem rude not to. It's a story written in 1958. I've read it before, but it brings a curious sense of comfort to slip it inside my bag. As I leave the shop, and the world of fiction, behind, it feels as if I'm taking a little bit of fantasy with me. A talisman made of paper and words to help ward off reality.

I stroll out with a little more hope in my heart than when I entered. I'm starting to think that everything might be okay after all. Then a woman grabs my arm, pulling me backwards out of the road, just as a double-decker bus hurtles past. A blur of red rushes right in front of my face as the driver's horn fills my ears.

"Watch where you're going!" snaps my rescuer, with a shake of her aggressively permed head.

I mumble a thank-you, not quite able to form the words or catch the breath that seems to have been stolen from me. That was close. Too close. Sometimes I just don't know what is wrong with me; I seem to have spent my whole life looking the wrong way.

I walk the final couple of streets to my agent's office, then take the lift to the fifth floor. The lift is empty, so I check my reflection in the mirror and spray myself with Chanel No. 5, not because I want to smell nice, but because this particular perfume has always made me feel calm when I'm most scared, I'm not sure why. Seeing myself reminds me of the CCTV of the bank Detective Croft showed me earlier. It wasn't, but it really did look like me. I didn't close our account and then forget about it. I'm not crazy. I'm more convinced than ever that Ben is working with someone else to try to destroy my career, but I have to lock these thoughts about him and her—whoever she is—away for now. Bury them both.

I stare at the fancy sign behind reception that says TALENT AGENCY and, as usual, wonder what I am doing here. I'm not talented and I don't fit. I always thought it was just a mistake when Tony signed me, so I suppose it was only a matter of time until he figured that out too. I wait, trying not to fidget, while someone goes to tell him that I'm here.

It's a big place. A tightly packed warren of glass-fronted offices, like a zoo of agents feeding on a healthy mix of talent and ambition. Dream makers one day, heartbreakers the next. The woman on the front desk smiles at me when we make eye contact. She's been staring at me since I walked through the door. She's new. I haven't seen her before, and I wonder if she knows why I'm here. I wonder if they *all* know.

Agents dump their clients all the time.

I thought about checking Tony's client list online on the way here, but I couldn't make myself, just in case my name and photo had already been removed from the page. The eye in the needle of my confidence has shrunk so small that I can no longer see a way through it, and even the tiniest threads of hope can't find their way inside. Alicia was right: I didn't fit with his other clients in the first place and I still don't. A couple of movie roles was never going to be enough to change that.

My nerves get the better of me and I think I'm going to throw up. Just as I stand to go to the bathroom, Tony's latest assistant appears to take me to his office, so I make myself smile and follow her instead. I'm convinced that everyone is looking at me as we walk down the maze of corridors, every step forwards requiring the most enormous mental, as well as physical, effort. As though I were fighting gravity itself.

Tony is middle-aged, middle-class, and always in the middle of something. He wears a permanent tan accompanied by an expensive suit, and his frown is a fixed feature, unless someone is looking his way, then he switches it off and lights his face with a mischievous grin instead. His hair has turned prematurely white recently, and I'm hoping that representing me didn't cause it. He looks busy through the glass wall, hunched over his desk, glaring at his screen. His assistant asks if I want a drink and I say no, even though I'm thirsty. I've never got used to other people doing things for me, it feels wrong. Tony sees me and it takes a second longer than it used to for his frown to convert into a smile. I try not to take it personally.

"So, how are you?" he says, closing the door behind me as I take a seat.

I'm fucking fucked and you know it.

"I'm great, how are you?"

I bet he says busy.

"I'm busy, real busy. The film is finished, right? I didn't want to have this conversation until it was all wrapped up."

Fuck. I knew it. I'm toast. Bastard, why couldn't he have just told me by email? I can get another agent, maybe, but it won't be the same. I'm sure I only got the parts I did because he represents me. I trust Tony, or at least, I did. I don't trust anyone else. I'm fucking fucked.

"Aimee?" He interrupts my internal monologue. "Are you all right?"

No.

"Yes, sorry, just . . . tired."

"I'll get straight to the point then. Do you know why I asked to see you today?"

Because you are going to dump me and I hate you for it.

I shake my head. My fear dictates what I will say now. And what I won't. I find myself staring down at my feet, unable to watch or listen while this person I trusted sharpens the knife. The nausea rises to grab my attention once more, and I think I might be sick right here in his office. My knees start to do that thing where they tremble when I'm scared. It's such a cliché. I use my hands to try to keep them still, while wondering if there is anything at all I could say that would change Tony's mind. He speaks before I get the chance.

"Well, it's two things really . . ."

I always listen to what he says, but most of my efforts are currently focused on trying not to cry or throw up.

Please don't do this.

"I received an email from your husband."

Time stops.

"What?"

"He wanted to let me know that you weren't coping with the pressure you've been under. I'm aware that you've basically made two films this year, which is a lot, even for an experienced actor. I want you to know that you can tell me if it's ever all too much. It is okay to say no to things from time to time. There are things, and people, I can protect you from."

"I don't know why he got in touch with you, I'm fine. Honestly."

He stares at me for a long time. "Is everything all right at home?"

"Yes." I've never lied to Tony before, it feels all wrong. "Actually, no, but it will be, soon. I hope."

He nods, looks down at a script on his desk. "Good, because the other reason I wanted to see you is that a director has been in touch about another movie. They wanted you to fly out to L.A. for an audition last week, but I said no on your behalf, seeing as I knew your filming schedule wouldn't allow it. So, the director and his team are coming to London next week, specifically to meet you. I think the part is pretty much yours already . . . if you want it. The job won't start for at least a month, so you'll get a little time off . . ."

"Who is the director? Is it someone I've heard of?"

"Oh, yes." He smiles.

"Who?"

"Fincher."

I wait a moment, wanting to be sure I've heard him correctly. I conclude I haven't.

"Fincher?"

"Yes."

It must be a mistake or a really mean trick of some kind.

"Are you sure it's me he wants to meet? Maybe they meant Alicia?"

I stare at him, looking for something in his face that isn't there. "I don't represent Alicia White anymore. There's no mistake. What is it going to take for you to start believing in yourself?"

I travel back through time and space. I'm at school, in my drama teacher's office, just after he gave me the part of Dorothy in *The Wizard of Oz,* even though I was too scared to audition. My agent reminds me of that teacher a little bit. I don't understand why either of these people took a chance on me, but I'm so grateful that they did. My life might not have turned out exactly how I wanted, but sometimes I feel so lucky I swear it hurts. And this is one of those times.

"Thank you," I say eventually, finding my way back to the present.

Tony is pulling that face he pulls when he has another meeting fast approaching and needs me to go away, but doesn't know how to say it. I stand to leave, relieved that he hasn't read any of the online nonsense written about me today.

"Aimee." I turn back. I can see from his face that I've got that wrong, too, of course he's read it, he reads bloody everything. But I'm surprised to see that he's wearing his kind face, not the disappointed-father one I expected. "If you only remember one thing that I tell you while I'm your agent, then I hope it's this. You should always fight, especially when you think you are going to lose. That's when you should fight the hardest."

"Thank you," I whisper, and leave before he can see me cry.

Thirty-three

Essex, 1988

Today is my birthday.

Not my real one in September, Maggie said I had to forget about that. Today is my new birthday, the one in April, and she says that I am seven years old. Even though I am only really six.

I don't mind that I have a different name and birthday now, I'm starting to like it here. Maggie buys me little presents all the time, and even John got me something today. Maggie got all upset when he gave it to me, and he looked at the floor and played with his new beard, the way he always does when she gets cross. Then he said something that I can't get out of my head, as if his words got stuck between my ears or something. "A child needs company." I understood what he meant, but I think he's wrong about that. I like being on my own.

I was still happy that he bought me a hamster though. I've named him Cheeks.

Cheeks doesn't do much. He lives in a cage and sleeps a lot. Sometimes he likes to go for a run on his wheel. He runs and runs and runs, but he never gets anywhere. I wonder if he minds. Maggie does not like the hamster; she refuses to call him Cheeks and calls him Vermin instead, which does not sound like a nice name to me.

Maggie got me something called a Walkman, so that I can listen to my Story Teller tapes and elocution lessons without her and John having to listen too. I'm getting pretty good at sounding English so that I can go to school in September, and my Walkman is *very* cool. I've worn the headphones all day long, even when I wasn't listening.

John got Maggie a present today, too, even though it is my pretend birthday, not hers. It was wrapped in the same She-Ra paper as my presents, and I felt a little bit funny about not being allowed to open it. She-Ra is a princess of power and my new favorite thing. She lives in a castle, flies around on a horse, and stops bad people from doing bad things. I would like to be like She-Ra when I grow up.

John said that Maggie deserved a present, too, because today is a special day for her as well. He said it is the day she brought a life into the world. He looked at me when he said that, but it wasn't me he was talking about. I might only be six or seven, but I'm not stupid. Maggie didn't look at me when he said it, she looked at the picture of the little girl inside a frame on the mantelpiece. She cried a little bit, but pretended it was her hay fever that made her do it, then she wiped the lie away with a tissue. I suppose it was just a white one.

When Maggie unwrapped her present, I didn't know what it was. It's called a Deep Fat Fryer. I don't know why I think that's a funny name, but every time John calls it that, I giggle. Maggie asked if he got it off the back of a lorry, and that seems like a strange place to buy presents to me. John ignored her and said that the Deep Fat Fryer would change our lives. I didn't believe him at first, but he was right. We always ate everything on toast before, but now we eat everything with chips instead. It's wonderful! Maggie has only had the Deep Fat Fryer for one day, but already we've had eggs and chips for lunch and burgers and chips for dinner!

It works like magic. Maggie peels potatoes, chops them into chip shapes, then throws them into the machine. When it beeps, it means that the potatoes have magically turned into chips! I'm not allowed to touch the Deep Fat Fryer. It has oil inside that gets very hot, so hot that Maggie burned her finger badly the first time she used it. John offered to kiss it better, but she pushed him away. It made me think that maybe sometimes kissing something better is really kissing something worse.

We're having a special dessert tonight for my birthday, and Maggie says it is a surprise. I hope it is one of her nice ones. She makes me sit in the front room on the sofa beside the electric fire. The lights go out, but it's because John has turned them off, not because the meter needs feeding. Maggie comes into the room carrying a cake with candles on it, then puts it down on the coffee table where we only drink tea. I've never had a birthday cake before. She tells me to make a wish and blow out all the candles, so I do, and John takes a picture of me on his Polaroid camera. There were seven candles, but I know I'm only six, so I don't know whether my wish will still come true.

After we have all eaten two slices of chocolate cake, John stands up and walks over to the mantelpiece. He takes the picture of the other little girl; she is blowing out candles on a birthday cake too, but I only count six. He opens the frame and starts to put her photo in his pocket, but Maggie says no, so he puts it back and slides the new photo of me over the top. It's strange seeing a photo of myself in the frame. The other little girl is tucked just behind me, I can't see her anymore, but I know that she's still there.

Thirty-four

London, 2017

I sit on the Central Line, trying but failing to read the book I bought earlier. It's an old story, but it's putting new thoughts in my head that I don't currently have room for. Books can be mirrors, too, offering a reflection of our worst selves for appraisal; lessons tucked between pages, just waiting to be learned. I put the book back in my bag and drink in the faces of my fellow travelers instead, wondering who the people wearing them really are.

Ben and I used to play a game on the tube. We would pick a couple of people talking in the distance, and we'd take it in turns to speak when they spoke, making up silly voices and amusing dialogues that didn't fit the faces we saw, finding ourselves hilarious. We were fun back then. It was good. The memory makes me smile, but then I realize I am grinning at strangers and a past I can never get back. It's rude of me to stare like this, but nobody says anything, people don't even see me doing it. They're all far too busy staring at their phones, partaking in the daily withdrawal from wonder and the world around them. We've all got so busy staring down at our screens that we've forgotten to look up at the stars.

I think it can be dangerous to spend too long watching the lives of others; you might run out of time to live your own. Technology is devolving the human race. Eating up our emotional intelligence, spitting out any remnants of privacy it can't quite swallow. The world will keep on spinning and the stars will always shine, regardless of whether anyone is looking.

Sometimes I think that every person might be his or her own star, shining at the center of his or her own solar system. I observe the changing expressions of my fellow commuters and am certain I witness an occasional flare on their surfaces, as they contemplate their past or worry about their future. Each walking, talking, thinking, feeling human star has its own planets revolving around it: parents, children, friends, lovers. Sometimes stars get too big, too hot, too dangerous, and the planets closest to them burn to oblivion. As I sit and stare at the galaxy of faces, trying to get from one place to another, I understand that it doesn't matter who we are or what we do; we're all the same. We are all just stars trying to shine in the darkness.

I get off the tube at Notting Hill and walk towards home, my neck seeming to hold my head a little higher than it has recently. I experience a trampoline of emotions with every step, bouncing from high to low then back again, before the mixed bag of feelings seems to collapse in an exhausted state inside my tired mind. I have an audition with one of my all-time-favorite directors, my agent is not dumping me, and despite all the problems in my personal life, there is a lot to be grateful for. This misunderstanding with Ben will get all cleared up. He's trying to hurt me, but he can't vanish forever, and I can't be accused of a crime that never happened.

I turn the corner onto my street, feeling as if everything might just be okay after all.

The feeling doesn't last long.

The two police vans that were sitting outside the house this morning are still there, but now they are empty. My front door is wide open. There is a steady stream of police officers going in and out of the building, and blue-and-white police tape forms a cordon between it and the rest of the street. I guess Detective Croft got her warrant.

This has to be a bad dream. Surely by now she must have realized that I'm telling the truth. I don't know where my husband is, why he said the things he did, or why he is doing this to me. I expect he just wanted to teach me a lesson, but enough is enough. I certainly didn't do away with him the way she keeps seeming to suggest. I might have been diagnosed with trauma-induced amnesia as a child, but the doctors were wrong, and either way, I think I'd remember if I'd done anything as dramatic as that.

I start walking towards the police tape. They'll have to let me in, it's my house, and besides, I need to get ready for the wrap party tonight, I can't go dressed like this. The wind in my newly hoisted sails dies an instant death when I see two men dressed in white forensic overalls. They are carrying what looks like a stretcher out of my front door. Something, or someone, is on it, hidden beneath a white sheet.

At first I can't believe what my eyes are seeing.

The image seems to burn itself onto my mind, leaving a permanent mark, and snuffing out my last remains of hope.

They can't have found a body, because that would mean that someone was dead. And if someone really was dead, then that would mean that someone else had killed them. I spot the shape of Detective Croft coming out of the house; she's pointing at something I can't see. If she really has found something, she'll never believe me about the stalker now; she didn't believe me in the first place. I can't make out the expression on her face from this far away, but I imagine that she is smiling. I turn and I run.

Thirty-five

Essex, 1988

I sweep and mop the shop floor every night now. I listen to my Walk-man while I do it and practice saying things like, *Peter Piper picked a peck of pickled peppers* or *Red Lorry Yellow Lorry,* or things about the rain in a place called Spain. Each evening, when I've finished sweeping, I refill the little plastic holders with new betting slips and blue mini-pens, ready for the next day. The betting slips are two pieces of paper stuck together, but when you write something on the top white page, it appears on the bottom yellow one, like magic. When people place bets, they give the whole thing to Maggie or John, then they get the yellow bit back along with their change. If they win, they take the yellow bit to the counter and collect their money. If they lose, they tend to screw the yellow bit up and throw it on the floor, along with their cigarette butts and other rubbish. Then, when the shop closes, I sweep them all up. This is what we do every day, except Sundays.

When Maggie yells that the shop is closed for the night, I take the broom and drag it behind the counter. She and John are still putting elastic bands around today's bundles of notes, and filling tiny plastic bags with coins, before throwing them all in the safe, which is almost as big as me, and very heavy. I tried to lift it once and it didn't budge, not even a little bit.

"Why aren't you married?" I ask, watching them count the money. I've just read about a princess marrying a prince in my *Story Teller* magazine. I know Maggie and John aren't married because they don't wear rings, and the envelopes that come through the letter box at the bottom of the stairs have different names on them.

Maggie looks up from a pile of twenty-pound notes. "Because marriage is a lie, Baby Girl, and we don't lie to each other in this family. I've told you that enough times for you to know it now." I don't understand what she means, but I don't ask again because Maggie is wearing her happy face tonight and I don't want that to change. John points at something I can't see over the counter. When I reach the shop floor, I see two great big fruit machines, side by side.

"What are—"

"English," says Maggie. I'm not allowed to speak like her at all anymore. I still have to think before making myself sound like someone else.

"What are they?" I ask with the right-sounding words.

John smiles, his gold tooth sparkling. "Bait."

"Shut up, John. They're for you."

"But what *are* they?"

"Well, one of them is just a plain old fruit machine, and the other one is . . . Do you know, I can't remember, can you, Maggie?" says John.

"I think it might be . . . Pac-Man!" she says.

Pac-Man is my new favorite thing. I play it every Sunday at the pub while they talk to the man who looks like Maggie and calls himself my uncle. They look the same and sound the same and say the same things. It's as if they are the same person sometimes, but he is a boy and she is a girl.

"Thank you, thank you, thank you!" I run back behind the counter to hug Maggie's legs.

She says that I'm only allowed to play on the machines after I have swept and mopped, so I do it extra quick. Then John gives me a bag of change from the safe and lifts me up onto a stool.

"Now then, I know all you really want to do is play Pac-Man, and I don't blame you, the little yellow chap is rather addictive. But first you have to play this machine, and you need to play until you win.

All you do is put the coin in the slot and press the button. When you get three lemons, lots of money comes out the bottom of the machine. After that you don't touch it again, at all, until tomorrow. Understand?" I nod. "Good girl. When you get the money out of the fruit machine, you can use it to play Pac-Man. I can empty that one anytime."

I play on the first machine for so long that my finger starts to feel sore from pressing the buttons, but then three lemons appear in a row and lots of money comes out the bottom, just like John said it would. He says the machine works best during the day if we empty all the money out of it at night, so perhaps that's why I have to play it. When I win, it makes a big crashing sound that seems to go on forever. I jump off the black leather stool and slide it across to Pac-Man, before climbing back up again. I play ten times so that my name, the new one, fills the leaderboard.

Then I hear Maggie's *EastEnders* program starting up in the flat, and she shouts down the stairs, "Dinner is ready in five minutes and you need to clean the hamster cage out first, like I told you."

I had forgotten about Cheeks. He does the same thing every day: eats, sleeps, and runs in circles. I don't know why Maggie hates him so much, but I'm hoping her TV program will cheer her up a little bit. I can smell the Deep Fat Fryer, so I know we're having chips. We have chips all the time now, with everything. Eggs and chips, sausage and chips, burgers and chips, cheese and chips. On Sundays we have chips with Bisto gravy on top, that's my favorite! I like eating chips every day, but I just got to Level 5 for the first time on Pac-Man, so I ignore Maggie for a little while.

When I hear the *EastEnders* music again, I realize that her program must have finished. I was so busy playing on the machine that I forgot all about going upstairs for my dinner. I hope Maggie isn't mad with me. I run up the stairs and into the kitchen; the Deep Fat Fryer is still on, so maybe I'm not too late.

"There you are." Maggie stands in the doorway. Her face looks strange, I don't think I like it. "Are you hungry?"

"Yes," I whisper.

"Really? Because I called you half an hour ago and you ignored me."

She steps forward and I take a step back.

"Dinner has all gone, I'm afraid. No chips for you tonight, Baby Girl. I'm cooking something else now. Something special. You want to see?"

I don't think that I do.

I turn and try to leave the kitchen, but she grabs me, lifts me up with one hand, and opens the lid of the fryer with the other.

The oil is hot and I can see something bubbling on top.

I scream when I see what it is.

I start to cry and try to look away, but she holds my chin with her hand, forcing me to watch.

Then she whispers in my ear, "Poor Cheeks. Never mind, I'm sure he's running in circles somewhere in hamster heaven. You don't need anyone except me, Aimee. It's a lesson you really should have learned by now. Next time I tell you to do something, I suggest you do it."

Thirty-six

London, 2017

People say we can be anyone we want to be in life.

That's a lie.

The truth is, we can be anyone we *believe* we can be. There's a big difference.

If I *believe* I am Aimee Sinclair, then I am.

If I *believe* I am an actress, then I am.

If I *believe* I am loved, then I am.

Destroy the belief, destroy the reality it gave birth to.

I'm starting to think maybe my marriage was little more than a lie. I find myself wandering around central London with no memory of how I got here. For a moment, I consider the possibility that the amnesia diagnosis all those years ago *was* correct, and that I've been kidding myself all this time, thinking that I could remember everything that has ever happened to me, and everything that I've done, but then I manage to shake the thought. It wasn't true then and it isn't true now.

I walk and I think and I try and fail to make sense of everything that has happened over the past few days. I don't know where to go, or who to turn to, and the realization that there is nobody I feel that I can trust at all makes everything seem even worse than it already is.

Ben can't be dead, because I don't believe it.

The unspoken thoughts rattle around inside my head, bouncing off the walls of my mind, looking for a way out. But there is no way out. Not this time. I think about the tide of hate I've had to swim against for the last few months. I think about what Ben did to me that night, and I think about my gun not being where I normally keep it, hidden beneath our bed. For the first time since this whole nightmare began, I sincerely start to doubt myself and accept that my grip on reality seems a little less firm than it used to.

Surely I'd know if my husband was really dead?

Surely I would have felt something?

Maybe not.

I feel as if I've been put in slow motion, and when I look around at all the people rushing by, everyone seems to be in such a desperate hurry. Most of them are too busy staring at their phones to be able to see where they are going, or where they have been. I find myself standing outside the TBN office where Ben works, without remembering the journey here. The sight of the place takes me back in time, to when we first got together. We used to meet here all the time when we started dating.

We were virtual strangers when we met online.

We were emotional strangers after almost two years of marriage.

I could never do that now—use my real name and picture on a dating website—but back then, nobody knew who I was, not really. My name meant very little to anyone, including me. Ben made the first move. He sent me a message, we exchanged a few emails, and I agreed to meet in real life. Everything was practically perfect until a few months after our wedding. Then we lived happily never after.

Ben loves his job. He's away almost as often as I am, traveling to any corner of the world that we deem to be more troubled than our own. The news is like an addiction for him, whereas I rarely pay any attention to it nowadays. If something bad had really happened, if he wasn't able to go to work, then his employer would know; I've never known him to be off sick for a single day. All I have to do is prove that my husband is still alive, and that he is the one trying to hurt me, not the other way around. He's trying to damage my reputation and destroy my career because he knows that's all I have left and that, without it, I am nothing.

I force myself to walk through the revolving doors and approach the reception desk. I wait for the woman staring at her screen to look up, then I open my mouth, but the question seems too afraid to come out. The receptionist's skin is a perfect black canvas, painted with critical eyes and an unsmiling mouth. Her hair is as restrained as her welcome, thick black strands pulled into a ponytail so tight, it results in an unnecessary face-lift. The lanyard around her neck displays a name badge reading JOY. From what I've seen of her so far, this seems a little ironic. My prolonged silence causes Joy to look at me as though I might be dangerously dim. Perhaps she's right. Perhaps I am.

"Can I speak to Ben Bailey please?" I manage at last.

Her eyes, which had narrowed, widen, before a frown makes itself at home on her face. "Can I take your name?"

I don't want to give her my name, I'd rather keep it to myself. I never give it willingly to anyone anymore.

"I'm his wife," I settle on eventually.

She raises a drawn-on eyebrow in my general direction, then taps something on her keyboard. The name *wife* seems to satisfy the system for now. "Take a seat over there."

I move to the red sofa where she wants me to wait. She doesn't pick up the phone on her desk until I sit down, and she watches me the whole time while saying words I can't hear.

I sit. People come and go. I watch the silver-colored lifts behind reception swallow some inside the building and spit others back out. Joy looks at and speaks in the same frosty fashion to everyone who approaches her desk, as though her thermostat is broken. The temperature of her tone is unchanging, and I think that it's sad how some people are predisposed to coldness.

When the shape of a young man pops out of the lift and walks in my direction, I presume his outstretched hand is on its way to greet someone else, until I remember that I'm the only person still waiting. His twentysomething-year-old hair is too long, just like his gangly limbs, which jut out at peculiar angles beneath his shiny suit. He smells of aftershave and breath mints and youth.

"Hello, I believe you were asking for Ben Bailey?" His deep, upper-class voice doesn't match his appearance. I nod and let him shake my hand. "I'm afraid Ben hasn't worked here for over two years now. I said the same thing to the police yesterday. Did you tell reception that you were his wife?"

I can't seem to form words just now, I'm too busy processing his, so I just nod again.

"How strange." He takes in my appearance as though seeing me for the first time. His features adopt the familiar expression people wear when they can't pinpoint how they know my face. He stumbles on, his sentences tripping over themselves in their eagerness to be heard. "I mean, Ben was the kind of guy who kept himself to himself, never came to the pub after work or anything like that. I didn't really know him, none of us did. I'm sorry I can't help. Is he in some sort of trouble?"

"You're saying that Ben Bailey hasn't worked here for two years?"

"Yes, that's right."

People are walking in and out of the building, the lift doors are opening and closing, the boy in front of me is still speaking, but I can't hear a thing. Someone has turned the sound of my world off, and maybe that's okay, because I don't think I want to listen anymore. It's true that I don't think I'd asked him about his work for a while, we only ever seemed to talk about mine. But surely, losing your job is something most people would tell their partner? My mind is finally asking all the right questions, but it's too late, and besides, I should already know the answers.

"Why did he leave?" It is a quiet question, but the young man hears me, and I hear his reply.

"He was fired. Gross misconduct. He didn't take it too well at the time, I'm afraid."

Thirty-seven

Essex, 1988

It's a Saturday and I am sitting in the back room of the shop counting the coins and putting them into clear plastic bags. I check I've counted right with the red plastic coin shelf. I like to start with the ten-pence coins, stacking them all up until they reach the mark that says five pounds. Then I put them in the bag, it's easy. Just as I'm folding over the top of the last bag, to stop the coins from falling out, I think I see a shadow move across the little window, but I must have imagined it, because Maggie and John are both in the shop, and it sounds awful busy.

Saturday is always the busiest day; people seem to really like placing bets at the weekend, I'm not sure why. Maybe they think it's lucky or something. I think maybe I'm too young to understand why yelling at horses racing on a TV screen is fun. I get fed up listening to the sound of all the customers shouting, and smelling the stink of their cigarettes. The smoke creeps all the way to the back room from the shop, then hides in my nose so I have to smell it all day.

When I get bored, I play with the new Speak & Spell machine that Maggie gave me. It's a little orange computer with a keyboard that I can carry around, and she says it will help me do well at school, *if* I'm allowed to go in September. I turn the Speak & Spell on, it plays a little tune, then it speaks to me in a funny robot voice. I think maybe that's why I like it so much; nobody else has spoken to me all day.

"Spell *promises*," it says, and then it reads out each letter as I type them onto the screen.

"LIES."
"That is incorrect. Spell *promises*."
"PROMISES."
"Correct. Spell *mother*."
"NOTMAGGIE."
"That is incorrect. Spell *mother*."
"MOTHER."
"Correct. Now spell *home*."
"NOTHERE."

I see the shadow again, and this time I push my chair up against the window and look outside, but I can't see anything except our car, and that doesn't tend to move by itself. Sometimes it doesn't move at all, and John has to push it down the little hill out of the backyard and onto the road, while Maggie sits in the front pressing the pedals with her feet and turning the key. I just sit in the back and watch. I've learned that they both get more cranky with me and each other if I say something when the car won't start.

I look through the bars on the windows. All of our windows have bars, even upstairs. Maggie says it's because bad men once climbed up on the roof. I'm still looking out through the bars, daydreaming probably—Maggie says I'm always doing that—when a face appears right in front of me. If the glass weren't there, our noses would almost touch.

"Hello, little girl," says the man in the window. He sounds like John, not Maggie. "I've lost my dog, can you help me? I saw him run up inside your backyard, but now I can't find him."

Our back gates are always locked, always. They are taller than John, with bits of wire and broken glass on top. I don't know how the man's dog could have jumped over them.

"Have you seen him? He's a tiny little white fluffy thing, real cute, I'm sure he'd let you rub his belly if you help me find him."

I do like dogs. I climb down off the chair and look up at the back door. It has so many bolts and chains and a great big lock, but I know where the keys are. Then I remember what Maggie said about never

opening the back door, ever. So I decide I should ask her what to do.
I walk through the phone room and stand behind the stripy-colored
curtain that hides the back of the shop from the front. A fan is on
because the shop is too hot today, and the colors blow around like
plastic hair in the wind.

"Mum," I whisper.

She's serving a customer who is standing on the other side of the
glass, and she doesn't answer. The customer looks old and mean; he
has a pipe in his mouth and looks like he needs a bath.

"Mum," I whisper again.

She does a sideways look in my direction. "Not now, Baby Girl,
can't you see I'm busy?" She serves the next customer. He is too white
and too tall, as if somebody flattened him out with a rolling pin, then
hid him away from the sun for a long time.

I walk back to my little room, wondering what I should do, hoping that maybe the man will have found his dog and gone away by
now. But when I stand on the chair and look out, he's still there.

"I'm so worried about my dog. Won't you be a good little girl? Why
don't you come outside and help me find him?" he says in a sad voice,
which makes me feel awful bad.

"I don't think I'm allowed."

His face looks even sadder than his words sound. "It's okay." His
face moves quite close to the glass again, so that I lean back a little,
even though I know he can't touch me. "I understand. It's a shame
you can't help me though, he's such a good dog, I don't want anything
bad to happen to him. You don't want anything bad to happen to him,
do you?"

"No."

"Of course you don't, I can tell you're a good girl. So, if it's not too
much trouble, can I use your phone, so that I can call the police and
they can help me find him?"

We have plenty of phones. We've got a whole room full of them,
for when people want to place bets without coming to the shop, but
it feels as if I need to have a think. Maggie says the police do not care
about people like us, so people like us don't care about the police and

must never talk to them. But Cagney and Lacey on the TV are the police too, and I like them a lot, so maybe some police are okay? If this man is a bad man, he wouldn't want to call the police because they would throw him in jail. I feel confused and I'm still not sure what to do, so I decide to ask Maggie, again.

I walk back to the stripy curtain and peek through the gaps, twisting one of the long red bits of plastic around my finger. Maggie still looks awful busy, and so does John.

"What is it, Pipsqueak?" he asks, counting some ten-pound notes out on the counter. I watch as he slides the bundle underneath to the waiting hands I can see on the other side. That means a customer won a bet. John hates it when they win.

"I don't know what to do about something."

He turns to me and shakes his head. "Can't you see how busy your mum and I are? You're old enough to make some decisions for yourself, Squirt. Time to grow up. Who's next for the two-forty?" he says to the men lined up behind the glass.

I take the keys from the hook next to the phones, then push my chair up against the back door, unlocking one bolt at a time, from top to bottom, before turning the key.

The door pushes open a bit from the other side, and I can see the man's boot. "You forgot the chain."

I unhook it and he comes in, smiling and closing the door.

"Good girl," he whispers. "Now, where's the safe?"

"I don't think your dog is in there."

He laughs, then pushes me out of the way. I hear the race start in the shop and it's so loud. I think I might have made a mistake.

"Who the fuck are you?" asks John, standing in the doorway behind us.

The man grabs me and I see the knife in his hand. He points it at my neck and lifts me off the floor so that my legs are dangling.

"Put her down," John says in his normal voice, as though he isn't scared at all. But I am scared and I wet myself, my pee running down my legs, stopping at my socks, then dripping down onto the stone floor.

"I want the contents of the safe, right now, or I'll slit her fuckin' throat."

I start to cry. I can hear the race still going on out front. The voice of the man on the TV seems to get louder and louder inside my ears: "Rhyme 'n' Reason is still in the lead, closely followed by Little Prayer on the inside, Dark Knight bringing up the rear . . ."

Maggie appears behind John. She looks at my face, then at the man who is holding me. Her face doesn't change, but her eyes do.

"You can have the money, I don't care about that, we have insurance. Just don't hurt our little girl," says John.

"Don't play games with me," says the bad man, I know that's what he is now. I feel him press the tip of the knife against my neck.

"Aimee, don't be scared, sweetheart," says John. "We're going to give the man what he wants and nobody is going to get hurt, I promise."

"You shouldn't make promises you can't keep." The man's breath smells like the pub on Sundays.

"Maggie, go and fill a plastic bag with whatever is in the safe, and give the man what he's asking for." John's eyes seem to have forgotten how to blink, and they look different somehow, darker.

Maggie disappears. I hear the sound of the safe opening, then her high heels on the tiled floor as she comes back again, holding a plastic bag full of bundles of notes. She hands it to the man with one hand, and when he reaches to take it, her other hand comes out of her pocket holding a gun. She shoots, and this time, she doesn't miss. I fall to the floor, and when I look over at the bad man, half his face is missing.

Thirty-eight

London, 2017

Ben was fired two years ago.

That's the last thing I hear before standing up and walking out of the reception of the building he used to work in. The boy who broke the news is still speaking to me, but I can't hear him anymore, the voices inside my head are far too loud, drowning everyone and everything else out. The questions they keep asking terrify me, because I'm no longer sure I know the answers. How can my husband have lost his job two years ago and I didn't even know? It must have been just after we met. What has he been doing all this time? Where has he been going when he was pretending to go to work? Where was he getting money from?

I should have asked what Ben did wrong. What constitutes gross misconduct?

I'm starting to think that I don't know the man I am married to at all.

Maybe I don't know myself as well as I think I do either.

Did I kill my husband?

Did I take the gun from under the bed and shoot him?

Did I drive to a petrol station and buy lighter gel to try to hide the evidence of what I'd done? Why was it in the bin, and why is there CCTV of someone who looks like me buying it?

I don't remember doing those things, but I'm no longer sure that is sufficient proof that I didn't. I feel more lost and lonely than ever before. Who can I trust if I can no longer trust myself? When life holds up its final mirror, I hope I'll still be able to look.

My phone beeps and I stare down at it. Jack's name is on the screen.

What time are you getting to the wrap party tonight? I'm missing you already! X

I had forgotten about the party.

I can't possibly go to that now, I can't *go* anywhere.

I grasp the truth of that, realizing I can't go home now with police swarming about the place. If they have found . . . something, then what if they arrest me? It doesn't matter that I haven't done anything wrong, it matters how it will look to others. Unpleasant rumors are like leeches: they stick. I swing awkwardly between the options like a broken hinge and conclude that I only have two. I can run and hide, proving to myself and everyone else that I am guilty of something I cannot remember. Or I carry on as though none of this is happening. If I don't go to the wrap party, I'll be missed. Not in a sentimental way, but there will be repercussions. Bad things have happened to me before, and I've always found a way to get through them.

I just have to *act* normal.

Faced with the option to sink or swim, I choose survival. Every. Single. Time. I'll teach myself to breathe underwater if I have to.

I did not kill my husband.

I tell myself that as I walk into the department store and as I ride the escalator to women's fashion. I tell myself again as I select a size-ten black dress from the rack and take it to the fitting rooms. And again, when I ask the shop assistant to remove the tags because I want to wear the dress now. I ignore the puzzled look on her face when, after paying for my purchase, I pass her the clothes I had been wearing before and ask her to put them in the bin.

I am not crazy.

When you plait truth and lies together, they can begin to look and feel the same.

Back on the ground floor of the department store, I stop at my favorite cosmetics counter and pay for a makeover.

"Look up for me," says the woman applying black liner to my eyes.

"Do you know you look just like that girl in that TV show . . . anyone ever tell you that?"

"All the time." I tell my face to smile. "Wish I was!"

"Don't we all. Look down."

I stare at my feet and notice my trainers. They don't go with the rest of my look, so once my face is taken care of, I hurry to the shoe department. I start to feel a little paranoid that other people might recognize me now that I'm all dressed up like the on-screen version of myself. I stare at the endless rows of footwear and spot some red shoes on the shelf, outshining everything around them. They remind me of a pair I wore in a school play once. I'm fairly sure they don't go with the black dress, but I try on the display shoe anyway, standing like a flamingo in front of the mirror. It's perfect.

While I wait for the assistant to bring me my new shoes, I observe the hordes of shoppers, all hoping to score their next consumer high. I feel sure that people are staring at me now. Who knows how many of them might have read Jennifer Jones's online article or, even worse, whether the news has leaked about Ben and what he accused me of. When the assistant finally returns, a queue of people are waiting, accompanied by a chorus of tutting and synchronized rolling of eyes. She apologizes for the delay and retreats back to the stockroom before I've even taken the lid off the box.

I slip the brand-new red shoes onto my feet and take another look in the mirror. Something about them delivers a sense of comfort I can't explain, then I think of Ben again. He knew how much I loved shoes and bought me a designer pair every birthday and Christmas we were together; something I could afford, but could never justify spending on myself. He would always choose a pair that I had secretly wanted, he knew me so well. It was kind and thoughtful, and he delighted in watching me unwrap them. Every marriage is different, and no marriage is perfect. It wasn't all bad between us.

I snap back to the present, see the enormous line of people snaking behind the tills, and again feel the eyes of others on me, like a weight on my chest making it difficult to breathe. I take one last look at my reflection, then swallow my fear down inside me like a pill. I decide to do something I've never done before, and walk out of the shop without paying, leaving my trainers and that version of me behind. If I'm about to be accused of murder, a little shoplifting can't hurt me too much. I'm terrified of the police and what the future has in store for me, but that woman I just saw staring back at me in the mirror, she's not afraid of anything or anyone.

All I have to do is remember to be her from now on.

Thirty-nine

Essex, 1988

"You just have to remember who you are," says Maggie.

She holds my hand tight the whole time the police are in the shop, as if she is scared of letting me go. I was worried that maybe everything was my fault because I opened the back door when I knew I wasn't supposed to, but I only wanted to help the man find his dog. I didn't know that he didn't really have one.

Maggie wears her kind face the whole time the police are here, even if it does look a little bit broken. She said before they arrived that we all had to act a little bit, and that it was very important for me to learn my lines. She made me say them over and over in my best English accent.

I had three to learn:

1. The bad man tricked me to open the door.
2. The bad man had a gun (not a knife) and pointed it at me.
3. Dad (John) gave him the money, but the bad man still wouldn't let me go, so they got in a fight and the gun went off.

I'm not allowed to say anything else at all. I have to say I can't remember, even though I can. I must not talk about Michael, the man who says he is my uncle; I don't know why they think I would. I must not say that the gun was Maggie's, or that she was the one who shot the bad man. John said it was important to "stick to the script" because of Maggie's record. I don't know which one he means, she has lots; she likes listening to music.

The police have been here for hours. The lady who asks me questions says that I'm a "very brave girl" and gives me a lollipop, but I don't want it. I don't feel brave, I feel scared. Maggie's kind face seems to follow them out the back door, no matter how much I wish that it wouldn't. I don't know what time it is when they leave, but it's dark outside, and I know it is late. I wonder if we'll still have dinner, and I wonder if it will be something with chips. But then I remember that we don't have a Deep Fat Fryer anymore, not after what happened to Cheeks. Maggie threw it away.

She picks me up, carrying me through the shop, with my legs wrapped around her waist and my arms wrapped around her neck. She smells of her number five perfume and it makes me feel safe. The screens in the shop are still on, but the volume has been turned right down, so that silent horses are racing and jumping over fences like secrets. Looking over Maggie's shoulder, I can see that there is litter all over the shop floor, but she doesn't tell me to sweep up tonight; instead she carries me all the way upstairs to the flat, through the kitchen, into the green bathroom, and puts me down in the bath.

"Take your clothes off," she says, so I do.

I always do what I'm told now.

Maggie disappears for a moment, then comes back holding a box of Flash powder, which is what I pour in the mop bucket before cleaning the floors each night. "Sit down," she says. Her face looks strange. It's twisted a little the wrong way, and looking at it makes my knees feel wobbly. She puts the plug in the bath, then turns on the hot tap and waits. The water is cold on my feet at first, but by the time it reaches my ankles, the water is warm. A bit too warm.

"Can I put in some cold please?"

"No."

"The water is hot."

"Good." She pours some of the powder onto a wet flannel, before pouring the rest into the bath until the whole box is empty. The water is burning my skin and I try to stand up, but she pushes me down. "Close your eyes." She starts to scrub at the skin on my face awful hard; it feels like the powder is scraping my cheeks right off. I scream, but Maggie doesn't seem to hear me, she just keeps scrubbing and the water keeps burning. "You have blood on your hands, you need to get clean." She scratches away at my arms, my legs, my back. The water is so hot, and the flannel hurts so much, that I'm screaming more than I have ever screamed before. The noise coming out of my mouth doesn't even sound like me. I hear John banging on the bathroom door, but Maggie has locked it so that he can't come in.

When she puts me to bed, all of me hurts.

She doesn't kiss it better, or kiss me good-night.

My skin is red and my throat is sore from screaming, but I am quiet now.

I am alone in the dark, but inside my ears I keep hearing the last thing that Maggie said, as though she is whispering it, over and over. She has locked me in my room and taken the bulbs out of the light in the ceiling and the lamp next to the bed, even though she knows I get scared. I am hungry and thirsty, but there is nothing to eat or drink. I close my eyes and I put my hands over my ears, but I can still hear her words:

That man is dead because you didn't do as you were told. I didn't kill him, you did.

She says I killed him, so it must be true, Maggie doesn't tell lies.

I killed my mummy and now I've killed the bad man.

I keep doing bad things without meaning to.

I cry because I think I must be a very bad person, and I cry because I think Maggie doesn't love me anymore, and that makes me feel sadder than anything else in the whole world.

Forty

London, 2017

The wrap party is being held at a private club in the heart of London. Even as a child I hated parties. I never had anyone to talk to and I didn't fit in. I've never known who to be when I'm supposed to be me. I don't want to go tonight, but my agent says I should and, given everything that is currently going on, it seems wise to do as I am told. He doesn't seem to understand that social gatherings, with people looking at me all night, fill me with the most horrific and inexplicable fear.

Perhaps I'm just scared of what they might see.

I think about the version of me I need to be tonight, then flick a switch and turn her on, hoping she'll stay with me for as long as I need her to. She doesn't always.

I pass a McDonald's and remember that I haven't eaten. I double back and order a Happy Meal, hoping it might work in more ways than one. I choose the same things I used to as a child thirty years ago: chicken nuggets and french fries to take away. I don't get far. I don't even open the box. I see a homeless girl lying in a doorway on a folded-up piece of cardboard and I stop. I know that could have been me. She looks cold and hungry, so I give her my coat and my Happy Meal, then carry on towards the tube station.

I stare at the floor of the train carriage, avoiding eye contact with my fellow travelers, pretending they can't see me if I can't see them. When I was a little girl, I was always afraid that I might disappear, like the little girl who lived in the flat above the shop before me. I still don't have children of my own, despite wanting them so badly, and time is running out for that dream. The only way I can now live on after I die is through my work. If I could star in the perfect movie, a story that people would remember, then a little bit of me might continue to exist. Someone once said that people like me are born in the dirt and die in the dirt, and I don't want that to be true. The Fincher audition might save me, and if I get the part . . . well, then maybe I won't have to be scared of disappearing anymore.

I get off the tube and fight my way to the surface, walking up the escalator, through the barriers, and up the stone steps, until I am in the open air again. I'm cold without the coat I gave away, but it feels better to be above ground and I remind myself to breathe.

It's just a party.

I let go of the me I need to be for just a moment and lose her in the crowd. My fear turns the volume and my terror up to maximum. I stare down at my new red shoes; it's as though they have become stuck to the pavement. I wonder if I click my heels together three times, if I might magically vanish, but there's no place like home if you've never had one, and I was only ever pretending to be Dorothy in that school play all those years ago. Just as I've only ever pretended to be Aimee Sinclair.

The closer I get to the venue, the worse it gets. I haven't slept for days now, and it feels as if I'm losing my grip on reality. I lean a trembling hand against a wall to try to steady myself as the rush-hour traffic roars past. A black cab races by, then a red double-decker bus seems to charge straight at me, its windows morphing into the shape of evil yellow eyes in the darkness, and even though I know it can't be real, I turn and try to run away, pushing through the crowds of pedestrians marching in the opposite direction. It's as though they link arms and deliberately try to block my path. I cover my head with my hands and close my eyes; when I peer out between the fingers I'm hiding behind, it feels as if the whole world is staring at me. The canvas of multicolored faces starts to twist and blur with the streetlights and traffic, as though someone has taken a paintbrush to this scene of my life and decided to start again. When I lower my hands, I see that they are the same color as the bus, dripping in what looks like red paint. Or blood. I close my eyes again, and when I next open them, the world has reset itself to normal. I switch *her* back on and force my feet to start walking in the right direction once more.

I can do this.

We are all capable of the most fantastical fiction in the aid of self-preservation. A shield of lies can protect from the toughest of truths.

The club wears a disguise, hidden inside a terrace of three Georgian town houses within an elegant square, a short walk from Soho. I cloak myself in a cocoon of forged confidence, then press the buzzer. The huge, shiny black door opens, revealing yet more eighteenth-century architecture and an overly opulent design within. It's certainly atmospheric. A man with a tray of champagne glasses is standing at the bottom of an elaborate circular stone staircase. I take one and enjoy a quick sip, hoping the alcohol might help neutralize my anxiety a little. I remind myself that I'm the lead actress in the film we're here to celebrate working on, and that I deserve to be here, but inside my head the words sound like lies.

The film company has hired the whole place, all three floors. I memorized the entire layout before I came by looking at the venue's website. I find that helps when I'm this scared of an event; knowing what a place is going to look like before I get there. I wander through the rooms, each one decorated in a different but distinctive style. I feel like a guest at a club I'll never be a member of in more ways than one.

I nod and smile when people wave in my direction, and exchange my empty champagne flute for a full glass at the bar, before wandering through to another room. The walls in this one are blue, and I like the color, I find it calming. Then I see her strutting towards me like a trainee catwalk model, and any brief sense of serenity evaporates.

Alicia White should not be here.

"Aimee, darling, how are you?" she purrs, and kisses the air on either side of my cheeks.

She's wearing a red flouncy dress that looks as if it might literally take off, and heels I'd never be able to walk in. She's all tanned skin and bone, and I look even bigger and paler than I am standing next to her. With her hair looking scarily like mine now, it's as though we're the before and after in some fucked-up slimming contest. I'm the before.

"I'm great. It's so good to see you. Again." I mirror her fixed fake smile.

It is not good to see her, it never is. She shouldn't be here, she's not in the film. It makes no sense, as if she just invited herself along to piss me off.

"It's so strange to think that I could have been in this movie"— she shakes her head—"if I hadn't turned them down."

She's crawled so far up her own arse, she can't find the way out.

"Yes, you mentioned that last time."

I so badly want to punch her in the face. She deserves it, but I've never punched anyone in the face, and I'm not sure I'd know how to do it without hurting myself. Her red lips part, and I dread to think what is going to come out of her poisonous mouth next.

"I know how daunting it can all feel when you don't have much experience, but Tony knows what he's doing. I'm sure he wouldn't have put you forward for this if he thought he could get you something better. Sometimes you just have to take what you can get."

Fuck you and your egotism poorly disguised as empathy.

"I saw Tony today actually," I manage, unsure where I'm going with this.

"How lovely. How is he?"

"He's good. He mentioned he doesn't represent you anymore."

Her smile falters so fleetingly I almost miss it. "That's right, it was time to move on."

It must be quite something to love yourself as much as she does; I wouldn't know. But something about her is a little tragic and broken. The spotlight led Alicia somewhere dark, and she couldn't understand when the light went out. I guess nobody explained to her that even the sun disappears for a while, once its turn to shine is over. All stars are born to die.

"Oh, look at your little red shoes, so sweet. It's like you're trying to be Dorothy in *The Wizard of Oz* all over again," she says. "It took me a while, but I think I've just about forgiven you for stealing a part that should have been mine at school." Her words sound a little slurred. I never knew she'd auditioned for the part; she must have *hated* me, especially given I was in the year below. Alicia was always queen bee and always got her own way.

"I . . . I had no idea that you—"

"Of course you didn't."

"No, really. If I'd known, well, I think you would have been terrific."

Water doesn't melt witches in real life, best to kill them with kindness.

She laughs. "I know I would, but it really doesn't matter to me now. It was over twenty years ago! You're probably wondering what I'm doing here tonight . . ."

You probably just invited yourself like usual.

She doesn't wait for a response, which is good, because I can't come up with a polite one.

"We've been keeping it a secret, but I don't think he could stand to be apart any longer, I know I couldn't. He's here somewhere. It can be so hard maintaining a relationship when you're always away filming, but I don't need to tell *you* that. How is your husband?" She looks around the room. I really have no interest in meeting her latest boy-friend. I'm about to make my excuses and walk away when she speaks again. "Jack, darling, come on over here and say hello to your co-star."

I feel physically sick.

Jack emerges from a huddle of men in the corner of the room and strolls over in our direction. She snakes her skinny arm around his waist as soon as he's within touching distance, but he only looks at me, as though he knows he's standing next to Medusa. She kisses him on the cheek, watching for my reaction the whole time, her red lips leaving their mark. My smile is in serious danger of sliding off my face, and holding it there is exhausting.

"Now, I know those pictures in the papers weren't real, but I can't

stay too late to keep an eye on the pair of you tonight, so don't go getting any funny ideas. I need my beauty sleep for my audition for the
next Fincher film tomorrow," she says. My face gives me away for less
than a second, but she sees it. "Oh, *you* have an audition too? You
didn't think you were the only one, did you? Bless, always *so* sweet
and naïve."

"I've just seen someone I just must say hello to, will you excuse
me?" I say to them both, with the best smile my face can manage.

I walk away without waiting for either of them to reply. I find myself in a red room this time—red walls, red furniture, my red shoes
scurrying across a plush red carpet—unable to stop thinking something that I shouldn't. The thought is only on loan, a temporary rental
that I already know I will have to give back sooner or later. I mustn't
hold on to it. But for now, for just a little while longer, I permit myself to indulge the idea. I get myself another glass of champagne, the
words repeating themselves over and over, loud and clear inside the
privacy of my own mind:

I wish Alicia White was dead.

Forty-one

We have carpet.

Brand-new red carpet all over the flat, except in my bedroom, which already had pink carpet, and in the kitchen and the bathroom, which both have a new floor with a name all of its own. It's called lino, and I like to skid across it in my socks. Maggie says the carpet is red so that I can practice being a film star, but for now my favorite thing to do is to slide all the way down the stairs from the flat to the shop on my bottom. John laughs at me and does it, too, yelling he's going to race me down the apples and pears. He does that a lot, makes up silly rhymes that mean something else. *Apples and pears* means "stairs." *Dog and bone* means "phone." Sometimes I don't know what he's talking about, like when he says *brown bread*—we only ever eat white. Maggie looks over the banister at us racing down the stairs and takes a picture on John's camera.

"Eejits," she says, but she smiles, so it's okay. I hear her put on the TV upstairs, leaving John and me laughing, but then there is a knock on the outside door and we both jump. It is Sunday. It is always just the three of us on Sundays, unless we go to the pub to see Uncle Michael, and we're not going there today because John says we need to *lie low*. I thought that might mean sleeping on the floor or something, but Maggie said it means something different without telling me what that was. There is a tall basket at the bottom of the stairs next to the outside door, and we keep umbrellas in it. There are also golf clubs, and a baseball bat, even though we don't play either of those things.

John picks up the bat before pushing me behind him, then moves closer to the door. "Who is it?"

"It's Mrs. Singh," says a voice outside, and I recognize the sound of the beautiful woman from the corner shop, with her brown skin and red spot. John opens the door a little, still holding the bat out of sight behind him.

"How can I help?"

"Someone has left something outside your shop, and I thought you should know." She sounds sorry, but I'm not sure what for.

John leans out of the doorway and stares at something that I cannot see.

"What is it?" I ask, but he doesn't answer.

"What is it?" Maggie asks, like a grown-up echo. She has reappeared at the top of the staircase, and I know he won't ignore her; nothing makes her more cross.

John's mouth opens but the words don't come out at first, as though they got stuck. Then he takes the cigarettes he gave up giving up from his pocket and lights one. It seems to help him speak again.

"It's a box."

Maggie comes down the stairs superfast. "Well, open it."

John thanks Mrs. Singh and brings the box inside, dragging it through to the betting shop, where there is more room. It's large and looks very heavy. He takes a penknife from his pocket, cuts the cardboard, and lifts the lid right off.

Maggie's face turns white and cross. "Go upstairs," she says in my direction, but I don't move, I want to see what it is. "I said, go upstairs!" She pushes me. She seems very upset all of a sudden. I start to walk away, slowly, and when I turn back, I see an empty white coffin. Not a big one, like I've seen at funerals; this one is about the same size as me.

Forty-two

London, 2017

I imagine what Alicia would look like dead as I make my way around the party.

I realize that these thoughts are neither normal or healthy, but they are the only ones currently occupying my mind, and I'm rather enjoying them. I need another drink. The club is full of bars, so that at least is one desire that shouldn't be too hard to satisfy. I climb the spiral staircase and head for the third floor, the place physically farthest away from Jack and Alicia.

I don't know what I'm so upset about or why I'm so surprised. Men fall for women like that all the time; as if they can't see the bitch behind the beauty. Why should Jack be any different? It isn't as though I thought there was anything real between us; obviously the sexual tension was just an act for when the cameras were rolling, and any friendship that developed as a result of spending all those months filming together was just the product of time shared, the camaraderie of a common experience.

As for the audition, I think I'm justified in feeling upset about that. Tony made it sound as if the part were already mine. I guess agents, like normal human beings, occasionally tell people what they want to hear. Maybe he was trying to boost my confidence after the online article about the affair I'm not having. Maybe he could see that I was falling apart and was simply trying to stitch me back together, protect his investment.

The drinks are all free, paid for by the film company, so I have another. I feel like I've earned it. Anxiety changes my relationship with food and drink; it comes between me and food, forcing me closer to alcohol. I know I need to slow down, but sometimes the advice we give ourselves is the hardest to hear. The barman looks surprised to see me again so soon. I tell him this glass is for my friend, and he nods politely. My acting skills are clearly fooling nobody tonight.

I head down to the floor below, another room, another design. This one is all about black leather sofas and low lighting, with modern art clinging to the walls. There are black blinds hiding the outside world from us, and us from it. And there's another bar, housing a barman who hasn't served me yet, one who can't judge me the way I'm currently judging myself. This will have to be the last glass for now.

Down another flight of steps and I'm back where I started on the ground floor. I won't make myself stay too much longer, but I can't leave just yet. Besides, where would I go? I need to be seen to say hello to a few more people for the sake of my future self. So much goes on behind the scenes in this industry that the general public doesn't know. Perhaps it's for the best. When magicians reveal how they do their tricks, it's hard to still believe in the magic.

Beyond the imposing façade of the Georgian architecture, I see a room I've yet to explore. This one is purple, with a metallic bar and lighting so low that the faces in the room are more like shadows. I feel a breeze, and I see something beyond the purple room: a garden. I step out into the secluded, yet spacious, hidden gem, such an unusual find in central London. A white tent in the middle of the walled courtyard is decorated in gold stars, with a champagne bar in the far corner. This is where everyone has been hiding—out in the open. I get myself another drink, ignoring the stern voice inside my head strongly advising me not to, then I scan the faces all around me and spot the director and his wife. They're talking to some people I don't know, but I join their group anyway, feeling a little safer surrounding myself with at least some familiar faces. I make an effort to listen to their conversation, hoping it might drown out the thoughts inside my head. I think I see the flash of a camera, but when I look up, I can't see anyone pointing anything in my direction. Besides, there shouldn't be anyone here from the press tonight, it's not that sort of party.

The director's wife takes a packet of cigarettes out of her bag. The smell of cigarette smoke can still transport me back in time, and the memories it invokes are not always good. I watch as she puts one between her gloss-covered lips and notice how unusual it looks—long and thin and completely white, as though there is no filter.

"They're fancy-looking cigarettes," I say as she lights up.

She removes it from her mouth with manicured fingers. "Would you like one?"

I haven't smoked since I was eighteen.

"Yes, please," I hear a voice say, before realizing it is my own.

She lights it for me, shielding the flame from the wind with her free hand, and I listen to her Hollywood stories without really listening. I inhale deeply, enjoying the temporary high of the nicotine. I'm starting to think there isn't much I wouldn't do to be the version of me I could live with. The version of me who could be forgiven for all the terrible things I've made myself do to get where I am today.

My attention is easily drawn away from the conversation, choosing instead to focus on the back of a smartly dressed man on the other side of the courtyard. His height, build, and the way his hairline tapers at his neck are all a little too familiar.

It's him.

I can't see his face, but every fiber of my being is telling me it's my husband.

I feel a lot colder than I did before, and my fingers holding the cigarette start to tremble. My eyes are willing him to turn around, to prove to my mind that it's wrong, but he doesn't turn to face me; instead he starts to walk away. I follow, as quickly as I dare without drawing attention to myself, but I can't keep up and soon lose him in the crowd. I retrace my steps, through each of the different-colored rooms, scanning wildly for another glimpse of Ben, before coming back to the courtyard, still unable to see him.

I must have imagined it.

I'm tired, a little drunk, my mind is playing tricks on me again, that's all.

I return to the group I was standing with before—safety in

numbers—then allow myself to get lost inside my own thoughts once more, the alcohol and the tobacco joining forces to coax them out of me. I'm still wondering whether I have just seen a ghost of a man or a memory.

Ben can't be dead.

Because I didn't kill him, I would remember if I had.

I remember everyone else that I've killed.

Forty-three

Essex, 1988

Today I'm learning how to shoot a gun.

Some bad people want to hurt me, and Maggie and John. Maggie says we need to be ready. I'm not sure what it is we need to be ready for, but I know that I'm scared. Maggie says that it's all right to be scared, but that I have to hide my fear somewhere I can't find it. I think that must be what she does with the car keys, because she loses them all the time. Maggie says I have to learn how to turn fear into strength. I don't know what she's talking about. I just want to go home, and I realize that home is the flat above the shop. I don't think about my old home much anymore, I don't ever want to go back there now. I have nice things here, and I don't want to "die in the dirt," like my brother once said that I would.

We drive to a place called Epping Forest. It's morning, but it's so early that even the sun isn't up yet; the moon is still doing a sideways smile in the black sky. We walk for a little bit, Maggie, John, and me, crunching over leaves and twigs, and I decide that I like the forest. It's nice and quiet, not like the shop. John says if we see anybody else, we have to say we are going for a picnic. I think that's silly, nobody goes for a picnic this early in the morning and we don't have any food with us.

The police took the gun that Maggie shot the bad man with, but we have two new ones now, presents from the man we call Uncle Michael. He gave them to us at the pub last Sunday. I think he needs a haircut—it's grown so long he looks like a girl. I must have pulled a face when Maggie said I had to learn to use a gun, but then she promised it would be fun, like my Speak & Spell machine. The one I am going to learn to shoot is called a pistol—even guns have lots of different names, like people. It looks nothing like my Speak & Spell—it is silver, not orange—and it feels heavy in my hand.

Maggie opens up the bag she has been carrying and takes out some tins of Heinz baked beans. I wonder if we are having a picnic after all, but then I see that they are empty. She puts the tin cans all over the place; some on top of the leaves on the ground, and some in the branches of the trees. Then she comes back to show me what to do. John doesn't do or say much. Maggie tells him, "Keep watch," but I'm not sure what he is meant to be watching—there is nobody else here.

Maggie can hit the tin cans from real far away; they make a funny noise when she does and topple over. She puts them all straight again, gives me back the pistol, and says that it is my turn. The pistol is so heavy it's hard for me to hold it straight. I close one eye, just like Maggie did, then I squeeze hard and fall backwards when the gun goes off. John laughs at me, but Maggie doesn't. She makes me do it again, and again, and again. Until my arms ache and my ears are hurting from all the loud bangs. I start to cry because I don't want to do this anymore.

Maggie tells me to stop, but I can't.

She tells me to stop crying again, and when I don't the second time, she takes the pistol from my shaky hands, pulls down my trousers, and smacks me hard on the bum with it. I scream and she does it again.

John is looking the other way. He's staring at a perfect-looking tree and has been smoking one cigarette after the other since we arrived. I see a pretty letter *A* carved into the bark and wonder when he had time to do that.

He turns to face us both. "I really don't think this is necessary."

"They sent a *coffin* as a warning, John. I won't lose her too," Maggie replies through her teeth.

"She can't do it."

"Yes, she can."

"I'm telling you, she can't."

"And I'm telling you to shut the fuck up."

He stares at the ground.

I stop crying because I know Maggie won't stop hitting me until I do.

She gives me the gun back without saying anything, then pulls up my trousers. I'm so mad I think about pointing it right at her, but she'd probably kill me if I did that. I don't want to disappear, and I don't want to die in the dirt in a place called Epping Forest. I know she loves me really. She must do, she says so all the time.

I point the gun at the lowest tin can in the tree. I close one eye and hold the gun still, just like Maggie showed me. Then I pull the part she calls a Tigger, like in *Winnie-the-Pooh*, and the tin can falls to the ground.

Maggie smiles, and her happy face looks at me for the first time all day. She picks me up, as though the bad stuff she just did to me didn't happen, so I pretend that it didn't happen too and put my arms around her neck. She smells so nice. When I grow up, I'm going to wear number five just like her. I don't even care what the other numbers smell like. When Maggie wears her happy face, I like to pretend she doesn't have another one.

"I knew you could do it, Baby Girl." She looks at John, even though she is speaking to me.

I do it again, and this time John takes a photo of me on his Polaroid camera. I don't get to see what I look like holding a gun though, because Maggie snatches the photo from his hand before the picture even appears, then uses John's lighter to burn it away into nothing.

"Idiot," she says, and he stares at his feet as though they are something interesting.

I hit the tin cans ten more times, and when Maggie says I have learned enough for one day, John drives us home. Maggie sits in the back with me, instead of next to him. She holds my hand and smiles, and I'm glad that she loves me again. When we get back to the shop, Maggie shows me where the gun is hidden and tells me that I must never, ever, touch it unless she tells me to. She says now that I'm a big girl, we need a code, and the code is "Say your prayers." I think this is funny because we never pray, but she tells me off for giggling. I can see she is wearing her most serious face, so I stop. She gives me the best present ever for being a good girl—a Wonder Woman costume, and I am allowed to wear it all day.

In the evening, after the shop is closed, the three of us watch *Cagney & Lacey* together in their bed, eating cheese on toast. I like this program, it's my favorite TV show ever. Both of the women are pretty and clever and they shoot guns. In my head, I pretend that Maggie and me are Cagney and Lacey, chasing all the bad men.

When the program ends, Maggie switches off the TV with the remote control and looks at me.

"If I said, 'Say your prayers,' right now, what would you do, Baby Girl?"

I think real hard because I know that I must not get this wrong. I know it's important.

"I would go and get the gun from the hiding place real quick."

She nods. "Then what would you do?"

"Shoot it."

"Shoot it and what?"

"Shoot it and keep shooting until nobody moves."

"Clever girl, that's the right answer."

Forty-four

London, 2017

I see it out of the corner of my eye as I take another sip of champagne. A flash. I'm sure I didn't imagine it this time.

For as long as I can remember, I have hated having my photo taken. I'm not sure why. I didn't even want a photographer at my wedding, not that Ben seemed to mind. There was just one little photo of our big day, taken by a stranger on the street outside the registry office. In some places in the world people believe that having your photo taken steals a part of your soul. My fears don't stretch quite that far, but I do worry that a camera can capture something in me that I would rather remained hidden.

I try to listen to the conversation I am pretending to take part in, and I see it again, the flash of a camera phone. If I was in any doubt before, the sight of the person holding it confirms my suspicions. Jennifer Jones stares in my direction; she has the audacity to smile. I don't know what to do. I look around wildly in search of some form of assistance.

Just like Alicia, *she* should not be here.

I don't just despise Jennifer Jones, I *hate* her, and everyone like her; disgorging all my secrets, one by one, forming a tower of truths I would rather nobody else could see. My secrets are my own, and I don't like them being shared. I look around again, and then, perhaps because of everything that is happening in my private life, or perhaps because I've consumed far more alcohol than was wise this evening, I decide to deal with the matter myself and march across the courtyard.

"How dare you come here tonight," I spit at her.

She laughs in my face. "I'm just doing my job. If you're looking for someone to blame, try the woman who tipped me off about you. You were set up by someone you know and it's the easiest money I've ever made!"

Her words wind me. "Who?"

"What's it worth?"

"It's worth me not smashing my glass in your face." For a moment I think I might mean it, but she doesn't look worried at all. If anything, the whole exchange seems to delight her.

"I thought I saw her here earlier," she says, looking over my shoulder.

Her.

"Who?" I look around the room, expecting to see Alicia in her line of vision.

"She wouldn't tell me her name. She looked a bit like you, dressed like you too. Same hair, trench coat, dark glasses, red lipstick. A little older than you are. Ringing any bells?" She's describing the stalker. This proves it, that everything that has happened is all connected. The woman pretending to be me *was* having an affair with my husband, it was her red lipstick I found under the bed, and she used my laptop to send emails calling herself Maggie to frame me.

"Of course, a journalist needs more than one source, and I needed photographic evidence, but luckily Jack was only too happy to help, taking selfies of the two of you together in your dressing room and sending them to me."

I can't believe what I'm hearing.

"Are you quite all right? You've turned very pale. You're not going to throw up, are you? That would ruin the video . . ."

I look and see her phone still tilted up in my direction. "You're filming this?"

"I'm afraid so, honey. They're making redundancies at TBN again, and a journo's gotta do what a journo's gotta do to survive in this business nowadays. It's not personal."

It *is* personal.

I grab the phone out of her clawlike hand and throw it onto the stone floor, then I smash the face of it with the heel of my red shoe. Quite an audience gathers around us, including the director, who has summoned security.

"I guess you won't be filing a story about me tonight after all."

As she is led towards the exit, she turns to look over her shoulder, still smiling. "Oh, I already filed a piece about you tonight. I had a tip-off to visit your home address this afternoon, and I got it all. It will go live in an hour or so. I'd say it's the showbiz scoop of the month, but I might be biased. Either way, it's a *killer* of a story."

She disappears into the crowd of faces all staring in my direction.

Forty-five

Essex, 1988

I do not like people staring at me.

Maggie and John have hired someone to help today. She is called Susan. Susan keeps staring at me and I wish that she wouldn't.

Today is something called the Grand National. John says it is the busiest day of the year. He keeps saying that, as though he is worried I might forget. He doesn't need to worry, my memory works just fine, and the only time I forget things is when I do it on purpose. Even then, I don't *really* forget. I can remember my old name, the one I'm not allowed to use. Sometimes I still say it inside my head when I'm in bed at night. Sometimes it feels like something I maybe ought to remember.

Ciara. Ciara. Ciara.

I don't like the idea of people forgetting me, it scares me a little bit. Sometimes it scares me a lot. As though if I am forgotten, then maybe I didn't exist in the first place. John said the little girl who used to live here disappeared. I don't ever want to disappear. I want people to remember who I am, even if the me they remember isn't the real me. I haven't figured out how to do that yet, but I'm sure if I think about it long enough, then I will. Maggie says that I am smart, and she says that I can be whoever I want to be when I grow up, and I like the sound of that.

John says that this is the busiest day of the year for the hundredth time, then tells me to be kind to Susan. They hired her to help answer the phones, I don't know why, I could have done it but Maggie says I sound too young. I'm going to start practicing sounding older, as well as sounding English, so we don't have to hire strange people to help out again.

I do not like Susan.

I think it's better when it is just the three of us.

Susan brought in a tin of Quality Street for us all to share, pretending to be kind, but she'd already taken out all the toffee pennies, which are the best ones. So she clearly can't be trusted. Maggie says that Susan is an old friend, so to be nice to her, but I don't know about that. She is definitely old. She has gray hair and lots of little lines around her eyes, and her teeth are yellow. I think it might have been all the toffee pennies she ate that did that. She's short and round, a bit like a toffee penny. I'm going to keep an eye on Susan, maybe both eyes, I think she's sneaky.

Today is so busy that I am helping too. We have to go to the bank three times instead of once today, I'm not sure why. John says it's important for the safe not to be too full. I think maybe he is worried he won't be able to close it if too much money is in there. We drive to the bank nowadays, even though it isn't far. The third time we go, I ask if we can get a McDonald's, but John says no. He gives the woman the bundles of cash out of the HEAD bag and gets cross when she takes too long to give him the bags of change he asked for. I'm cross too, because I'm hungry, and because he isn't being nice. Nobody is being nice to me today. It's just a bunch of horses jumping over fences and I don't understand it, I'd rather read a book.

John kicks the car outside the bank because it has a flat tire, but I'm not sure kicking it will help. We walk super fast all the way back to the shop, with no talking allowed. John tells me to lock the gates, then he makes sure the back door is locked twice, before disappearing behind the stripy curtain to serve all the customers that are waiting. It's very noisy today, even more than normal, and I can see them pushing each other to get to the till. The smoke from their cigarettes has turned into an indoor cloud, and it stings my eyes.

I turn back towards my little room and see Susan sitting by the phones, eating. She's always eating. I'd forgotten she was here and

I give her my best evil stare, because I don't care whether she knows I don't like her.

She stops chewing her lunch and smiles. "Would you like some of my sandwich?"

I am hungry, but I don't know whether I do.

"What's in it?"

"Just Flora and corned beef."

I do like corned beef, so I say yes. Her sandwich is cut into triangles, she gives me one from her plate, and I dislike her a little less than I did before.

"I know today isn't much fun for a little girl like you. You should be outside playing in the fresh air."

I ignore her and go sit in the little back room, then I watch TV without watching it. Susan appears in the doorway, and I wish one of the phones would ring so that she would just go away. They haven't rung for ages, which is strange.

"I don't think you locked the gate properly," she says, looking out the window.

"Yes, I did," I say with my mouth full.

"No, I don't think so, and I think your dad is going to be real mad when he finds out."

I'm sure I locked it.

"Do you want me to go check? It can be our little secret?" I notice a little bit of corned beef stuck between her yellow teeth.

"We're not allowed to open the back door," I say, remembering the bad man with the knife.

"It will only take me a minute. Otherwise, when they find out you didn't lock it, you'll get in such big trouble. I'm only thinking of you."

I don't want to get in trouble. "Okay."

I watch as she takes the keys, unlocks the back door, then walks down to the gate. I can't see what she is doing, but when she comes back, she says that I *had* locked it properly after all. I *knew* I had. I do not like Susan.

She starts to lock the door. I see her put the key in the hole, but then she stops. "Do you like Dairy Milk chocolate?"

"Only if it doesn't have nuts or raisins in it."

She smiles, and I stare at the corned beef in her teeth again. Maggie says that it is wrong to stare at people's imperfections, but I can't stop my eyeballs from looking at what they want.

"See, I brought a big bar of Dairy Milk with me today, one of those giant ones, but then I realized I couldn't possibly eat it all by myself. Do you think you could help me?"

I love Dairy Milk. I like putting the little squares on my tongue and sucking on them until all the chocolate melts away inside my mouth. I nod, hoping she won't change her mind because I've been so unfriendly all day long.

"Thank you, you are a good girl. It's no wonder your mum loves you so much. The bar is in my bag. Why don't you go on through and open it for me, while I make sure this door is properly locked."

I walk into the phone room and find the chocolate straightaway. I open it, careful not to tear the purple paper or foil, then snap off a little bit and pop it in my mouth. I think about what Susan just said, about Maggie loving me, and I realize that I love her, too, and that makes me feel happy.

It's late when the shop finally closes, and I am tired and hungry. Maggie has promised we'll get fish and chips for dinner, as soon as all the money has been counted and put away.

"Cod and chips, my favorite," says John. I look over at him and he pulls a codfish face, so I do too. Both our mouths are open, our lips like the letter O, and then we smile at our silent Mary Poppins joke. Maggie doesn't smile because she doesn't think it's funny, even though it is. She says we've made so much money today that I don't have to sweep up tonight, we'll do it all tomorrow.

Susan leaves through the front door, she says that it is quicker to get to her bus stop that way, and Maggie locks it behind her. Susan was invited to stay for supper but said no, and I'm glad. I still don't like her, despite all the chocolate she let me eat, and fish and chips is what the three of us do. As John always says, we don't need nobody else.

Maggie helps John count the money behind the counter. I can hear the adding machine going clickety-click. I decide to build a fort in the shop while I wait, dragging some of the leather stools together, and laying the newspaper pages that have come down from the walls over the top.

It all happens so fast and the sound is so loud.

The car crashes through the front of the shop, almost smashing straight into my fort. Time stops for a tiny moment. I look at Maggie and John behind the counter, both their mouths are wide open, staring at the blue car, and I realize that my mouth is open too. I think we must all look like codfish now. Maggie's eyes are awful wide, and she is shouting something at me, but I can't hear her; the sound of glass smashing and car doors opening is all too loud. My eyes are staring at the two men with masks on their faces getting out of the car, but then my ears remember how to work and I hear Maggie.

"Run, Aimee!"

So I do.

I run behind the counter, and John locks the door that separates us from the shop. Maggie grabs me with one hand and picks up the phone in the other, holding it to her ear with her shoulder. She keeps stabbing the 9 button with her red nails, but then slams it down, saying that it's dead.

"Fuckers," says John, but Maggie ignores him and looks down at me.

"Say your prayers," she says, and I know what that means.

I always remember everything Maggie teaches me.

I run towards the little back room, but before I even reach the stripy curtains, I hear the men smash through the counter. One of them is swinging a giant hammer, it's bigger than me.

"Open the fuckin' safe," says the other one, and I see him point a gun at Maggie's head. John bends down to the safe and I run. I crawl under the desk, and my fingers find the pistol that is taped underneath it. Even though my hands are shaking, my fingers seem to know what to do. The back door bursts open, and another bad man comes inside. He doesn't see me under the desk. I don't understand how he got in because I know I locked the door when we got back from the bank. But then I remember Susan, and the gate, and the Dairy Milk, and the silent phones. I know she tricked me, and I am so confused and cross all at once.

I am not afraid anymore, I am just angry. More angry than I have ever been about anything. I stand behind the stripy curtain, trying to hold the gun steady, not sure who to point it at first—there are three of them now. One of the bad men is holding Maggie, another is pointing his gun at John, who starts to open the safe, just like they told him to. Then everyone is shouting again and I hear a loud bang.

I see all the red on Maggie's white jumper before she falls to the shop floor.

John runs to her, and they shoot him, too, twice in the back.

I stand perfectly still while they kick my mum and my dad with their dirty boots, and I hear them say that they are dead. Nobody has seen me, as though I have already disappeared. Two of the bad men bend down next to the safe, laughing and filling their bags with our money. I look back at Maggie and can see that her eyes are open again, looking at me.

I fire my gun.

I'm so close behind them, I cannot miss.

I do what she taught me to do and shoot until nobody moves. Then I carry on shooting anyway, until I don't have any bullets left.

"Come here, Baby Girl." Maggie sounds croaky and far away. I cuddle up next to her on the floor and try to stop the blood from coming out of her tummy with my hands, the way I've seen people do on TV. But it won't stop. There's a great big red puddle of it now, and my fingers are all red.

"Give me the gun," she whispers, so I do. She wipes it on her trousers, then takes a white hankie from her sleeve and wraps it around the pistol. "Don't touch it again, don't touch anything. Now go and put this in John's hand, go on, hurry up now, careful not to touch it." I'm crying and shaking, but I do what Maggie tells me to do, because I've learned that bad things happen to me when I don't. John doesn't move when I put the gun in his hand. I don't like touching him, and I run back to Maggie as soon as I've done it. She puts her arm around me and I lay my head on her chest, the way I do when we cuddle in bed. Then I close my eyes and listen to the sound of her breathing, and her voice in my ears.

"When they come, you just say you hid out back and found everyone like this. You don't tell them about the gun. You don't tell them nothing. I love you, Baby Girl. You tell them your name is Aimee Sinclair, that's all you say when they come, and you remember that I loved you."

I'm crying too hard to speak. I lie in her arms, her blood all over my face and clothes, and when I manage to say, "I love you too," her eyes are already closed.

Forty-six

London, 2017

I emerge from the bathroom at the club, coercing my head to hold itself high, and planning to just get the hell out of here as fast as I can. I feel as if everyone at the party is looking at me after my exchange with Jennifer Jones, and although she has been escorted from the building, I can't stay here now. She's confirmed what I suspected from the start: I'm being set up by my husband and a stalker who is pretending to be me. I remember all the vintage postcards I found in the shoebox in the attic, all written by her, all with the same short message:

I know who you are.

Well, I don't know who *she* is, but I know that they're working together, I'm sure of it.

If the woman looks older than me, then it can't be Alicia, and I don't know anyone else who hates me enough to want to destroy me like this. And as for Jack . . .

"There you are, I've been looking everywhere for you! I heard what happened," he says, crossing my path right on cue. His face is doing such a good job of portraying concern that I almost believe it is genuine.

"How could you?"

His mouth opens and closes repeatedly, whatever he is trying to say experiencing a series of false starts. *"Je ne comprends pas,"* he eventually says with a childish grin, accompanied by a theatrical shrug.

I try to push past him, but he stops me. "I'm not in the mood for your silly French phrases."

"No. Right. Of course, I'm sorry. If you mean sending the photos to the press, well, then I did that for you as well as me, you'll thank me one day. All publicity is good publicity, did nobody teach you that yet?"

"I'm going to leave now."

"No, you're not." He blocks my path. "Stay for one more drink. Journalists and politicians aren't the only people who need to spin for a living. You need everyone here to think this little incident was nothing, laugh it off. Let them see that you don't give a shit. Then, and only then, can you leave this party."

"I hate you right now."

"I hate me all the time, but I think you should put that to one side for a moment. Think with your head, not your heart, then you can go back to hating me again tomorrow."

"No, I want to leave."

He sighs in mock defeat. "Okay, then let me take you home, I'll call us a taxi."

"I don't need you to take me home. Go hang out with Alicia." He smiles at this, and I feel childish, wishing I could take back the words.

"It's nothing, it never was. I'm not sleeping with her, regardless of what she might have told you, and I don't plan to. Christ, she'd probably swallow me whole afterwards, like one of those spiders who eat the male after mating. I'm just being kind because she's going through a bad patch. Her mother died a few weeks ago, and her grief seems to have consumed her. It surprised me a bit at first, because it sounded like they had a difficult relationship. I always remember this horrible story she told me, that happened when she was a teenager. Apparently, her mum didn't speak to her for over a week once, just because she didn't get the lead in some stupid school play, can you imagine?"

He's talking about when I got the part of Dorothy instead of her, I'm sure of it.

"Alicia ended up running away from home because she thought her mum didn't love her anymore after that. She slept in a cardboard box on the street for three nights before going back. Even then, her mother never forgave her, said that she had let her down because she didn't get the part. It's funny, isn't it, why we do the things we do? Why we become the people we become? I've reached the conclusion that our ambitions are rarely our own. Her mother might have died, but I swear Alicia is still trying to make her proud, desperate for forgiveness. Imagine that; having a ghost for a muse. A few days after her mother's funeral, her agent dropped her. It wasn't his fault, he didn't know, and to be fair she hasn't even had an audition for months."

No wonder she hates me so much.

"She said she has an audition for the new Fincher movie tomorrow."

"Ha! See what I mean! Now, Alicia is someone who knows how to spin! From now on, in any given situation, I want you to think, 'What would Alicia do?' Then you should at least consider doing that, instead of being so nice all the time. Nice wins in the movies, but rarely in real life. There is no Fincher audition; rumor has it he's already decided on the female lead and the deal is practically signed off."

I feel a moment of pure joy rush through me but say nothing. I've learned to keep quiet about everything in this business until contracts have been signed and exchanged. Promises and hearsay are worthless. But I can still feel people staring at me and I want them to stop.

"I need to go home." The words come out of my mouth wrapped in a whisper, but Jack hears them.

"Let me help you." He takes my hand, and I let him lead me through the crowds and different-colored rooms towards the exit.

A waiter carrying a tray with a single glass of champagne blocks our path in the middle of the red room.

"No, thank you," I say, avoiding eye contact.

"It's Dom Pérignon, not house," the waiter says. "We don't normally serve it by the glass, but this was paid for by the gentleman at the bar. He also wanted me to tell you that he likes your shoes," he adds, looking more than a little embarrassed. I peer behind him, but don't see anyone I recognize. Everyone I do see seems to be staring in my direction; I don't think I'm imagining it anymore. My phone beeps inside my handbag, and I let go of Jack's hand, my fingers frantically searching for it, scared of what it might say—some news alert about what the police think I have done, or Jennifer Jones's latest online article. But it's just a text, albeit from a number I don't recognize. At first, I think it must be a mistake when I read the two words on the screen accompanied by a link. Then I feel my body turn icy cold.

"What date is it?" I ask Jack.

He twists his wrist to consult his Apple Watch. More people seem to be filling the room with every second that passes.

"September sixteenth. Why?"

I read the two words on the screen again, blinking, unsure whether I can trust my own eyes.

Happy Birthday!

I have celebrated my birthday in April for most of my life. Nobody knows that I was really born in September. Except Maggie. But she's been dead for years.

I watched her die.

I look wildly around the room.

Who bought me this drink?

Who sent me that text?

Who is it that knows who I really am?

It isn't her that I see, it's him. Just a glimpse of his eyes watching me from the corner of the red room. My not-so-missing husband finally found. He raises a glass in my direction, but then someone walks right in front of him, and when I look again, he's gone. Like a ghost.

Did I imagine it?

More and more people are staring at me, I'm not imagining that.

I turn to Jack, but he is busy looking at his phone, and when he looks up, his expression is not unlike all the others being worn by the faces in the room. He looks at me as though he were staring at a monster. I look back at the text message and click the link. It redirects me to the TBN news app, and I see my face on the screen and read my name in the headline.

The sensation is disorienting.

It's like thinking you were sitting in the audience, only to discover you were actually on center stage the whole time. Surrounded by expectant eyes, but unable to remember your character, let alone your lines. I feel dizzy. I think I might be sick right here in front of them all. The crowd is almost completely silent as I see the now-familiar shape of Detective Alex Croft walking towards me, the sea of expectant faces parting to allow her through.

"Well, isn't this a nice party," she says. "Aimee Sinclair, I am arresting you on suspicion of murdering Ben Bailey. You do not have to say anything, but it may harm your defense if you do not mention when questioned something you later rely on in court. Anything you do say may be given in evidence."

Each one of her words seems to be punctuated with a further loss of hope, until I have none left.

She smiles her crooked smile, then leans forward and whispers in my ear, before cuffing my wrists, "I always knew you were a killer actress."

Forty-seven

Essex, 2017

Maggie O'Neil sits in her flat reading the Sunday newspapers. She wears cotton gloves on her hands because the flat is cold, and because she hates the sight of them; they are hands that have spent a lifetime working for a living, not *acting*. Her hands have worked hard because her life has been hard, and nothing about any of it is fair, because life just isn't. Maggie has been waiting a long time to tell her side of the story, and now that her turn has finally come, she's enjoying every minute.

She removes her gloves temporarily, to look at the picture of Aimee as a child she keeps on the little side table next to the telephone. The frame is covered in a thin layer of dust, the wood a little chipped and scratched in places. The photo inside the frame is old now, and a little faded. Maggie shakes her head, unaware that she is doing so, and narrows her eyes at the smiling face of the child in the picture. *After all I did for you,* she thinks, and tuts. Maggie believes that she is responsible for Aimee's success; she helped raise her as a child after all, taught her things, gave her opportunities that Maggie herself never had. And what did the child ever do for her in return? Nothing, that's what. Doesn't even acknowledge her existence.

She holds the frame right up to her face, as though she might kiss the glass. Then she breathes on it and wipes the dust and grime with the sleeve of her hoodie, to get a clearer view of the face beneath the dirt. Aimee was only five or six when the photo was taken. She was a good girl back then. She did what she was told.

Not like now.

Maggie prefers to remember Aimee as the child she used to be, rather than the woman she grew up into; a woman who *acts* as though Maggie doesn't exist. She spent years wondering what happened to the sweet little Aimee in this photo, but she knows the truth about that now, too, no matter how badly it still hurts. Sweet little Aimee found a new home for herself with a series of foster parents and started *acting*. She was so good at pretending to be someone she wasn't as a child, she went and made a career of it—a lifetime of lying to everyone, including herself. But Maggie knows the truth. Maggie knows who Aimee really is. Perhaps that's why Aimee acts as though Maggie is dead.

Maggie reads all the online articles about Aimee, checking Twitter *and* Facebook *and* Instagram for updates at least once an hour. She buys all the newspapers and cuts out all the reviews, then saves them in her giant red album of Aimee. She's read every single interview, and despite searching for some scrap of gratitude or recognition, Aimee has never, ever, mentioned her. Not once.

Maggie looks down at her ugly hands again and sees that she is doing that thing that she does from time to time. She can't remember when she started doing it, but wishes she could stop. She holds the three smallest fingers of her left hand inside her right one and closes her eyes; it's easier to pretend she's still holding the little girl's hand when her eyes are closed. Aimee used to like holding Maggie's hand, but then she went and grew up into someone who didn't look or sound like Aimee at all. The children we raise are supposed to love us, not leave us behind.

Maggie keeps that picture of Aimee by the telephone because she knows that the girl will call her up one day, she just *knows* it. Her eyes move from the smiling child in the picture back to the sight of her own ungloved hands holding the frame. She is equally disgusted by what she sees and puts her white cotton gloves back on.

You can do all sorts of things to your face and your body to make them look younger and more beautiful. A variety of potions and lotions for the amateurs, a wide range of procedures and operations for the more dedicated followers of self-preservation. But the hands are always a giveaway. She stands and stretches, her back aching from leaning over today's newspapers for too long.

Maggie walks around the tiny front room, negotiating a path around the clutter. Some of it her own, most of it inherited from people who didn't need whatever they had wherever they were going. She runs a house-clearance company now, a rather successful one too. She often has to turn down work lately; she can only do so much on her own, and she likes working alone; she learned a long time ago that other people can't be trusted. Clearing out the homes of dead people is hard work, not like *acting*, but it does have its rewards.

She stops pacing to examine her reflection. The mirror on the wall is nice, with a good, solid frame. She *recovered* it from an old lady's house in Chiswick last week. Maggie only takes things she knows won't be missed. She is mostly pleased by what she sees when she looks in the glass. *Mostly*. She's worked hard on this face and body, really hard. She's had some help: a nose job, liposuction, eye-bag removal, Botox, fillers. Her face looks very different from how it used to, but it still isn't quite right.

She pulls her long black curly hair across it like a curtain, then flicks it back over her shoulder before lowering her gaze, unbuttoning her shirt a little. Her chest is still her worst feature, the sight of it inflicting daily damage on her self-confidence, but the doctor in Harley Street is insisting on yet another meeting before going ahead with the procedure. She closes her eyes, touching her chest with her fingertips, imagining what her body will feel like when everything has been done.

Technically she is middle-aged now, and it's about time she had what she wanted in life, everything she has worked so hard for. She leans closer to the mirror, sees a black hair on her chin, and reaches for a pair of tweezers on the mantelpiece—there are several pairs all over her home. Maggie only sits down to relax on the sofa again when the face she has tried so hard to perfect is hair-free.

She refreshes her laptop and smiles at the new tweets she reads about Aimee, taking screen grabs of each one. Then she checks her emails, but there is nothing new. Maggie has tried dating websites in the past, but true love is a luxury that she has never quite been able to afford. And she hasn't spent all these years, working hard on this body, just to share it with some loser. She glares at the letter on the mantelpiece from the Harley Street doctor because she often thinks that her current situation—being alone—is his fault.

Maggie returns her attention to today's newspapers, slipping her glasses up onto her nose and licking her finger before turning the pages. She sips her lukewarm green tea with a series of loud slurps. She hates the flavor, but the proven antiaging and antioxidant benefits far outweigh any displeasure experienced by her taste buds. She reminds herself as she gulps it down that green tea can help delay several signs of skin aging, such as sagging skin, sun damage, age spots, fine lines, *and* wrinkles. Maggie thinks the idea that what is on the inside of a person counts the most, is nothing more than a myth invented by ugly people.

Her gloved hands hover in midair when her eyes find what they have been looking for, forming a bird-shaped shadow on the wall. A picture of Aimee Sinclair is staring right back at her from the newspaper: Aimee the actress, all grown-up, with a big smile stretched across her stupid, lying face. It must be an old picture; she's quite certain that Aimee isn't smiling anymore.

Maggie's eyes stick to the words written in the headline, as if she's fallen under a spell. She removes her glasses and wipes them on her hoodie, ignoring the stains from last night's spilled baked beans on toast. Then she rests them back on her nose to get a better look. She stares at the words as though she were in a trance, translating them into something that makes her smile so hard it hurts.

AIMEE SINCLAIR ARRESTED
FOR HUSBAND'S MURDER

Maggie reads the story three times. Slowly. Some meals for the mind are too delicious to rush. She picks up her left-handed scissors and takes her time cutting out the article, careful not to tear the thin paper. Then she lifts the heavy photo album from its place on the coffee table, and turns to one of the few empty pages at the back. She peels away the transparent sleeve and sticks the new Aimee Sinclair clipping right in the middle of the page.

Forty-eight

London, 2017

"Name?" says the prison guard behind the desk.

"Aimee Sinclair," I whisper.

"Speak up, and look at the camera," he barks, and I repeat my name, while staring at the small black device attached to the wall. It feels a bit like being at an airport, except that I know I'm not going anywhere nice.

"Place your right hand in the middle of the screen," he says next.

"What for?"

"I need to process your fingerprints. Place your right hand in the middle of the screen." He sounds weary. I do as he says. "Now just your right thumb." I move my hand. "Now the left . . ."

I feel strange as I follow a female guard through further airport-style security. A little light-headed, as though perhaps I am dreaming and none of this is real. I walk through a full-size scanner and then stand with my arms and legs spread, while two guards pat down every single part of my body.

"Remove your clothes, all of them, and put them on the chair."

I do as I am told.

At first I feel violated because I haven't done anything wrong, and they shouldn't be treating me like this, but then I start to question everything again, unsure whether I can trust myself and my memories of what did or didn't happen.

Ben *is* dead.

They found his body buried beneath the decking in our garden. His remains had been burned using some kind of accelerant, just like the lighter gel I discovered in our kitchen bin, which the police found in the bin outside, along with my fingerprints. They say I bought it in the petrol station, then burned him somewhere else, before burying his remains at home.

What they are accusing me of is unthinkable.

I wouldn't believe what they said at first, but dental records confirmed that it was Ben. I thought I saw him, just for a moment at the wrap party before I was arrested, but I must have been mistaken about that, too, because my husband is definitely dead, and the whole world thinks I killed him.

Detective Croft said that the bullet wound in his skull was consistent with those from the bullets that fit my gun at home. The gun I bought, legally, to try to make myself feel safe. The gun they can't find because I won't tell them where to look.

They think I'm hiding evidence, but I did *not* kill my husband.

Did I?

What if I did?

No, that's not what happened. *It can't be.* I shake the thought and stick to the script I already wrote for myself: I'm being framed, I just don't know who by.

I've been in a police station, then a police cell, then I was cuffed inside a white security van, and now I am here. I don't know how long it has been, a couple of days perhaps; time has stopped working inside my head, I don't know how to tell it anymore. They said I could use the telephone, but I didn't know who to call. I have got myself a lawyer though, a good one. He's handled a lot of high-profile cases over the last few years, and he seems to know what he's doing. I told him I didn't do it, and when I asked if he believed me, he just smiled and said it didn't matter. His answer keeps replaying on a loop inside my head: "What I believe is irrelevant; it's what I can make others believe that dictates the future." It's as though his words might have been written for me.

I pull on the green prison-issue top and jogging bottoms I've been told to wear, and every inch of my skin starts to itch. The feeling makes me want to scratch myself out. I catch a glimpse of a strange-looking woman in the mirror; she doesn't look like me. When you dig down, deep enough inside your own despair, you usually meet the you that you used to be, but I don't remember her. It feels as if I have to be someone different now, someone strong and brave, a role I'm not sure how to play.

I've never been inside a prison before. It's a lot like how you might expect: high exterior walls topped with barbed wire, a lot of doors, a lot of locks. The place feels cold, and everything seems to look grayish green. The people I see don't tend to smile too much. I follow another guard as he locks yet another gate behind us, before opening the next with the enormous bunch of keys attached to the belt of his uniform.

The keys remind me of Maggie, and the set she used to carry around the shop. I've thought about her a lot since I was arrested. It's as though someone hit my reset button when I wasn't looking, and I feel like a little girl again, a little girl who was taught never to trust or talk to the police. The only person I've spoken to since they took me away is my lawyer, a complete stranger.

I think he thinks I did it.

I've retreated as far inside myself as it is possible to go, and locked my own door with a key I thought I'd thrown away. I look at the other women I pass and can't help thinking that I am not like them, that I do not belong in here.

But what if I do?

We walk across a yard and I see a series of buildings, all with barbed wire on the walls and bars on the windows, to keep the bad people in, not out. The guard unlocks another door with another key, and we enter one of the smaller buildings; the sign says BLOCK A. I wait while he locks the door behind us, then we walk in communal silence, up some stairs and along another corridor, past endless closed metal doors with tiny windows. I'm starting to think that life is little more than a series of doors: every day we have to choose which ones to open, which to walk through, and which to close behind us, leaving them forever locked.

What if I did do what they're accusing me of?

It seems increasingly difficult to prove that I didn't, even to myself.

What surprises me the most is my grief. My husband is dead, not just missing anymore, but dead. Gone. Forever. And I feel *nothing,* except sorrow for myself and for the child I know I'll never have now. Perhaps they're right, with all their doctors' reports and theories about my memory and mental state.

Maybe there is something wrong with me.

"Here we are then, home sweet home for now," says the guard. He unlocks a blue metal door and pushes it open, introducing me to my future. I step forward, just a little, and peer inside. The cell is tiny. There is a bunk bed on the far right, and just in front of that is a dirty-looking curtain, barely hiding the stained toilet bowl and small sink behind it. On the left is a desk, with what looks like a computer, which surprises me. There's also a small cupboard covered in someone else's things: a can of baked beans, some books, some clothes, a toothbrush, and a kettle.

"There is someone in this cell already," I say, turning back to the guard.

He is old and weary looking, with dark circles beneath his beady eyes, and an overfed belly hanging over his belt. His crooked teeth are too big for his small mouth. He has a substantial gathering of dandruff on his shoulders, and an impressive collection of gray hairs protrude from his nostrils, which flare in my general direction.

"I'm afraid the penthouse suite was already booked, along with all the single-occupancy guest rooms, so you'll have to share. Don't worry, Hilary is *very* friendly, and you'll only be here until your court appearance, then they'll find you a more permanent home." He ushers me inside.

"I didn't kill my husband." I hate the pathetic sound of my voice.

"Tell it to someone who cares." He swings the cell door closed with a loud bang.

Forty-nine

Essex, 2017

Maggie decides to celebrate Aimee's incarceration with a curry.

It's been three years since she had her gastric band fitted, and that little silicone belt changed everything. She had let herself go in her thirties; it was a difficult time. She'd given up on life ever being what she'd hoped it might be, and she turned to food for comfort in the absence of anything else. But then, in her forties, she found Aimee.

The best thing to ever happen as a result of joining all those dating websites was finding her again after all those years. What a surprise that was. Aimee's face might have changed a little, but Maggie would have recognized it anywhere; she saw those eyes whenever she closed her own. That's when she started her self-improvements. The NHS paid for her gastric band, but she's paid for all the other work herself, not that she minds; Maggie thinks investing in yourself is the smartest use of a person's assets.

She calls ahead to place her order, so that she doesn't have to wait when she gets to the Indian restaurant. She doesn't like the way they look at her in there sometimes, like she is some kind of loser. Maggie is *not* a loser. She proves it by correcting the man with the Indian accent on the other end of the phone when he says the total cost of her meal will be £11.75. She has already calculated that the amount *should* be £11.25, according to the prices listed on the current takeaway menu. The man agrees that her maths is correct without an argument. It might only be fifty pence, but it's *her* fifty pence, and Maggie does not like thieves.

Maggie thinks that all immigrants are illegal and crooks. She reads stories about them in the newspapers, and it makes her worry about the future of this country. She is Irish by birth, but does not consider herself to be an immigrant, even though some people might say that she is. She is not like them.

She puts on her coat, ties a giant silk scarf around her head, securing it tightly under her chin and tucking it into her collar, until she is sufficiently wrapped up to be seen by others. She pulls on her boots and picks up her keys. She has quite a large collection of them, all different shapes and sizes, but they are not all her own. Most of them are for the houses of the deceased that she has been commissioned to clear—keys to unlock the secrets people think they'll never have to share.

Her food is ready when she arrives to collect it.

"Chicken Madras, plain rice, garlic naan, and chips?" says the man behind the counter as soon as she walks through the door, as though that were her name. He sounds the same as the man she spoke to on the phone, but she can never be sure, and he looks so much younger than she imagined, little more than a boy.

"Beef Madras. It should be *beef*, not chicken." Her voice sounds strange, deeper than it should.

"It's beef, yes, sorry. Beef Madras." He hands her the flimsy white plastic bag containing her celebration supper. She tuts, mumbles that she can't eat chicken, then shakes her head at the boy's accent while he continues to apologize for his mistake. Maggie wonders why nobody taught the boy to speak proper English. She pays the £11.25 using the exact change, so that there can be no further confusion.

She watches the news while she eats, hoping to see something about Aimee's arrest on the television. She records it, pressing the red button on the remote, just in case. Sometimes she talks at the screen, maybe because there is nobody else to talk to. Maggie has never had much luck meeting the right people, even with the help of dating websites.

She still remembers the first time she came across Ben Bailey. She didn't think much of him initially, had no idea of the role he was going to play in her life and the story of Aimee Sinclair. Sometimes, at our lowest moments, life lends us a signpost, and Maggie was smart enough to follow its directions, once she'd thought the journey through and realized where it might lead. She's glad that she did, very glad indeed.

Ben Bailey was the kind of guy who kept himself to himself. Didn't have any family or friends to speak of, at least none that Maggie could find after trawling the internet. His house was a mess. Shame really. Neglectful even, given its value and location on a nice street in Notting Hill. She thought it was strange that he didn't tidy up after himself a bit more, didn't seem to mind that people would see all his clutter when they came to the house, but then, there are some strange folk out there, people who are actually comfortable wearing the skin they were born in.

Ben Bailey's garden was the biggest travesty of all. It had the potential to be a beautiful, secluded oasis, in the middle of an overpopulated city. But instead, it was a jungle of overgrown grass, dirty white plastic chairs, and an ugly patio. Maggie had always been keen on gardening and right from the start thought decking would be much easier on the eye.

It was obvious that Ben Bailey was a clever man; there were lots of fancy-looking books on his shelves. Most of them looked as if they'd actually been read, too, not like when you visit some people's homes and you can tell it's all for show. He didn't have a single photo on display, not one. She still sometimes wonders what he did to push everyone around him so far away that he seemed to be completely alone in the world. But she tried her hardest not to think ill of the man; he had helped her in ways she had never previously dared dream possible.

The planning had to be meticulous: one mistake and the game would have been over before it ever began. It was so hard keeping it all to herself the whole time, but she knew she couldn't tell *anyone* what she was doing if she wanted the plan to work. And Ben Bailey couldn't tell a soul either.

He'd lost his job.

Gross misconduct the letter on his desk had said. She felt bad reading it, as though she were intruding during that first visit to his house. But then she figured he'd left it out knowing it would be read, as though he wanted her to see it. She'd googled *gross misconduct* when she got home that night; she had felt embarrassed to not really know what it meant. She didn't enjoy feeling as if she knew less than other people just because she didn't have a fancy education and hadn't been to university.

Maggie had worked hard for everything she had; she might not have a degree, but she was smart in ways that couldn't be learned in any school. Anything she didn't understand, she taught herself, with the help of the internet.

Gross misconduct is behavior, on the part of an employee, that is so bad that it destroys the employer/employee relationship.

The definition reminded her of Aimee straightaway. Aimee had behaved badly and destroyed their relationship. Aimee and Ben were both guilty of gross misconduct in Maggie's eyes, the only difference being that Ben had been punished for his behavior, and Aimee had got away scot-free. Until now.

Maggie couldn't stop thinking about Ben Bailey those first few days; it was like an obsession, and she wanted to know everything about him. She visited the building where he had worked as a journalist and took one of his shirts home with her after her second visit to his house. She wore it in bed that night, thinking about him and everything he was going to help her do to teach Aimee a lesson she'd never forget.

Maggie puts down her knife and fork, feeling very uncomfortable now that she has eaten everything on her plate. She should not have ordered rice *and* chips. She turns off the television, disappointed that there was no mention of Aimee or Ben, and makes a mental note to watch the later bulletin on a different channel, hoping they might have better news judgment.

When she cannot wait any longer, she walks to the bathroom and vomits up her dinner. All of it. Thanks to the gastric band, she doesn't even have to stick her fingers down her throat. She feels much better afterwards. She knows she can't eat a big meal like that anymore, but she did it anyway. It's okay to sometimes do the wrong thing in life, so long as you accept the consequences, that's what Maggie believes. You do something bad, you pay the price, them's the rules. Maggie has done some very bad things, but she doesn't regret any of them, not a single one.

Fifty

London, 2017

I sit on the lower bunk inside the cell and don't touch a thing. I've done some bad things in my life, so perhaps I deserve to be locked away. Maybe this is where I belong: a place where I might finally fit. There is no clock on the gray walls, I have no idea what time it is or what happens next, so all I can do is wait.

I wait a long time.

The light through the tiny, barred window diminishes, until the cell is almost completely dark. I close my eyes and try to shut it all out, switch myself off. I perform an exorcism of the truth and a curfew of the mind, and it works, for a little while at least. I'm exhausted but I daren't sleep, and when I hear the jingle of a set of keys outside the door, I don't move. The light switches on, it is blindingly bright, and I shield my eyes.

"Jesus Christ, you scared the crap out of me! Who the fuck are you?" asks a squat middle-aged woman, as the cell door slams back closed behind her. The sturdy shape of her body is clearly visible beneath the strained waistband of her green prison jogging bottoms. She resembles a lump of white Play-Doh that has been dropped from a great height. Her head is partially shaved at the bottom, and scraped back into a short shiny black ponytail on top. Her hands have balled into fists by her sides, and she has tattoos on each of her fingers. I don't wish to judge an intimidating book by its cover, but I'm so scared I think I might be sick.

"S-sorry," I stutter, then the rest of my words come out all at once in a rush. "They put me in here, I haven't touched anything or moved any of your things."

She looks around the cell, as though conducting a silent inventory, before staring back down at me. I don't know whether I should stand up. I feel small and vulnerable sitting on the bunk. A little bit cornered, a lot trapped. My indecision paralyzes me, and before I can decide what to do, she crosses the cell with three strides and leans down, her face within spitting distance of my own. Her piggy eyes stare hard, focusing first on my left eye, then my right, then back again, as though she can't decide which one to look at. She opens her mouth and I get an unpleasant whiff of garlic.

"I know who you are."

I swear I stop breathing altogether.

My mind conjures up an image of this woman sending me anonymous notes written on vintage postcards, but the picture is crooked and refuses to straighten out. It can't have been her, I'm quite certain we've never met.

She waits for a reaction I'm determined not to give. Then she stands back up straight and starts looking through her tiny cupboard, as though still checking I haven't stolen something from her. "You're the actress that killed her husband, shot him in the head, and buried him in the garden." She continues to rummage about, then turns and smiles. "I've read about you!" She thrusts a notepad and pen in my direction. "Give us your autograph." The experience is slightly surreal, but I do as she asks and sign my name. She looks at it, seems pleased, then turns the paper to reveal a blank page underneath. "And again."

"Why?"

"They're not for me—what would I want with your paw print? They're for eBay, so I can sell them when I get out. Maybe sell my story, too, about how I had to share my cell with a dangerous celebrity murderer. How much do you reckon a newspaper would give me for that? You must know how these things work—"

"I didn't kill my husband."

"Doesn't matter what you did or didn't do, it only matters what they *think* you did. And this ain't *Shawshank*. You don't want to walk around here saying you're innocent. Best to let people think they ought to be a little bit afraid of you. I'm Hilary, by the way." Her tone suggests that she thinks badly of me for not inquiring about her name already.

"What did you do?" I ask.

"Me? Nothing as exciting as you. Online fraud. This time. I'm guessing this is your first time inside?" I nod. "Thought so. It really ain't as bad as it seems, you get used to it. It normally takes at least twenty-four hours for them to set you up on the system." She turns on the computer screen. "They give you your code yet?" I shake my head. "Thought not. Once you get your code, you just type it in like this." She uses the same index finger to slowly type each letter. "Then you get this menu, so that you can apply to do a class: art, computers, hairdressing—that's really popular, long waiting list for that one—we even have yoga now too. You can watch a TV show or whatever film they are streaming. You can join the library. That's one I'd recommend, the guard who runs it is one of the good guys around here. It's also how you book your meals, tell them what food you want, and they deliver it to the cell at mealtimes. A bit like doing an online Tesco shop, or, I guess, Waitrose for someone like you. I'll tell you now, there's never any fruit or salads. You'll get a ten-pound credit on the system once a week for extras, a little gift from the government to help make sure you don't starve."

"You don't eat in a canteen?"

"Hell no! There are some mean bitches in here, but the thing that starts most of the fights is *always* food. I guess some people just don't understand the concept of queuing, and I've never seen folks get so crazy violent as they do about someone else getting more mashed potatoes on their plastic plate. Canteens are too dangerous when women are hangry."

"*Hangry?*"

She smiles again. "Yeah, *hangry*. Ain't you never heard that expression? It means when you're so hungry you get angry. Speaking of which, when did you last eat? I don't want you attacking me in my sleep." I think about the question for a while and realize I don't re-member. "You want some baked beans?" She holds up a tin but doesn't wait for a response. "I can heat them up for you, and you can just owe me a tin when you get your own allowance."

I watch with peculiar fascination as she boils the little travel kettle and opens the tin can. Just seeing the Heinz logo makes me think of Maggie. Even if I'm not guilty of killing my husband, I *have* killed before. I just never got caught.

Hilary tears off a square of cling film from a battered-looking box, spoons half a tin of beans into the middle, then twists the bundle to seal it, before dropping it inside the kettle.

"Does that really work?" I ask.

"I guess you'll find out."

Five minutes later, she serves me my first prison meal in a chipped Wonder Woman mug with a plastic teaspoon. It tastes like something resembling home, and for just a moment I close my eyes and remem-ber what it's like to feel safe. I notice a new notch on her face, mas-querading as a smile, and I feel so grateful for the kindness she has shown me.

"You're pretty—without the makeup, I mean," she says, and I re-member what a mess I must look. I haven't had a shower or washed my hair, or even brushed my teeth for at least forty-eight hours. "You look different in real life to how you look on the internet."

"Can you search the internet on this?" I point at the computer in the cell.

"Don't be daft. This is prison, we're not allowed internet in our cells or anywhere else."

"How then?"

"I get it on my iPhone."

"You're allowed iPhones in prison?"

"Of course not. Are you thick or something?" She reaches down inside the front of her trousers, and it looks as if she removes a phone from her knickers. "I like to make friends with people. I do some-thing for them, they do something for me. Being in here isn't so differ-ent from life on the outside. *This* prison is just a little smaller than the one you're used to, that's all. The modern world has made prisoners of us all, only fools think they are free. There's 4G in the corner of Building D, that's why so many people sign up to do the art classes, so they can get internet. It sure ain't about wanting to paint pretty pictures. I can't refresh the page in here, but look, here's you on the TBN website." She holds out the phone for me to see. I'm reluctant to touch it at first, knowing where it has been, but I soon forget all about that when I see the pictures on the screen. "There's you on the left, wearing all your makeup with your hair all fancy, and there's your husband on the right. Why *did* you kill him?"

I don't answer. I'm too busy staring at the photo that is captioned *Ben Bailey, husband and victim.*

My hands are shaking so badly, I'm scared I might drop the phone. I hold it tight, not willing to give it back yet, then sit down on the bunk, unable to articulate or process what my eyes have just seen.

"Are you okay?" she asks.

If I could answer, it would be no.

I look at the faces on the screen again, but nothing has changed. I barely recognize myself, but I don't know the man pictured next to me at all.

I don't recognize the man they claim I killed, because the man in the picture is not my husband. It isn't Ben.

Fifty-one

Maggie is supposed to be clearing a house in Acton, but she can't resist slowly driving past Aimee's Notting Hill home a couple more times first. A magpie swoops down in front of the van, and Maggie pulls over and salutes before it flies out of view.

"One for sorrow, two for joy," she mutters, then takes a noisy sip from her flask of coffee, while quietly observing the scene just ahead. The blue-and-white police tape is still flapping in the wind, sealing off the building, but the police vans and the press are gone. She supposes that they have found everything they need for now; everything that she left for them to find, including the lighter gel, the poorly cleaned bloodstains, the body.

She remembers the first time she visited the house with such fondness. He'd shot himself in the head, the real Ben Bailey. Suicide. He'd lost his job and was quite upset about it. Bits of blood and brains were still on the wall when Maggie was contracted to clear out his possessions, but she didn't mind that. It wasn't her job to clean up, only to get rid. She had only recently started the business, which was probably why she got the job: she imagined most people would have turned it down because it was too gruesome and gory. But Maggie had never been afraid of ghosts, at least not dead ones. She had a strange feeling as soon as she stepped inside, as if it were meant to be. Ben didn't have any real family waiting to argue over his prized possessions. He didn't have many of those either.

She took her time going through his things, learning all about the man he had been. She found his passport, driver's license, bank statements, and utility bills. Identity fraud is so easy when you work in Maggie's business, everything was right there, just inviting her to play God and bring the dead man back to life. She fell for the house he lived in, as well as the idea of him. Not how the house was back then, but how she knew it could be, with a little work. Some people just can't see the potential in things, but she could, Maggie had always been good at that. Just look at the potential she saw in Aimee as a child. She was right about Aimee, and she knew that she was right about Ben too.

Maggie knew that Ben Bailey would make the perfect pretend boyfriend, and then the perfect pretend husband for Aimee the actress, so she wasn't going to let a little thing such as his being dead get in the way. All she had to do was find the right person to play his part, and she didn't have to look very far.

Fifty-two

I don't know how anyone can sleep inside a prison cell. It is never quiet. Even in my dreams I hear the murmurs, shouts, and sometimes screams of strangers beyond the gray walls. It's even noisier when I find myself alone inside my head. The familiar cast of my bad dreams delivered a stellar performance this evening. A standing ovation of insomnia was the only suitable response to the story on the stage of my mind. I won't get the part in the Fincher movie now, that's for sure. I've lost *everything* and everyone.

I feel stiff, so I stand and stretch a little, getting a whiff of my own body odor as I raise my arms. The small frosted-glass window in the cell is open just a fraction. As I lean my face against the bars in front of it to gulp the fresh air, I spot a magpie on the lawn outside. I salute the bird, unable to remember when or why I started doing such an odd, superstitious thing.

As Hilary predicted, she has been allowed out for various classes, and to exercise in the yard, but I have been confined to my cell while I wait to be successfully added to *the system*. I appreciate I haven't been here long, but I think it's safe to say that *the system* is broken. If it weren't for my cellmate's generosity, I still wouldn't have had anything to eat or drink, but luckily Hilary seems to have a never-ending supply of tinned beans and cartons of Ribena. I normally avoid sugary drinks, but I daren't risk the water coming out of the tap. I've already been ill, and having to go to the toilet with nothing but a thin curtain to separate me from a complete stranger is worse than degrading. I keep thinking about the photo of Ben that Hilary showed me on her phone. It wasn't him. I realize now that the reason I've been unable to slot all the pieces of what has happened together, is because they don't fit. Not that I've been able to tell anyone, not that they'd believe me if I did.

I hear the increasingly familiar sound of keys jangling behind the cell door, and I presume that Hilary has been escorted back from her latest excursion. But it isn't Hilary. It's a prison guard, the same one who brought me in yesterday. He looks as though he hasn't slept either. The collection of dandruff has disappeared from one of his shoulders though, and I wonder whether he or someone else brushed it away.

"Well, come on then, I haven't got all day," he says in my direction, without actually looking at me.

I get up and follow him out of the cell, retracing the journey we made yesterday. It takes longer than it should, waiting for him to lock each door behind us, before taking a few more steps, then stopping to unlock the next.

"Where are we going?" He doesn't answer, and my chest starts to feel tight, as though the air has become hard to breathe. "Can you tell me where you are taking me? Please?" As I add the word *please*, I am reminded of my childhood and of Maggie. I remember how she conditioned me and rationed her love, only ever giving a little at a time. It's as though she has come back from the dead to haunt me. I stop walking in protest to being ignored, and finally the guard turns around, sighs, then shakes his head as though I have done something far worse than ask a simple question.

"Keep. Moving."

"Not until you explain where you are taking me."

He smiles, a twisted shape fracturing his facial features, which were already so unpleasantly arranged. "I don't know or care who it is you think you were on the outside. In here, you are nothing. You are nobody."

His words have an undesirable effect on me. I used to think that I was nobody, I still do, but not in the way he means. I think we're all nobodies, but I won't have some jobsworth in a cheap uniform, with an overinflated sense of empowerment, and a bad case of halitosis, speak to me that way. Sometimes you have to fall hard enough for it to hurt, to know when to pick yourself up. You can't start to put yourself back together if you don't even know that you're broken. I lift my head a little higher and take a step closer before giving him my reply.

"And *I* don't care about you losing your job, your home, your pet porn collection—from your appearance I doubt very much you have a wife—if I have to make a formal complaint and have your arse fired from this establishment. I know people who can end you with one phone call."

He glares at me through narrowed eyes. "You have a visitor."

"Who?"

"I'm not a fucking secretary. See for yourself."

He opens another door and I see her there, sitting at a desk waiting for me.

"Sit down," says Detective Alex Croft.

I stay exactly where I am. I'm a little tired of people giving me orders.

"Please, take a seat. I'd like to talk to you."

"I did *not* kill my husband," I say, fully aware that I must sound like a broken record.

She nods, leans back in her chair, and folds her arms. "I know."

Fifty-three

"You know?"

My words come out as a whisper in the cold prison room.

Detective Croft leans forward in her chair, no sidekick today. Her young face, as always, so completely impossible to read.

"Yes, I know you didn't kill your husband."

Finally. I think I could laugh, or cry, if I weren't so exhausted and angry.

Funny how life does that sometimes—throws you a line when you're drowning, just as your head is about to completely disappear below the surface of your darkest troubles.

"Do you know this man?" She slides her iPad across the table. It's the same picture from the online TBN article.

"No. Who is he?"

"He's Ben Bailey."

"That's *not* my husband."

"No, it isn't. But that is his name, and it was *his* body that was found buried in your garden. TBN have verified that *this* is the Ben Bailey who worked for them, land registry confirmed he owned your house for ten years before *you* bought it, and *this* man had already been dead, and buried, for over two years, albeit somewhere else. He committed suicide when he lost his job, was laid to rest in Scotland, and someone decided to dig him up and replant him beneath your decking in West London. There are things I understand about this case, but mostly there are things I don't. I don't understand your involvement in it for starters."

She stares at me as though she expects me to say something, but my mind is busy processing everything she just said, trying to make sense of something that simply doesn't make any. I feel as though this can't possibly be real, and yet it is. A contradiction of thoughts and feelings jumble themselves up inside my head, folding into conclusions I can't seem to iron out.

"Someone has gone to a lot of effort to set you up," she says.

"And you fell for it." Hate loosens my tongue. "I tried to tell you I was being framed and you wouldn't believe me."

"Your story was a little far-fetched."

"You fucked up!"

I watch as she tries the idea on for size, before deciding it doesn't fit and shrugging it off.

I turn my voice back down to its normal volume. "What happens now?"

"You'll be released. We can't keep you here for killing a man who was already dead."

"Then what?"

"Well, we're trying to find him. The man who pretended to be Ben Bailey, the man who married you using a dead man's birth certificate and persuaded you to buy the same dead man's house. To even try to begin to understand the who and what of this case, it would be really helpful to know the why. Why would someone go to such lengths to do this to you?"

"I don't know."

"If the man you were married to wasn't really Ben Bailey, then who was he?"

"I. Don't. Know."

She stares at me for a little while and appears to conclude that I am telling the truth.

"How did you meet him?"

"An online dating website."

"*You* were on a dating website? Using your own name?"

"Yes. It was before I got my first big role a couple of years ago. My name didn't mean anything to anyone then."

"Who contacted who?"

"He contacted me."

"Then I guess maybe your name meant something to him. Whoever did this to you was planning it for some time. Maybe the dating website was how he found you. And he told you from the start that he was Ben Bailey?"

"Yes."

"Was there a picture of the man you married on the dating website?"

"Yes, of course."

"Good, we'll check that out and see if it might still be there. I'm guessing now that the reason you couldn't find any pictures of him in the house was because he deliberately removed them all. And he told you that he worked for TBN?"

"Yes, we even met outside the TBN offices, several times."

"But you never went in? Never met any of his colleagues?"

"No."

"What about his family?"

"He said he didn't have any left. It was something we had in common."

"And you didn't meet any of his friends?"

"He said his friends were all back in Ireland. He hadn't been in London that long, and it just sounded like he'd been too busy to make any."

"Why would you agree to marry a practical stranger after just a couple of months?" She looks at me as though I'm the most pathetic and stupid person she's ever come across. I share the sentiment and start to wonder if maybe I am. I should have learned to let go long before now, but I held on too tight to what I thought I wanted: a chance to start again. This is all my fault. Your past only owns you if you allow it to.

"He said we'd wasted so many years being apart before we found each other. He said there was no need to wait when you knew that you'd met the one," I say eventually.

She looks as if she might throw up. "You've clearly made an enemy out of someone. The stalker you mentioned, the name she used . . . Maggie. What does that name mean to you?"

"Maggie is dead. It can't be Maggie. I watched her die."

Detective Croft leans back, looks unsure about what she is going to say next, which makes me quite certain I won't want to hear it.

"I've read about what happened to your parents when you were a child . . ."

Her words wind me a little. I don't talk about this. I can't. I never have and I never will. *She told me not to.*

"I know how your mother died. It must have been a horrific experience."

"My father died too," I say, remembering my lines.

"John Sinclair?" A deep frown folds itself onto her forehead.

"That's right."

"John Sinclair didn't die in the robbery. He was in hospital for three months, then he went to prison."

"What? No. John died. He was shot in the back, twice. I was there."

She reunites her fingers with her iPad, swipes a few times, then reads from the screen, "'John Sinclair was sentenced to ten years in Belmarsh prison and served eight.'"

I try to keep up with this new information. "What for?"

"He killed the alleged burglars with an illegal firearm. The gun was found in his hand and was linked to three other serious crimes."

John is alive. John went to prison because of me. I put that gun in his hand.

"Where is he now?" I ask.

"I don't know. And I don't know what to think about this case anymore. You'll be released later today." She stands to leave, waving to the guard on the other side of the door to let her out.

"That's it?"

"For now, yes."

"Well, where am I supposed to go?"

She shrugs. "Home."

She doesn't seem to understand that I don't have one.

Fifty-four

Maggie steps back inside the flat and slams the door closed behind her without meaning to. She's aware that it isn't the door's fault she had a bad day—the dead can be so bloody demanding. She puts on her white cotton gloves to cover her hands. She knows they aren't to blame either, but they are still an ugly reminder of who she is and who she isn't. Maggie was taught to toughen up at a young age, but she is not impervious to pain. A thick skin can wear thin when worn too often.

She remembers that she hasn't eaten all day, so eases her tired feet into her slippers and shuffles to the kitchen to examine the contents of the fridge. Everything she sees is disappointingly healthy, and that isn't what she wants or needs right now. She walks back out to the lounge to use the phone and dials a familiar number. The framed photo of childhood Aimee stares back while she waits for someone to answer. Maggie glares at the child, twisting the phone cord around her gloved hands as she becomes increasingly impatient.

"Fuck you," she says to the photo, turning it facedown so she doesn't have to look at Aimee anymore. "Not you," she adds, realizing that someone has finally answered her call.

She leaves the exact cost of the pizza in a recycled white envelope on the doorstep, along with a Post-it note that reads, *Leave food here*. She has taken off her makeup now and does not want to see anyone else again today. She closes her tired eyes and holds the three smallest fingers of her left hand inside her right, pretending she is comforting Aimee as a child when she was scared of something. Maggie wishes she could go back to that time. After a couple of minutes, sitting waiting in the darkness on the other side of the front door, she opens it, bends down, and adds the words *Thank you* to the Post-it note. She doesn't want to be rude or take out her bad day on someone else.

After she has eaten almost an entire large pepperoni pizza, with extra cheese, she vomits it all back up in the bathroom, flushes the toilet twice, then wipes her mouth with a square of quilted toilet tissue. She makes herself a green tea, adding a little cold water from the tap, then settles down on the sofa to watch the news.

She feels sick all over again when she sees Aimee's face.

Even worse when she watches the report.

Aimee has been released from prison.

Fifty-five

I stand on the doorstep, wearing the same black dress and red shoes I was wearing when I was driven to the prison. I didn't know where else to go, and I didn't have anything else to wear after they released me; the street outside the house where I used to live is full of reporters and satellite trucks. It seems my celebrity status might have increased over the last few days, for all the wrong reasons.

The door swings open and he hesitates for just a moment, making me worry that he's changed his mind since I called from the taxi.

"Come on in." Jack looks behind me theatrically, as though I might have been followed. "I'm so sorry, I didn't hear you at first, the doorbell is broken. I broke it. Reporters kept ringing the damn thing."

His house is beautiful. The layout is almost an exact copy of my own just a couple of streets away, but this house is a home. There are books, and photos, along with all the general clutter of life that you would expect to find, and I struggle to take it all in. It's warm and feels safe, if not familiar. I wait to be invited to sit down. I feel dirty, as though I might accidently infect all his beautiful things if I touch them.

"Do you want to have a shower?" he asks as though reading my mind. I guess I must smell even worse than I look. "There are clean towels and plenty of hot water. You're welcome to use anything you find in the bathroom. I have argan-oil conditioner." He smiles, stroking his own graying but glossy hair.

I stand beneath the rain showerhead for a long time, letting it pummel my body, and I wonder how I ended up in this situation: almost completely alone in the world. I don't know Jack, not really, he's just a colleague, not a friend. Some people don't know the difference, but I do. Right now, it feels as if I don't have anyone left in the world who knows the real me. Nobody I can be myself with.

I never had much of a family, but I did used to have friends. There are people I could call, names in my phone that used to mean something. But if I did call, or text, they wouldn't come for *me,* they would come for *her.* The me you become when you spend your life being someone you're not. They would come to see her, then gossip afterwards about her with everyone they knew, while pretending to be my friend. Sadly, that's my experience, not my paranoia speaking loud and clear inside my head. Sometimes self-preservation means staying away from the people who pretend to care about you.

I suppose family is who most people turn to when the world closes in, but I don't have any of them left either. I went back to Ireland when I was eighteen, having never once been in contact with my father or brother since the day I ran away. I'm no longer sure what I expected or hoped to find there; I think I just wanted to visit what I had left behind. I found out that my real father had died a few years earlier; he was buried in the same plot as my mother, at the church we used to attend every Sunday. I visited their grave, unsure how to feel about it as I stared down at the overgrown plot and simple headstone. A neighbor confirmed that my brother still owned the house that we used to live in, but nobody had seen him for a while. I wrote him a letter and slid it under the front door before I left. Either he never read it or I wrote the wrong words. He never got in touch and it made me realize that sharing the same blood does not necessarily make you family.

After Maggie died, I was taken into care, although calling it that always seemed a little ironic to me, because most of them didn't. I was sent to live with lots of foster families, but never really felt that I belonged with any of them. I think the feeling was mutual. I wasn't a bad child, I didn't get into trouble, and I was good at school. I was just *quiet,* at least on the outside; the characters I wanted to be were so noisy inside my head that, for me, it was practically deafening at all times. People don't always trust quiet; they didn't then and they certainly don't now. The world we live in today is too loud, so that most people think they have to shout all the time just to fit in. I've never been great at fitting in, and when I look at the world around me, I'm not sure I even want to.

I think about all the years I spent believing John was dead, when he wasn't. What if I'm wrong about Maggie too?

I'm not.

I watched her die.

But I also saw John die, or so I thought. I don't know what to think anymore.

I wish I could erase what happened that day; the memory of it has never stopped haunting me, and I've felt alone in the world ever since.

Every time I film a movie or a TV show, I am surrounded by people, all of them fussing over me, and telling me what they think I want to hear. But, when filming stops, they go home to their families and I am left abandoned. That will never change now, it will always be this way. I'll never marry again; how could I even meet someone else? I'd never know whether he was with me for me, or for *her*. Sometimes I hate her, the me that I have become, but without her, I am nothing. Without her, I am nobody.

Life is a game that few of us really know how to play, filled with more snakes than ladders. I'm starting to think that maybe I've been playing it all wrong. Perhaps, when all is said and done, and the world decides to turn against you, people are more important than parts. Somebody hated me enough to do this to me, and whoever it is is still out there. It isn't over until I slot the pieces of the puzzle together, and I won't be safe until I do.

I wash the remaining fear and dirt away, then step out of the shower. I wrap a thick, soft white towel around my body, and another around my wet hair, then creep out onto the landing, leaning over the banister at the top of the stairs.

"Jack?" I call.

He doesn't answer. The house is completely silent except for the sound of the oversized metal clock ticking in the hallway. I walk down the stairs, enjoying the feeling of the carpet beneath my toes, telling myself that everything is going to be okay, because if I can make myself believe that it will be, then maybe it might.

"Jack?"

I wander through the rooms, ending at the kitchen at the back of the house, cold tiles beneath my feet now, sending a shiver all the way through me. It's strange, walking around a house that has the exact layout as your own. I double back to the lounge and freeze when I see the coffee table. Panic paralyzes me as I stare at the items on it, as though they were dangerous. It feels as if they are.

"Jack!"

Nobody answers.

It's happening again.

His phone and keys are here on the table, but Jack is gone.

Fifty-six

Maggie arrives early for her appointment in Harley Street.

Thanks to Aimee, she has more work than time in which to do it today, and she is not in the mood for a so-called doctor to feed her any more excuses or lies about why they need to delay her surgery. It's her body, she should be allowed to do whatever she wants to it. She isn't asking others to pay for her self-improvements, so why should she need their permission?

Maggie thinks the whole country has tied itself in knots with red tape, so consumed with checks and bloody balances that nothing gets done anymore. She tuts and shakes her head and only realizes that she has been muttering beneath her breath when she notices a woman in the waiting room staring at her. Maggie lifts her chin and stares back, until the woman's eyes retreat and look down at the magazine she is pretending to read. The next person to look at Maggie the wrong way today is going to regret it.

Everything in the clinic is white. The walls, the floor, the strange modern chairs in the waiting room, the staff, the patients, and the lengthy invoices she receives after each visit. All white. Sterile. The place is too white and too quiet. There is no music, just the maddening and monotonous sound of the receptionist tapping away on her keyboard, with her pretty little hands. Maggie always thinks there ought to be music, something to help take your mind off your present, forget your past, and daydream about a fantasy future. Without anything to listen to, she kills her time observing the other people waiting for their appointments, wondering what they are here for, wondering what they want to have *done*. She finds them all rather fascinating and tries to guess from looking at their faces and bodies— nose job, tummy tuck, hair transplant. Almost anything is possible nowadays, you can completely reinvent yourself. Start again.

"The doctor will see you now," says the receptionist, fourteen minutes after Maggie's appointment should have started. *Doctor. Doctor my arse,* thinks Maggie, hearing the cracking sound her knees make when she stands up from the uncomfortable white chair, wishing the clinic had invested in some white cushions. Maggie can see that the receptionist has also had some work done. Her crease-free brow screams Botox, and the face-lift is good, subtle, the skin on her cheeks hasn't been pulled too tight. Only the skin on her neck gives the age game away. Maggie wonders whether the receptionist gets a staff discount, but thinks it might be rude to ask. Instead, she forces herself to smile and say, "Thank you," before shuffling along the white corridor to room three.

He smiles when she walks into the room. He's practiced that white smile so often, it almost seems real. "Hello, how are you?" he asks, as though he cares.

He's younger than her and has already made far more of his life than she can ever hope to now. His tan is real, unlike his concern for her well-being, and his floppy blond hair looks as though it might have been blow-dried. Photos of a smiling wife and two perfect-looking children adorn his desk, reinforcing the image of all-round success.

Maggie knows the man is busy, she has seen all the people waiting in reception to become better versions of themselves. Maggie is busy too; she might not be a doctor, but she has things she needs to fix and mend, important things, so she would rather they didn't waste any more of his time or hers with unnecessary small talk.

"Why have you postponed my surgery again?" She leans as far forward in her chair as she can without falling off, as though she might hear his answer sooner if her ears are closer to his mouth.

He sits a fraction backwards in his own chair, but keeps his eyes fixed on hers. They are deep blue and look wonderfully wise for such a young man.

"Having some excess breast tissue is incredibly common after dramatic weight loss, like you experienced after having a gastric band fitted—"

"Yes, well, I don't want to look *common,* I want to look more like this." She thrusts a crumpled magazine page from her pocket onto his desk.

He gives the glossy picture of a celebrity he vaguely recognizes a cursory glance. "The surgery you wanted is relatively noninvasive, and I would have been happy to go ahead, but do you remember the scan that we did the last time you were here?" He carries on without waiting for an answer. "And do you remember the unexpected mass that we found, and the biopsy I performed?"

Maggie does remember, she's not senile. It was how she imagined it must feel to have a staple gun used on your naked flesh: a sharp stabbing pain and then a dull ache for the rest of the day.

"There is nothing wrong with my memory . . . thank you." She's even more cross with him now, but tries to remain polite; she needs this man to help her become who she wants to be. "You said the biopsy was just a precaution, nothing to worry about."

The doctor looks down, as though he's forgotten his lines and thinks they might be written on the palms of his hands. His thumbs revolve around each other in some hypnotic spinning dance.

It is all Maggie can do to stop herself from tutting. *He is going to say no to my surgery again*, she thinks, and can feel her crossness inflate inside her. She has never been good at controlling her temper; when she is cross with someone, it can literally last a lifetime. She knows that this is neither a clever or a kind way to be, but she cannot help it. She inherited her anger from her father, who inherited it from his, like a genetic disorder of wrath. She sits up a little straighter, trying, but failing to remain calm.

"If you won't perform my surgery, then I'll find someone who—"

"I'm so sorry, but what we found was a tumor."

The room, and everything in it, has become perfectly still and silent, as though his words have created a vacuum and sucked anything she might have had left to say clean away.

"Right. So then take it out at the same time as the procedure."

"I'm afraid that isn't possible. You have breast cancer." He says the words so kindly, she thinks she might actually cry.

"I don't understand," she whispers.

"Tests on the tissue sample have confirmed the cells are malignant. From what I can tell, it has spread further than your chest, but there are treatments that might be suitable for you either on the NHS, or privately . . ."

"I don't understand."

"I've written to your GP. I recommend that you make an appointment to see them as soon as possible."

"I don't understand! How can this be happening to *me*?" Maggie's voice is louder than before, cracking a little, as though some part of her just got broken. Her eyes fill with tears, and she permits them to spill down her cheeks. It must be over thirty years since she let a man see her cry, but she doesn't care about that right now, she doesn't care about anything.

The doctor nods. She can see him trying to arrange some words inside his head, trying to press and fold them into something a little neater, before letting them out of his mouth.

"It's a lot more common than people realize."

Maggie hates that word, *common*. She wishes he would stop using it.

"How long have I got?"

"Your GP will be able to advise you on—"

Maggie leans across the table. "How. Long. Have. I. Got?"

He looks away, then shakes his head before meeting her eyes again.

"It is impossible for any doctor to tell you that, but based on what I have seen, not very long. I'm so sorry."

Fifty-seven

Men keep disappearing from my life and I don't understand it.

I run around Jack's home in just a towel, calling his name repeatedly, as though I've developed some unique form of anxiety-induced Tourette's. I search each of the unfamiliar rooms, stopping inside a child's bedroom on the first floor. The carpet is pink, and the furniture is white, with a colorful bookshelf in the corner and toys on the bed. The little girl's bedroom drags me back in time and holds me there for a moment; it looks so much like my bedroom above the betting shop, it's uncanny. I stand and stare, completely mesmerized. Distraught. Disturbed.

Am I losing my mind?

I lean against the wall, my breathing uneven and rushed, until the stress of my current predicament breaks the spell. I force myself to stand up straight and close the door, as though the memories the room invokes need to be locked away. I search the rest of the house before returning to the lounge, but Jack is not here. I stare at his keys and mobile, left redundant on the coffee table, and feel as if I'm going completely mad. How can this be happening to me *again*?

I find my own phone and for a moment consider calling Detective Croft, but then I remember where that got me last time: prison. I cannot call the police. I cannot trust the police. I can't trust anyone. I notice that I've missed five calls, then see that they are all from my agent. I could tell Tony that Jack has gone missing, but what would that achieve? I decide against it. I'm quite certain my agent already thinks I am crazy. I see that he's left two messages; I've obviously lost the Fincher film, so it seems pointless to listen. Before I get the chance to hear whatever he has to say, there is a knock at the door and I freeze. I don't know what to do. I'm convinced it's the police, that maybe I'm being set up all over again for something I did not do.

The knocking at the door resumes almost as soon as it stops, louder this time, more insistent, as though whoever is out there has no intention of going away. I walk into the hall and see the shape of someone bigger than me behind the frosted glass, but that's all. What if it is him? The man I was married to for nearly two years, who didn't even tell me his real name.

It could be him.

I walk to the kitchen, take a knife from the stainless-steel block on the counter, then return to the hallway holding the blade behind me. I open the door, just a fraction, enough to see who is standing on the other side.

"I forgot my keys, can I come in, *s'il vous plaît?*" says Jack.

I let out the breath I hadn't known I was holding and step back from the door, watching as he passes by with a collection of shopping bags in each hand. I follow him into the kitchen, replacing the knife without being seen, and pulling my towel a little tighter around my body. Jack puts a carton of milk in the fridge, then turns around, his eyes lingering on my legs beneath the towel before making contact.

"I thought we might need a few supplies, and I also thought you might need something to wear. Apologies in advance if I've got your size wrong. It's all from Portobello market, just some bits to keep you going for now." He hands me one of the bags, and I can see a couple of dresses, some loungewear, and some new underwear inside. "And I got you these, I know how much you like to run." He opens a shoebox, revealing an expensive-looking pair of trainers.

"Thank you." I feel overwhelmed by his kindness, so I don't know why I can't stop myself from saying something I shouldn't. "I didn't know you had a little girl." The words come out of my mouth like an accusation, and I can see I've caught him off guard.

"Yes, I have a daughter, she's called Lilly. I don't get to see her as often as I'd like, with the job, you know how it is."

Not really. I would have given it all up if I'd had a child.

"Does she live with your ex-wife?"

"No, my daughter was a result of my first marriage. She was born in France and lived there until she was five, that's why I've been trying to teach myself the language. She moved here last year and lives with my sister when I'm working, or here with me when I'm not. It isn't a secret, it's just that the whole single-dad thing tends to put people off. I'd love for you to meet her one day."

He cared what I thought enough to hide the truth from me.

I don't blame him for not telling me before now. We learn to future-proof our hearts, building a maze around them until they are almost impossible for others to find. I imagine myself becoming a mother to someone else's little girl. I could do that, but deep down I still want a child of my own, my flesh and blood. I can tell Jack wants to change the subject, but I'm not ready to yet.

"Why doesn't she still live with your first wife?"

He looks away briefly. "Because she died."

"Oh, I'm sorry—"

"Don't be, you weren't to know. Cancer took her. She fought a good fight. Sometimes I wish she hadn't, she was ill for a long time and it was hard. For all of us. It broke my heart, broke my everything actually, but I had to carry on for Lilly. We're okay now." His face changes, as though a filter has been applied to my view of him. "By the way, your agent called. He said you need to call him back, urgently."

"My agent called *you*?"

"Yes, he said you weren't answering your phone."

"But how did he know I was with you?"

Jack frowns. "Darling, do you ever check Twitter? Facebook? The news?"

"Not if I can help it, no . . ."

He walks back into the lounge and picks his phone up from the coffee table, tapping it a few times before holding it in my face. He's opened the TBN app, and there I am, headline news, again, along with a photo of me embracing Jack on his doorstep less than an hour ago.

"Did you tell her I was here?" I ask.

"Not guilty this time." He looks a little hurt. "I am sorry about that. I made a terrible mistake a few years ago, did something I shouldn't have when my first wife was ill. It was such a dreadful business, watching her fade away. I was dealing with it all on my own, and I'm not making excuses, but I was scared and so . . . lonely. Jennifer Jones knew about what I did and threatened to spill the beans; she's been blackmailing me ever since. If I'd felt like I had any choice, I would never have done what she asked, and you have my word that nothing like that will ever happen again. If I hadn't let her into your dressing room that day, and then sent her the pictures of us, she would have destroyed me. Not just my career, my relationship with my daughter too; I can't have Lilly read about what I did online one day, she'd never forgive me."

"You slept with someone else when your wife was ill?" I guess, hoping that I'm wrong.

He stares at the floor. "Yes. There's really no need to look at me like that, we all make mistakes when we are under enormous stress and strain. I was drunk, emotionally exhausted, it meant nothing."

"Who did you sleep with?" I whisper, not sure I want to know the answer.

"She had a tiny part in the film I was in, it was so stupid, but life at home was so hard and—"

"Who?"

"Jennifer Jones. That's how she knew I'd cheated on my sick wife, because it was with her. Maybe she thought I could help her nonstarter of an acting career, I don't know, but I couldn't do that, and I couldn't see her again either. I knew it was a mistake at the time, but I didn't know it would haunt me for this long. She gave up on acting shortly afterwards and became a showbiz journalist, but she never gave up on getting revenge for our one-night stand."

The revelation makes me feel a little sick. I don't like the idea of Jack sleeping with anyone, not that I have any right to think that way, but *Beak Face,* of all the people. No wonder she hates us both so much. Something else occurs to me, interrupting my revulsion.

"If you didn't tell her that I was here, then how did she know?"

He shrugs, and we both stare down at the latest Jennifer Jones headline:

AIMEE SINCLAIR BACK IN THE ARMS OF HER LOVER AFTER BEING CLEARED OF HUSBAND'S MURDER

Fifty-eight

Maggie arrives home, barely able to remember any of her journey from the clinic. Coming back to a cold, empty flat after news like this is far from ideal, but she doesn't have anyone she can call. At times like these she wishes she had some sort of pet for company; she has always preferred animals to people, animals know what they are. She feels smaller than she did before. As though having the fragility of life thrown at her this way has made her shrink a little.

She's hungry, but she can't eat, not now. She suspects that knowing the end is coming is worse than the end itself. Her parents didn't know when their time was up, and she wonders what they might have done differently if they had. The answer is one word, and she believes it to be true: *everything*. *When things don't look right, sometimes you just have to change your perspective*, she thinks to herself, then reaches a more positive conclusion:

This death sentence is an opportunity to fix things before it's too late.

She decides to eat after all, knowing she'll need her strength to make this work. The fridge is practically bare, so she makes beans on toast. "Nothing wrong with that, packed with protein," she mutters to herself, while stirring the orange contents of the saucepan.

Once she has eaten, she lights the fire. It will help to warm the place up, and she should probably start burning all the things she doesn't want anyone else to find when she is gone. In her hurry, she forgets to put on any gloves before picking up a piece of wood and gets a splinter in her finger. She tries to get it out with a pair of tweezers, but it snaps in half, leaving most of the fragment still buried beneath her skin. She ignores the pain and strikes a match, lighting a small bundle of newspaper and kindling, watching the worthless words written on the paper smolder and burn. She unexpectedly finds herself smiling. Life might have moved the goalposts when she wasn't looking, but she's confident that if she adjusts the plan and her aim just a little, she can still win the game.

Maggie has some regrets, but doesn't want to share them, not even with herself. When you've spent your whole life living a lie, it can feel a little late to start telling the truth. She checks her emails, then checks Aimee's; she knows all her passwords. She can also see exactly where she is, thanks to the phone tracker app she installed on Aimee's mobile. She just knew that Aimee and Jack Anderson were having an affair. She imagines him fucking her right now and squeezes her eyes shut to try to delete the image. *Slut.* Maggie has tipped off a journalist and is pleased to see that the story has already been published online. Jennifer Jones has come in very handy indeed so far.

Maggie closes her laptop and sits quietly in front of the crackling fire, trying to silence the thoughts that seem so loud and profound to her now. Perhaps it's the clarity of knowing that her journey is coming to an end. She looks around the room and concludes that her life hasn't amounted to much. Her eyes come to rest on the pile of unopened mail sitting on the coffee table: white paper rectangles, with tiny plastic windows revealing her name.

Maggie O'Neil.

Except it isn't really hers.

Knowing a person's name is not the same as knowing a person.

She's used that name for so long now, sometimes she forgets it was secondhand, borrowed, stolen. She wonders if perhaps Aimee feels the same way too. Maggie stares into the flames and starts to think she has more in common with other people than she previously believed. We are born alone and we die alone, and we're all a little bit afraid of being forgotten.

Maggie wasn't always Maggie.

Maggie was just who she became in order to hide.

You can't find a butterfly if you're only looking for a caterpillar.

As soon as she is reunited with Aimee, Maggie will go back to being who she was before.

Fifty-nine

A meeting with my agent is something I could really do without today, but Tony was quite insistent on the phone and said it couldn't wait. I don't think I'm looking my best, but perhaps that doesn't matter anymore. The dress Jack bought for me isn't something I would ever have picked out for myself. The figure-hugging plum material is flattering, I suppose, a little more revealing than the sort of thing I normally wear. My hair has dried into its natural curls and I'm not wearing any makeup, because it is all still at my house, and I daren't go back there anytime soon.

I walk into the restaurant and see him straightaway. Tony eats out a lot, and he has a favorite table everywhere he goes. He's reading the menu, even though he always chooses what he is going to eat beforehand, and he looks a little stressed.

He's going to dump me.

I'm sure of it this time, and I don't even blame him after everything that has happened. Nobody will want to work with an actress accused of murder. Maybe *this* is what agents do when they decide not to represent you anymore—take you out for a slap-up meal to soften the blow. Just as I start to back away towards the exit, he looks up from the menu and sees me. I've left it too late to run away.

"How are you?" he asks as I sit down. He looks genuinely concerned, and I'm not sure how to answer. He carries on speaking without waiting for one, but I'm still thinking about the question. The truth is, I've never felt this close to oblivion before. I've never let myself. I've never let life break me, despite all the numerous occasions when it has tried so hard to. I'm proud of myself for that. Proud for staying strong, at least on the outside. The armor I've worn to hide what's on the inside has grown heavy over the years, weighing me down, so that it has become increasingly difficult to pick myself back up. People are always so jealous of me, but they wouldn't be if they knew the life I'd had to live to get the one I lead now.

"... so, I thought we could just have lunch and see what happens?" says Tony, as I tune back in to what he is saying. My tired mind has wandered again, leaving both me and it a little lost.

"Lunch?" They make great chips here, but I think I'm too anxious to eat.

"Yes, that's right, lunch. You look like you've lost weight, but you do still eat, don't you?"

"I thought you were dumping me."

He frowns. "Why would I do that?"

"I let you down."

He shakes his head. "You didn't let me down, and besides, I've told you before, all publicity is good publicity. I've had seven scripts offering you lead roles just this morning. Even JJ's people have been in touch."

I came close to working with JJ last year and was so excited, but then it didn't happen.

"I thought JJ said no?"

"I guess he's changed his mind. Four of the scripts that have been sent are worth you reading. I have a favorite, but, as always, I'll let you decide. I expect all this is the reason Fincher moved the meeting forward."

"Forward to when?"

"Lunch. Here. Now. Have you been listening to anything I have been saying?"

I stare down at the unfamiliar dress and see my hands resting on my lap, my unpolished nails reflecting my entire current appearance. I remember my messy hair and missing makeup. I've wanted to meet this man forever, but this isn't how I imagined it. I haven't rehearsed, I don't know what to say . . .

"I can't have lunch with Fincher now!"

"Yes, you can. Take the leap, Aimee. You'll only fall if you forget you can fly."

Sixty

Maggie feels as if she is falling.

Time is running away from her and she's no longer sure she can catch up. She's worked so hard, for so long, to make things right. She deserves for things to go back to how they should always have been. It's what would have been best for both of them; she just has to make Aimee see that. She can't wait any longer for the girl to figure things out for herself. Maggie turns the final page of her Aimee Sinclair album, having reread all the newspaper and magazine clippings she has collected over the years. It was almost full anyway, perhaps it is time after all.

The shade Maggie has spent her life hiding in just got darker. She can feel it, the lump inside her chest. She has a pain there now that she never noticed before, as though she were always able to feel the cancer growing inside her, but pretended not to. We all avoid the truth when we think it might hurt too much. She feels the lump with her finger, not knowing how she could have missed it when showering; it's huge. She feels a sharp pain and pulls her hand away, realizing that this particular discomfort is in her finger, not her chest. The splinter from the firewood is still buried beneath her skin, despite several attempts to remove it. She's read about how splinters can travel through the bloodstream, all the way to the heart and kill a person. She doesn't know if that's true, but she doesn't want to risk it.

She stands in front of the bathroom mirror and pulls at the pink skin with a pair of tweezers. She makes her finger bleed, but she still can't get the damn thing out. Her reflection distracts her from the discomfort, and she notices some tiny black hairs have sprouted from her chin. She starts to pluck at them instead, getting some small satisfaction each time she successfully removes one at the root. Extracting pleasure from the pain.

She wants to look her best this evening.

She can see from the mobile phone tracker app that Aimee is eating out somewhere special tonight, as though she has something to celebrate. She checked Aimee's emails and has read the three latest ones sent by her agent.

Maggie does *not* want Aimee to be in another film.

That is *not* part of the plan.

She's heard of the restaurant Aimee is at; it's the kind of place that requires a booking several months in advance, unless you are someone like Aimee. Or Jack Anderson. So Maggie knows she needs to dress the part.

She puts on Aimee's old trench coat, fastening the teeny tiny belt around the slim waist she has worked so hard to achieve. Then she blots her red lipstick one last time, with a piece of quilted toilet tissue, before admiring her reflection. She puts on her sunglasses, despite the fact that it is already dark outside, and leaves the flat. Maggie has thought a lot lately about whether grief was a price worth paying for love, and has decided that it was. Love is all Maggie has ever wanted, and she's going to get it, regardless of what it will cost her.

Sixty-one

"Cheers!"

"Here's to you," Jack replies, clinking his champagne glass with mine. "I want to hear more about the meeting. I want to know *everything*. Every single word he said."

I laugh. "No, I don't want to jinx it. I think the lunch went well, and now we'll just have to wait and see whether I get the part."

We're sitting at the bar of an exclusive West London restaurant, waiting for a table, and enjoying the taste of premature celebration until then. I let myself relax a little, appreciating the way the alcohol numbs my senses and diminishes the fear that has been growing inside me since this nightmare began.

I've already said more than I should about the meeting with my agent and Fincher. I couldn't help it, it's all too exciting. I embroidered the truth a little, just a few stitches here and there, to present the story how I have chosen to remember it. I might have let the waist of the story out just a tiny bit around the middle, to let it breathe, but that's okay. I think we all do that. The stories we tell each other about our lives are like snow globes. We shake the facts of what happened in our minds, then watch and wait while the pieces settle into fiction. If we don't like the way the pieces fall, we just shake the story again, until it looks how we want it to.

I used to think that everything happened for a reason, but I stopped believing in whims like that some time ago. That said, if there *was* a point to the hellish last few days, then maybe this was it. Maybe this is the part that will change my life for the better. I try to stay calm and steady and deny the excitement that I feel. I don't want to let the fantasy of fiction seduce me into a false sense of security; I've made that mistake before.

"There was one thing Fincher said that I can't get out of my head," I say eventually, aware of the weight of Jack's stare as I take another sip of champagne.

"Well?"

"He said that the character he wanted me to play was morally repugnant but fascinating, and I got to thinking that maybe I am too."

Jack stares at me for a few seconds, then the creases around his eyes fold, his mouth opens up into a wide white smile, and he laughs at me. Really laughs. Completely unaware that I wasn't joking.

"I'm so proud of you, do you know that?" He takes my hand in his.

"I don't have the part yet—"

"I don't just mean about today, I mean all of it. Most people would have crumbled or just crawled under a rock to hide, but you're so strong."

I'm only strong on the outside.

I'm not sure what we're doing anymore. Whatever it is, I'm quite certain that I shouldn't be encouraging it, my life is complicated enough right now. We're sitting facing each other on expensive-looking barstools, far closer than we should or need to be. My legs are tucked inside his, and I like feeling the warmth of his body against my own. Being this close to him makes me feel safe, and a little more willing to succumb to his charm-plated seduction.

Despite the alcohol, I'm fully aware that the comfort I feel from Jack holding my hand is nothing more than a placebo. It's not real, but I swallow it down anyway, wanting to hold on to the feeling for as long as I can. He downs his own glass of champagne before taking my empty flute and putting it next to his on the bar.

He looks serious all of a sudden. "I want you to know that you're safe with me."

I do feel safe in this moment, as though maybe everything that happened was nothing more than a bad dream.

"You can trust me."

I so badly want to that I don't pull away when he leans in to kiss me. Not the sort of kissing we've been doing on set, but something real, almost animal-like. It's as though I've wanted this for just as long as I suspect he has, but have been denying the truth until now. I know this is madness, to behave like this in a public place, but I can't help it. His hands cradle my face and I wish that I'd met him first, before I married the wrong man.

I hear someone tapping on the glass window directly behind us, and when I open my eyes, I see Jack frowning over my shoulder. "Who the fuck is that?"

I turn to see her standing right there, outside the restaurant. The woman who has been stalking me for the last two years.

I knew Ben wasn't working alone.

She's wearing what looks suspiciously like the coat I can't find, and her long black curly hair is blowing about her shoulders in the wind. Despite her dark glasses, it's pretty obvious she is staring right at us, and I wonder how long she has been there. She waves a white-gloved hand without smiling, and my scales tilt in an unexpected way; my anger far outweighing my fear. I run to the restaurant door, ready to confront this woman, whoever she is. Jack follows close behind as I burst out onto the street, but we're too late. The woman in the window has gone.

Sixty-two

Maggie always suspected that Aimee was having an affair with Jack Anderson. But seeing them together like that, watching him kiss her through the restaurant window, the whole experience has made Maggie feel utterly wretched and physically ill. She had to run away, there was no other alternative now that she knows for sure who Aimee Sinclair has become: a filthy, lying, cheating *whore*. She wonders what happened to the sweet, kind, innocent child she used to know.

She closes the door behind her and starts to pull off all her clothes, dropping them to the floor as she walks through the flat. She removes Aimee's trench coat first, then her jumper and skirt, until she is standing naked in front of the antique mirror in her front room. She cries a little, she can't help it, unable to get the image of Aimee and Jack out of her head.

Then she slaps herself hard across the face, three times.

Her finger stings and she notices that she still has a splinter, which brings a curious mix of pain and comfort. If it is still there, then it hasn't started to travel through her bloodstream to her heart. She might just live long enough to finish what she started and take back what should have been hers.

Maggie turns to stare at the photo of Aimee by the phone, and the tears continue to stream down her face. She holds the three smallest fingers of her left hand inside her right, pretending that the little girl she once knew had stayed that way, instead of growing into a *selfish slut*. She puts the picture facedown, unable to look at what she lost any longer, and returns her attention to the woman in the mirror.

Tomorrow she will get back to work, but for now, just for tonight, Maggie wants nothing more than to just be herself again. The tears have stained the face staring back at her, and she no longer likes what she sees. She starts to remove the makeup from her damp cheeks, washing away the woman she was forced to become. She feels a little better when the reflection shows someone she recognizes, someone real. It's as though Maggie O'Neil has left the building.

Sixty-three

"And you saw this woman too?" asks Detective Croft the following morning. I don't know why I let Jack persuade me to call her.

"Yes," he says. I can hear his patience evaporating with every question she asks. "*Yes,* I saw her too, *yes,* she is exactly as Aimee described. It seems to me you've bungled this entire investigation from beginning to end, no offense, but what are you actually *doing* to catch this person?"

Detective Croft stares at him for a long time. "It can be hard to solve a puzzle when you don't have all the pieces. We still haven't established that this woman is linked to what happened, or who she is. Have you thought of anyone matching her description who might have a grudge against you?" she asks me.

Jennifer Jones.

Surely not. The idea sounds so ridiculous inside my head, I can't say it out loud.

Alicia White.

Seems more plausible; she's hated me for such a long time now. Plus, she changed her hair color to match mine *and* she sometimes copies my clothes. The woman in the window was dressed just like me. She looked older, but then Alicia *is* an actress. I try to extract the memory of exactly what I saw last night. It's already a little frayed at the edges, but it's possible it could have been Alicia. I still can't say her name out loud because the truth is, it could have been anyone. I shake my head.

"Well, if you do think of someone, just let us know," says Croft.

"We still don't know the true identity of the man you were married to either; all we know is that he wasn't really Ben Bailey. Whoever he is, he closed down his profile on the dating website shortly after you met, and they no longer have a photo of him. Sadly for us, they purge their servers every three months, and unused profiles get deleted. It might be easier to put all this together if we knew the motive, and it might be easier to establish a motive if you started being honest with me. How long have the two of you been having an affair?"

"This is outrageous, I want to make a complaint," says Jack.

"Join the queue. How long?"

"I told you already, we're not having an affair," I reply.

"The night before the man you married disappeared, he accused you of cheating on him. Is that correct?"

"Yes."

"We've interviewed every member of staff at the restaurant you were at last night. None of them saw the woman you have described standing in the window, but several of them saw you two . . . kissing. Some of them even took pictures. Do you want to see?" She reaches for her iPad. I shake my head and feel my cheeks flush. "Now, unless you're going to tell me next that the two of you were just rehearsing for a new film together—"

"I really don't see how this is relevant," I say.

"It's relevant because whoever is responsible for what happened had to have been planning it for a long time. Which means they have hated you for a long time. And if we knew why, we'd have a far better chance of knowing who they are." She waits for me to say something, and when I don't, she expels an audible sigh. "We're done here." She stands to leave, her silent sidekick following close behind.

"You're done?" asks Jack. "Are you kidding me?"

She stops and turns. "One more thing." She ignores Jack and stares at me. "We managed to track down your birth father."

I sit completely still, and it's as though I feel my blood turn cold. *She knows I was born in Ireland. She knows I'm not really Aimee Sinclair.* "What do you mean?"

"John Sinclair." I try not to display the huge relief I feel. "He moved back to Essex when he was released from prison, stayed with someone called Michael O'Neil for a while, your uncle on your mother's side, I believe."

John is really alive?

I don't know what to say and stare back at her. As usual, Detective Croft doesn't waste any time waiting for me to find the right words. "Given you thought your father was dead all these years, and I've just told you he's alive, your reaction does seem a little strange."

I rearrange the expression on my face. "It's just a lot to take in. Where is he now?"

"We don't know. We think he moved to Spain, but that was almost twenty years ago. Would your father have any reason to want to hurt you?"

I put a gun in his hand and he went to prison for the murder of three men I killed in 1988.

"No."

She turns back towards the door. "Mrs. Sinclair, I know when someone isn't telling me the truth, and I know you're keeping something from me. When you're ready to tell me whatever it is, you have my number. Until then, please don't waste any more of my time."

Sixty-four

Time is a funny old thing, the way it stretches and folds and bends.

Maggie stares at the photo of Aimee as a little girl, thinking that it could have been yesterday. The look in the child's eyes dislodges memories of happier times and reminds her that there were some.

We weren't always the us we are now.

Maggie pushes the thought far away, wishing she'd never had it, but some memories are impossible to delete, no matter how hard we try.

Her back aches from a day of delivering antiques to shops along Portobello Road, and her hands are blistered from moving the larger items. Business is booming, and she had a lot of stock she needed to shift. The homes of the dead are dusty, neglected treasure troves, and the plunder is there for the taking; the dead don't miss what is no longer theirs. It's been hard work, and while she's all for equality, truth be told it is man's work; all that heavy lifting. She relaxes a little when she remembers it was the last time she'd ever have to do that job, there's no need now for her to work ever again; Aimee will call soon.

The girl has always had the most incredible memory, even as a child, and once she remembers her past, they can both get on with their future. Maggie's memory is a little less reliable. As far as she is concerned, none of us can remember every moment of every day of every year for an entire lifetime; the storage systems of our minds simply do not have that capacity. Yet. We select which memories to save and which to archive, and like everything else in life, it's about choices.

252 | Alice Feeney

We lead the life we choose to, based on what we think we deserve, and we hold on to the memories that mean the most to us, the moments we believe shaped the life we lead now. It's a pretty simple system, but it works. Unlike Aimee, Maggie might not remember it all, but she remembers enough.

Everything that has led them here was so carefully thought out, and soon, all of her hard work will have been worth it. It was always a good plan:

Identify a suitable partner for Aimee.

Someone nobody knew well enough to notice if he came back to life: Ben Bailey.

Cast someone believable to play his part.

Keep the keys to his home and delay clearing out his belongings until Aimee was in L.A. and could be persuaded to buy the property.

Dig up and rebury the dead man beneath the decking in what used to be his own garden.

Burn his remains in Epping Forest first, so that dental records would be used to confirm his identity.

Dress like Aimee to visit the bank and petrol station and make police believe she was violent.

Make it look as if she had killed her husband, to teach her a lesson: you should never forget who you are and where you came from.

No wonder Maggie feels so exhausted.

She stares at the framed Polaroid photo next to the phone again, reassuring herself that Aimee *will* call. All Maggie has to do is wait a little while longer. She knows this, because although Maggie might not have the best memory in the world, she knows Aimee better than she knows herself.

Sixty-five

The phone rings, waking me from a deep and blissful sleep. My dreams had taken me so far away from here that, at first, I don't know where I am. My mind struggles to identify the unfamiliar bedroom and the crisp white sheets. Then I remember that I am in Jack's house, and that the nightmare was real, but that I am safe again now. Safe enough at least. It's only 8:00 p.m. but I'd gone to bed early, exhausted and unable to fight the call of sleep any longer.

I stare at the screen on my phone and see that Tony is calling. My agent only calls with very good or very bad news; anything in between he does by email. It has to be about the Fincher film. I think it might be too soon for good news and let it ring, but then something inside me screams that I deserve this part, it *must* be good news. I answer, listening while Tony speaks on the other end. I don't say much. I don't need to.

As soon as I put the phone down, there is a knock on the bedroom door.

"Come in." I pull the sheets up over my bare legs. I'm wearing one of Jack's T-shirts; I still haven't been able to go back to my own house or get my things.

"I heard the phone ringing, I just wanted to check you were okay?" He peers around the door.

"Come in, I'm fine. It was Tony."

"Good news?" He sits down on the bed and I shake my head. "Oh, honey, I'm sorry."

"It's okay. I'm fine, honestly. I didn't really expect to get it."

"Bullshit, of course you should have got it. Do you know who did?"
I nod, wishing I didn't. "Who?"

"Alicia White."

His face experiences a freeze-frame. "You have got to be kidding me."

"No joke. Alicia got the part."

He looks genuinely appalled by this news, which does make me feel a little better. "Wait here," he says before leaving the room, as though I have anywhere else to go.

I let myself fold a little, now that there is nobody to see the creases. I didn't just *want* that part, it meant so much more than that. Acting is like taking a vacation from myself, and I need a break. I need to be someone else again for a little while, think her thoughts, feel her fears, walk in her shoes, with the help of a map-shaped script. I don't know how to explain it; sometimes I just get so damn tired of being me.

There's no secret ladder to reach the stars; you have to learn to build your own, and when you fall, you have to be brave enough to start the climb again. Never look back, never look down. I've put my broken self back together plenty of times before, I can do it again. I can handle not getting the part, I think. I just can't believe that *she* did. Of all the people. Tony says that she somehow knew where we were having the secret meeting with Fincher and followed him afterwards. I don't know what she said to convince him, or how she knew where he would be. The only person who knew where I was and what I was doing was Jack. *How did she know?* And why is it that so many horrible human beings succeed in life?

Jack returns with a bottle of whiskey and two glasses.

The anger I feel rushes straight to my head. "Did you tell Alicia where I was meeting Fincher?"

He looks as if my question has physically hurt him. "If you try hard enough, I think you'll remember that, like you, all I knew beforehand was that you were meeting your agent. I didn't know anything about Fincher until you got back. Even if I had known, I would never do that. Do you really not know how I feel about you?"

I do know. I just don't believe it.

"I'm sorry," I whisper.

He pours two large glasses and downs one of them. I don't even like whiskey, but I drink it anyway. All of it. It's as though we are out of words and wasted time. When he kisses me, I kiss him back. When he lifts the T-shirt up over my head, I don't stop him, even though I'm wearing nothing underneath. I reach down to unbutton his jeans, my fingers far more confident than I would have expected them to be. It's as if my body has taken over, no longer trusting my mind to make the right choices. When his hand reaches down between my legs, I open them a little wider. I'm not feeling like myself right now. I'm not feeling shy or anxious. I want this. I want *him*. I think I've wanted him since we first met, but I just wouldn't let myself be *that person*. I forget about everything that has happened, concentrating instead on the taste of him, the feel of his body on top of mine. If I'm honest with myself, as honest as I can be, I've imagined this moment for so long that now that it is happening, it feels completely natural. I don't even feel bad when it's over. I feel satisfied, I feel like a woman again and I feel alive.

I don't know whether it was the whiskey or the sleep or the sex, but I've remembered something. I know what I did with the gun and I know where it is.

But that can wait.

For now, I just want to lie in Jack's arms and pretend I might be able to stay here. I've spent too long equating love and loneliness; it doesn't have to be that way. And I've spent too long trying to be *nice*, always trying to do the right thing, doing what I thought I *should*. Turns out doing what you *want* to do feels pretty good.

Sixty-six

Maggie does not feel good. She can't sleep and she doesn't even want to eat. She stares at the photo of Aimee and wonders why she still hasn't called. She should have figured it all out by now, but maybe Aimee isn't as clever as Maggie has been giving her credit for all these years. Sometimes when we put someone on too high a pedestal, it only means they have farther to fall. Maggie checks the landline to make sure it is working.

It is.

She's cold, so she comes to stand in front of the fire, throwing another log on top. She notices that it didn't hurt to pick it up. When she looks down at the splinter in her hand, she sees that the black shape has risen to the surface, a halo of white skin separating it from the pink coloring of the rest of her finger.

It's formed a scab.

Her body knew that this part of it was harmful, so has rejected it.

Just as Maggie has rejected Aimee.

She takes a pair of tweezers from the mantelpiece—there are three different-colored ones to choose from. Then, slowly—because she wants to savor this moment and she already knows how much pleasure and satisfaction it is going to give her—she starts to lift the edges of the scab.

It feels *so* good.

When the whole thing has been gently torn away, she examines it on her other finger: a tiny black splinter of wood and a piece of her skin, conjoined. She puts the little piece of herself on the mantelpiece. She wants to keep it. She's not sure why.

The fire is hot now, crackling and spitting, yellow flames wildly dancing in the otherwise darkened room. Holding the tweezers in her hand makes her want to remove some more of herself, but she can't find any stray hairs on her chin. Looking back at the face in the dusty mirror, for just a moment Maggie feels like she doesn't know who or what she is anymore.

But she remembers her name, her real one, and wonders if Aimee remembers hers.

Maggie borrowed her name from a dead woman, just as Aimee borrowed hers from a dead little girl. The thing about borrowing other people's things is that, eventually, you have to give them back. She lifts her splinter-free finger and starts to write her *real* name in the dust, taking longer to write the *A* than any other letter.

Sixty-seven

I wake up to the annual sadness of autumn; it's pitch-black outside the bedroom window, yet my phone informs me that it is morning. The night sky has outstayed its welcome, and the darkness I can see seems to seep inside me, as though the color black is somehow contagious. It feels as if I have forgotten how to turn on the lights, and my life will be little more than a shadow from now on.

Alicia White.

Jennifer Jones.

John Sinclair.

Maggie O'Neil.

The names circle my mind because I'm certain the man I was married to didn't do this to me all on his own. Sometimes I wish I could go back in time to the day I ran away from home in Ireland. I wonder where and who I'd be now if I had stayed. I wouldn't have met any of these people, and my life might have turned out simpler, safer, more straightforward. I might have been happy.

I think about Detective Alex Croft. She was right, I have been keeping some things from her, I didn't have a choice.

I look over at Jack, still asleep on the other side of the enormous bed, the sound of light snoring escaping from his mouth. I take in the shape of his shoulders, the line of his spine, the tiny blond hairs on his neck. His eyes are closed and his hand has formed a fist, as though he might be fighting with his dreams.

Perhaps we all are.

I remember everything that we did last night; it would be hard not to. It felt so good I only wish I hadn't waited so long to give in to the attraction. I don't know what happens next. Maybe now that he's had all of me, his interest will fade away to nothing. I don't know whether he wants more. I don't know whether I do. I can't help thinking it would be nice to stay like this: the pleasure of intimacy without the pain of a formal relationship. Everyone wants something from someone, that's just how we are made. Most relationships, whatever their nature, are based on some kind of trade and compromise. I'm not naïve.

I climb out of the bed as quietly as I can. I want to be alone for a little while, make sure the thoughts inside my head are still my own. I want to get back to some vague kind of normal and do the things I used to do before this nightmare began. It feels like I need to do that, for me.

I want to run.

I look back at Jack before creeping out of the room, wondering if this might be the last time I see him like this; stripped back to being himself.

I run the short distance to my house. It's still early, and when I'm sure no reporters or police are outside, I let myself in. I grab an old rucksack and fill it with a few essentials: makeup, some clean underwear, and my phone charger. Then I walk over to the wardrobe and bend down to remove one of the bottom panels of wood. Ben designed the whole house and garden, but clothes are very much my department, and I had the fitted wardrobes especially made after we moved in. When you have as many secrets as I do, you need places to hide them. I find the gun where I'd put it to keep it from my husband. Concealed out of fear one night, when I was a little too drunk to remember. Afraid of him, and what he might do if he found it. I put the gun in my bag, then I replace the panel in the wardrobe floor and leave.

I take exactly the same route I always have—running past the pub on the corner, past the fish-and-chips shop and through the graveyard, until I reach Portobello Road. Along the way I pick up a thought or two about what happens next, and carry them with me for a while. I decide that I don't like them much, so put them back down and run on, without looking back, hoping they'll stay where I left them. As I reach the start of a long line of antique shops, I slow down a little, allowing myself the pleasure of longingly staring at the window displays. Ben always knew that I preferred older furniture to modern pieces with no personality, but he didn't listen to me, and I let myself be silenced. There were times I would have done almost anything to keep him happy, and try to convince him that we should have a child together, but I'll never let anyone control and manipulate me like that again.

I come to a halt, my brain taking a little while to process what my eyes think they have just seen. I turn back, retracing my last few steps, to peer inside the shop window I just passed. I'm no longer in any doubt about what I am looking at.

It's Ben. Or at least a photo of him as a child.

The black-and-white image I always hated.

The only picture of him I could find after he disappeared.

It doesn't make any sense. What is it doing here? I haven't touched any of his belongings yet, haven't removed a thing from the house we shared, masquerading as husband and wife. The thought stings a little, and I feel the need to defend us from it. I'm sure ours wasn't the only marriage that unraveled into separate lives, lived together out of habit or convenience. We each spin our own intricate web of lies, then get stuck and tangled inside them, unable to find a way out.

I bang on the shop door, but nobody answers.

It starts to rain, fast, fat drops falling from the sky without warning, soaking my clothes and skin, filling the network of veins on the paved street with dirty-looking water. I stare back at the picture, my vision a little blurred, but still sure of what I see.

I carry on down the road, retreating, as though a black-and-white photo of a child might come to life, smash through the glass of the shop window, and hurt me. I don't get far. The window of the next antique shop contains a different frame, but it's the same face staring out at me. I start to shiver. I walk to the next shop, and he is there again, malevolent eyes glaring in my direction.

I look up and down the street, suddenly in fear of being watched.

But there is nobody there. All I see is an empty pink-and-white-striped paper bag—the kind I used to get sweets in when I was a little girl—blowing along the pavement in the wind. I can see lights on inside the final shop, but when I try the handle, the door is locked. I bang on the glass, and eventually an elderly man comes to open it.

"I'm so sorry to bother you, but I need to ask a question about a picture in your window." I realize how crazy I must sound and feel a little surprised when he beckons me inside, my rain-soaked clothes dripping on the tiled floor.

The shop is overly warm and smells of toast and age. The man in front of me is at least eighty, perhaps older. His back is a little hunched and his clothes are too big for him, as though the years have caused him to shrink. It looks as if his smart tartan trousers might fall down altogether, without the help of the red braces holding them up, and the bow tie beneath his chin looks expertly hand-tied. His hair is white, but thick, and his eyes are smiling even though his mouth is not, as though glad of any form of company.

"You'll have to speak up, dear."

I walk to the window display and reach for the frame, careful not to knock anything over. "This picture, I wonder if you could tell me where you got it?"

He scratches his head. "I don't think I've ever seen it before." He looks almost as troubled by the sight of it as I feel.

"Is there someone else who might know?" I ask, trying not to sound impatient.

"No, it's just me now. I had a delivery from a supplier yesterday. She helped me bring the bits I wanted in from the van. I don't remember the frame, but it can only have come from her."

"Who is she? Who did you buy it from?"

"It's not stolen." He takes a small step back.

"I didn't say that it was. I just need to know how it got here."

"It got here the same way most of these goods do . . . dead people." The hot room seems to cool a little. "What?"

"House clearance. People's unwanted things after they've gone. You can't take it with you."

I think for a moment. "And this woman, she runs a house-clearance company?"

"That's right. All legit. Nothing illegal about it. She brings in some good pieces, too, knows her stuff."

"Who? Who is she?"

"I'm not so good with names. I have her card here somewhere." He shuffles behind a small desk. I can see that despite his dapper appearance, he is still wearing his slippers. "Here you go, I'm happy to recommend her, she's very good."

I stare down at the card he has put in my hands, not able to stop them from shaking as I read the name printed on it.

Maggie O'Neil.

It can't be.

"Can I buy this picture?" I can't hide the tremor in my voice.

"Of course," he says with a grin. I give him my credit card, not caring how much he plans to charge me, and remove the photo from the frame before I've even left the shop. I turn it over, unable to take another step when I read what is written on the back of it in a child-like scrawl:

John Sinclair. Age 5.

Sixty-eight

Maggie lets the phone ring and doesn't answer.

Whoever it is calls three more times without leaving a message.

She is sure it is Aimee calling. It's as though Maggie knows it. She holds the three smallest fingers of her left hand inside her right and squeezes them hard, until they hurt.

The ringing starts again. The caller has perhaps thought of something to say now, and Maggie leans right down, until her face is next to the answerphone, her ear turned and tuned to the little speaker. Pleasure ripples through her entire body when she hears that beautiful voice coming out of the machine; it's like a song she's missed hearing.

"Hello, my name is Aimee. I wonder if you could give me a call back . . ."

Maggie listens to the whole message thirteen times. She turns her face to kiss the phone, leaving red lipstick all over it, and starts to moan a little, as though the sound of the voice in the recording is caressing her in return. Giving the girl elocution lessons might not have been her idea, but it was a good one.

She pictures Aimee's face crinkling with confusion, dripping in disbelief. She is tempted to return the call, but she knows that she mustn't. She'd be willing to bet that Aimee will come to find her now, and the odds of that happening soon are quite high. She just needs to wait a little while longer. Some conversations are better had in person.

Sixty-nine

I let myself back into Jack's house and head straight for the shower, doing my best to wash the sweat and fear away.

I thought Maggie and John were dead but this is too much of a coincidence, it all has to be linked, I just don't know how. The police have already confirmed that John survived the shooting. *Why did he never get in touch?* I thought he cared about me, in his own way. Did he blame me for what happened? The memory of John's face had smudged over the years, but now that I've seen his name written on the back of the black-and-white photo, I know it is him, I recognize his eyes. Why would the man I married have a picture of John as a child and pretend it was him? I should go to the police, but I can't trust them. I can't trust anybody. I try to think it all through, but none of it makes any sense to me.

My husband was pretending to be Ben Bailey, but that isn't who he was.

I'm pretending to be Aimee Sinclair, but I'm not really her either.

Someone is pretending to be Maggie O'Neil; at least I *think* they are pretending. If John is alive, then what if she is too?

We're all just pretending to be someone we're not, but I still don't know why.

The bathroom fills with steam, and I'm so lost in my thoughts that I don't hear the door open. The shampoo stings my eyes, so I close them. I don't see somebody walking into the room, or hear them climbing into the shower behind me. A hand touches my body, I scream and the hand covers my mouth.

"Hey, it's only me, no need to wake the neighbors." Jack wipes the suds from my face, allowing me to see again. My heart is beating so hard I can hear it inside my ears. "Sorry, I didn't mean to scare you." I turn and he kisses me. The whole thing seems deeply inappropriate at first, as though last night didn't happen and this is somehow unexpected. I suppose I just didn't think this far ahead. His hands move down my body, and the feeling they generate is so good, I give in to it. I turn around, so that I am no longer facing him, and I love that he seems to know exactly what I want him to do without saying a word. I lean against the glass and let myself forget everything else except this. I'm enjoying things I thought I might never again experience, as though thirty-six were somehow old, and I were past my prime. He doesn't make me feel like that, he makes me feel new.

We eat breakfast afterwards, and when I say I need to pop out for a few hours, he doesn't insist on me telling him where. He doesn't act as though he owns me, and this newfound sense of freedom makes me feel hopeful about the future for the first time in a long time. I know I should tell him where I am going, but I can't. I don't want anything to spoil this, whatever this is. We all have secrets. Secrets from ourselves as well as from others. We bury them deep down inside because we know if they were to slip out, they have the power to destroy not only us, but everyone we care about.

I make some more coffee and pour him a cup.

"What did I do to deserve meeting someone as nice as you?" he says, before kissing me again. I can still taste our kiss goodbye as I leave the room, hoping it won't be our last.

I take my gun, my phone, and what little courage I can summon, then leave the house.

Nobody is nice all of the time.

Seventy

The address on the business card the antique dealer gave me should have been enough.

But it wasn't.

I never knew the name of the road until now. The journey through East London and into Essex gave me plenty of time to think, but until I stood in front of the building, I was still trying to convince myself that I was wrong; that this was just another coincidence.

It isn't.

It's been thirty years, but I still recognize this place, I still visit it in my dreams.

The little parade of shops is still here, but everything has been boarded up and closed down, except for the launderette. No more video rental, greengrocer's, or corner shop, nothing but bars on broken windows and graffiti; a consumer ghost town.

The betting shop is still here, too, boarded up, but with a hand-painted sign above the door:

BRIC-A-BRAC & ANTIQUES

There is also a CLOSED sign, sellotaped behind the frosted window. I hold my hands up to the glass to block out the light and try to peer inside, but all I can see is black.

I knock. Twice.

There's no answer, so I move to the door at the side of the shop, the one that leads to the flat. The paint has peeled and someone has sprayed the word LIAR on it in red. It always seemed so big when I was a little girl, but now I can see that it's just a regular door. I knock again, but nobody answers.

I bend down and push the rusted letter box open. "Hello?" I peer through the tiny rectangle, but am unable to see anything more than a huge pile of unopened mail and takeaway flyers. I bend my neck a little lower and can see the bottom of the stairs, covered in the old red carpet and new dark stains.

"Hello?"

There's still no reply.

Then I hear music start to play up in the flat.

I take out my phone.

I should call the police.

I should call *someone*.

But I don't. Instead I put my mobile back in my bag, check that I still have the gun, and walk down the road and up the alley to the back of the shop.

The back gate has gone, and a lot of the fencing has fallen down. Once again, everything seems so much smaller than I remembered. A battered old white van is parked outside on the tarmac, nothing of note visible through its grimy windows. The door to the little back room is slightly ajar, but I'm too scared of what might be behind it to go in.

I knock on the peeling, splintered wood, but the chances of anyone hearing me seem fairly minimal, given the volume of the music now blaring inside. I recognize the song—"Fairytale of New York." It seems strange to hear it when it isn't Christmas. I take a step forward, the lyrics about stolen dreams already a little too loud inside my head.

The little room where I used to sit and read my *Story Teller* magazines and listen to tapes is still here, but everything about it is different. There is no desk, it's just a room full of clutter. I walk through to what was once the shop, but it is more of a dusty storage space now. I press the sticky light switch and see that the place still has fluorescent lighting. It flickers to life, so that some squares in the ceiling are faintly illuminated. They give off an eerie glow, revealing pieces of antique furniture leaning against each other for support, all of it covered in dust and dirt. I make my way through the wardrobes, dressers, and stacks of chairs and eventually navigate a path to the side door, leading through to the flat. It's open, but the light switch here doesn't work at all.

"Hello, is anyone home?" I shout over the music, which sounds even louder than before. There's no answer, but I can definitely see light at the top of the stairs. I start going up in the darkness, feeling my way, surprised to discover that after all this time the walls are still covered in cork tiles. Each step seems to creak and groan, and although the voice in my head is screaming at me to turn back, I can't.

I need to know the truth.

When I'm halfway up the stairs, the music stops.

I hear a door open, some footsteps, then nothing.

The renewed silence swallows me, but I force my feet to keep going.

Then I hear a door up above slam closed.

When I reach the top, I see tealight candles flickering on the floor of the landing. They are the only source of light. I try a switch on the wall, but nothing happens, and I see the fixture on the ceiling has no lightbulb. The doors to the rooms are all closed, but everything looks the same. I follow the line of candles to what used to be the lounge, and my hand rests on the doorknob a little longer than necessary while I build up the courage to turn it.

The room looks nothing like it used to, and I feel nothing but relief. The old electric fireplace has been ripped out, and the original open fire haphazardly restored, with exposed bricks and a slightly wonky mantelpiece. The sight of the flames and the smell of the logs burning brings a peculiar sense of comfort. Everything is a little dated and dirty, but it's just a normal-looking room. Somebody's lounge with chairs and a table. No skeletons so far. No closet. The candles continue their path along the floor, stopping at an ornate-looking coffee table in front of the roaring open fire. There are candles on the table, too, surrounding a large red book. It's a photo album.

I pick it up. It feels heavier than it looks, and when I open it, I see my own face staring out at me from an old newspaper interview. I turn the page and see another picture of me, another article. I keep turning the pages, and it appears as if every interview, profile piece, or review of my work that ever existed has been collected inside. A part of me knows that I should leave now, that this isn't right or normal, but I just keep turning the pages, as though I'm in some kind of trance and can't stop.

But then I do.

Stop.

The music starts again. The same song as before. I know I need to get out of here, but the final page of the album doesn't contain a newspaper clipping. It's a letter.

One that I remember writing almost twenty years ago.

Dear Eamonn,

You might not remember me, but I remember you.

A long time ago, I was your sister, but I ran away and a woman called Maggie kidnapped me and took me to England, though I did not understand that at the time, or for several years afterwards.

I lived with Maggie and a man called John in their flat above a betting shop in a place called Essex, very close to London.

They told me that our daddy didn't want me anymore and, later, they told me he had died, though I know now that that was not the case.

I want you to know that I was not unhappy, living with them, but then they died too.

The police believed that I was their child.

There was a passport in the flat that belonged to a little girl called Aimee Sinclair. The police also found her birth certificate, which said she was the daughter of Maggie O'Neil and John Sinclair.

The police thought that little girl was me, everybody did, and I let them.

I've stayed with a lot of foster families, some good, some not

*so good, but I'm doing well now. I have a scholarship to a place
called RADA and I'm going to be an actress.*

*I'd really like it if you felt able to get in touch, meet up
sometime. You looked after me when our Daddy couldn't, and I
remember that. I remember who you were then and I'd like to
know who you are now.*

*I'm sorry I waited so long to get in touch. I was scared to tell
anyone the truth until I was eighteen, scared of getting in trouble. Even now, I'm only telling you. I remember you well enough
to know you would never hurt me. I'm happy as Aimee. Nobody
knows about my past and I'd prefer it to stay that way. I hope
you understand.*

*The girl you knew as Ciara no longer exists, but I'm still your
sister. A name is just a name.*

> *Lots of love,*
> *Aimee*
> *xx*

The fire spits and burns, its shadows wildly dancing to the loud
music. When I look up from reading the letter, I can see that the door
has been closed, and I am no longer alone.

"Hello, Ciara," says the woman with the long dark hair and red
lips.

Seventy-one

At first I see Maggie, my Maggie from the 1980s.

It's dark in the room, with only the light from the fire and the candles struggling to illuminate the face in front of me. She sings along to the song, a girlie Irish voice escaping her red lips, completely out of tune with the melody. As my eyes adjust to the light, I realize my tired mind is playing tricks on me again. It might look like Maggie, but it isn't her.

"Who are you?" I ask, struggling to make my voice heard above the music.

She laughs, and it's the smile that I recognize first. The person opposite me comes a step closer, then starts to remove what it now seems is a wig, before throwing it onto the flames. I hear it hiss and burn. The woman in front of me vanishes into the bewildered confusion that has taken control of my body and mind.

"Does that help?" the man left standing in her shoes asks, in a deeper voice this time. "What kind of woman doesn't recognize her own husband?"

His face looks different, but his eyes, although heavily made up, are still the same.

"Ben?" I whisper.

"Do try and keep up, my love. My name is not Ben Bailey. Just like your name isn't Aimee. Do you need to read the letter again?"

I stare down at the crinkled piece of paper in my hands.

"Eamonn?"

He smiles and claps his gloved hands. *"Finally."*

I try to process what is happening.

My husband has been dressing up as a woman and stalking me.

That same man, my husband, has just told me that he is my brother.

I shiver, despite the heat of the fire. I feel physically sick at what I'm seeing and hearing, and automatically back away when he walks towards me. It looks like him, but at the same time, it doesn't.

"Did you like all those vintage postcards I sent you?" he asks.

I don't answer. Can't speak.

"'I know who you are' in my very best handwriting, over and over again. But you *still* didn't know who *I* was! It's funny when you think about it."

"Your face," I say, unable to articulate anything more.

"Oh, the nose? Do you like it? I asked for one just like Jack's, showed them his picture, had my bags removed too . . . the things I do for you. Did the police show you what I looked like? I went straight there after the surgery, let them take a picture of my broken nose, black eyes, and swollen face as evidence of your abuse. Almost all healed now. Looks good, don't you think? Just. Like. Jack."

"Why?"

"Because you're in love with him and I wanted you to love *me*! Just like I loved you!" he shouts.

I take another step back.

"Come on, dance with me." He grabs my hands, as though wanting to embark on some demented waltz to the climax of the song. The music stops, but it's as though it is still playing inside his head.

I try to pull free from his grip and start to cry as he holds me closer, humming the tune. "Please, stop."

"Stop? Baby Girl, you and I are just getting started. Till death do us part, remember? Do the pictures make you feel at home?"

I follow his stare and see the framed image of us on our wedding day, next to the black-and-white photo of a little boy.

"Why do you have pictures of John as a child?"

He looks down at me, fake surprise drawn on his clownlike face. "Finders keepers."

"I don't understand."

His surprise ignites into anger. "I took *all* of his things because he helped her take *you* from *me*. Maggie O'Neil was already dead when you wrote me that letter, but *he* wasn't, so I tracked him down. To be fair, he *was* dead not long after that." He laughs and forces me into another embrace, as though we are ballroom dancers in some twisted horror film. "All those years I didn't know where you went, I thought you were dead too. Did you ever wonder what happened to the *real* Aimee Sinclair? The girl you replaced?"

He takes my head in his hands, forces me to look up at him.

"I made John tell me everything before he died. It was an accident, apparently. I said I'd spare him if he told me the truth, but I couldn't do that. An eye for a lie, and what's mine is mine." He twists my head and whispers in my ear, "They killed her, then buried her in Epping Forest. I made him show me where. The sick bastard had carved her initial into the tree they hid her under. They're together now."

I push him away and run for the door.

"I bought this humble abode for you shortly after I met John. Do you like what I've done with the place? Business has been booming, but times are tough, so I had to borrow ten grand from the joint account before I left. You didn't mind, did you?"

The door is locked.

"I've even dressed up like her, the woman you left me for. Does it bring back happy memories? I thought you'd figured it out when you found my lipstick under our bed . . ."

I bang on the door and call for help, already knowing it's pointless; all the other shops are boarded up and empty.

"You're not going to run away again before I give you your belated birthday present, are you?" He picks up an elaborately decorated box.

"Please, we can get you some help. Please let me go, please," I say.

"Don't you want to open it?"

"Please, Ben."

"I'm not Ben, I'm Eamonn! And you're not Aimee. You always were so ungrateful, Ciara. So spoilt. Don't worry, I'll do it for you. After all, I used to do everything for you, but that still wasn't enough. That's why I had to teach you a lesson."

He starts to untie the ribbon on the box.

"I like your hair better like that, by the way, natural. It suits you curly, you look more like . . ."

I'm trapped in the corner of the room, my back pushed right up against the locked door as he leans forward and kisses me on the lips.

". . . more like you."

His lipstick has smudged all over his mouth, and I can taste it on my own. I want to wipe my face, but I'm too scared to move, too scared to say or do anything. He strokes my hair, tucking a strand behind my ear, then kneels down in front of me and starts to remove the wrapping paper from the box.

"There was a girl, who had a curl"—he lifts the box out of the paper—"right in the middle of her forehead."

He opens the lid and I see a pair of red children's shoes. The exact ones I had wanted for my sixth birthday, before I ran away. They were missing from the shop window that day when I first met Maggie. Now I understand why—he had bought them for me.

"When she was good, she was very, *very* good."

He puts a hand inside each shoe and thrusts them in my face.

"But when she was bad . . . she was a *bitch*." He caresses my face with the red leather. "When our daddy found these shoes, he beat me so hard, I couldn't walk for three days. We couldn't afford to eat, but I got you these bloody shoes because I knew how badly you wanted them, and I loved you."

He throws the shoes on the floor and grabs me by the throat, then bangs my head against the wall in time with his words.

"I. Loved. You."

He lets me go and I fall to the floor. I sit on my knees and can't stop myself from sobbing.

"I did so much to protect you from him. *I* took the verbal abuse, *I* took the beatings, I made sure it was *me* he came to visit in the night and kept him away from you. Everything was fine before you were born. *We were happy.* But you killed our mother and it changed him. You may as well have killed me too." He starts to pace around the room, his large high heels clicking on the wooden floorboards. When his back is briefly turned, I try to reach inside my bag for the gun. "And what did you do to thank me? You ran away, left me with him and never looked back. Do you know what he did to me after you were gone?" He sees my hand inside the bag and comes storming over. He grabs the bag from me, reaches inside, and takes out the gun, shaking his head and smiling.

"Just like I was saying . . . when she was bad—"

He hits me hard across the face with the pistol and I'm knocked flat onto the floor, the taste of blood filling my mouth.

"I should really shoot you with this, it's what you deserve." He throws the gun onto the sofa, picking up something else I can't quite see. "But, seeing as we are *family*, I'm going to shoot you with something else instead. I got this little beauty at a house clearance in Notting Hill a few months ago. It's amazing how useful it is to know the dead. Now, this is going to hurt, Baby Girl. That's what you said she used to call you, isn't it? The woman you called *mother* after killing your own? I think that's the only true thing you told me about her."

I see a purple electric light, then feel incredible pain dance through my body. It's unlike anything I have ever before experienced, as though I am being repeatedly stabbed with a thousand tiny knives. I'm gasping for air, I can't seem to gulp enough down into my lungs. Before I close my eyes, all I see is Maggie's face, all I hear is her voice.

"I love you, Baby Girl."

Seventy-two

In my dream, I am flying.

I am a bird with outstretched wings, soaring and swooping above the waves of a turquoise sea. I am dancing in a cloud-free sky, looking down at the world below and thinking how very small we all are.

Consciousness stirs me a little, enough to permit the sound of a van door sliding closed to invade my dreams. The confusion it creates smashes the sky. Huge, jagged shards of it start to fall down all around me, as though the world were raining blue glass. I don't fly fast enough, and some of the fragments tear into my wings, red blood staining my white feathers. I start to feel heavy, as though I can't hold myself up. I decide to dive down into the sea, seeking safety beneath the waves, but they have grown rough, crashing onto the rocks below. The churning water has turned black, and as I continue to dive, getting closer and closer, white spray spits up in my face, blinding me from what lies beneath. I hit the surface hard, feeling the bones in my nose and cheeks shatter first. My body is bent and broken, and the impact has left me folded in on myself, so that I'm even smaller and more insignificant than I used to be.

I open one eye, just enough to make out that the sea has turned into green carpet liner, and that I have been rolled inside. I stay awake long enough to know that I am broken.

When I stir again, I can hear someone coming. I try to lift my birdlike self off the floor, but I can no longer move. I can't even lift my head and it feels like I'll never be able to fly again. I black out before I can see or feel any more.

Consciousness revisits and is a little less patient with me this time. My head is throbbing, and it takes a while to remember what happened, and then to wonder where and when I am now.

It's dark. Completely pitch-black.

My hands are tied behind my back and something is stuffed inside my mouth, so that I can't close it or speak.

My legs are bent at the knee, tucked up behind me, and when I try to move I realize that I am inside some kind of box. At first I think I am in a coffin, and the idea that I have been buried alive makes it hard to breathe. I start to cry. Tears and snot and drool from the sides of my open mouth stain my face in the darkness. I try to calm myself with logic; the box is too small to be a coffin, and for a brief moment I feel a tiny bit better, but the voice of fear is too loud inside my ears.

It could be a child's coffin.

I realize that although whatever is shoved inside my mouth has stopped me from speaking, I can still make a noise. The muffled scream that comes out of me sounds so primal that I think that someone or something else must be making it. It seems harder to breathe than it did before, and I wonder how much oxygen there can be in a space this small. I try to kick my feet against the side of the box, and when I scream again, the lid opens.

I blink a few times into the light, my eyes trying to translate the silhouette looming above me.

"Hold on, Baby Girl, we're almost home," says a voice that changes in my ears with every distant word. At first the voice belongs to Maggie, then to my brother, then back again. He holds a cloth over my nose. I try to keep my eyes open, but they're too heavy. I think it is Maggie who holds my hand for a little while before I hear the lid of whatever I am in slide closed, clicking shut.

I am a broken bird again.

I cannot open my eyes or sing or fly away.

I am sinking down farther and farther beneath the surface of a cold black sea.

Seventy-three

I wake up.

My eyes see that I am bathed in daylight, and I realize I am lying on a bed. I try to move and discover that my wrists and ankles are each tied to one of the four bedposts. I look around the room, twisting my head as far as I can, and I'm relieved to discover that I am at least alone. I stare at the crumbling, damp-stained walls, the dirty white net curtains crusted with mildew and age, and the elderly-looking wooden furniture. A faded painting of the Virgin Mary is on the wall in front of me, and a metal statue of Jesus is on the bedside table. I recognize this room. I'm in the house where I was born in Ireland; the sound of the sea in the distance confirms it. I haven't been here since I was five years old, but the smell of the place transports me back in time, as though it might have been yesterday.

There is a dressing table, covered in a lace doily, with a framed photo on top. It's me as a little girl, wearing a white blouse, red skirt, and white tights. My hair in the picture is tied in slightly uneven bunches and I look happy, even though I don't remember ever being especially happy when I lived here. It seems, even at that age, I already knew how to pretend for the camera. There is a mirror on the dressing table, and when I twist my body as far as the restraints will allow, I can see myself in it. I am wearing clothes I don't recognize. An adult-size white blouse, red skirt, and white tights. My hair has been tied into bunches. Red lipstick is all over and around my lips, so that they look twice as big as they should. The sight of myself like this makes me scream without thinking.

The door flies open and my brother rushes in. He's dressed as a man, the wig and makeup are gone. He is Ben again, but different.

"There, there, you're okay, Baby Girl. It was just a bad dream." He strokes my cheeks and I stare in horror at the alterations he has made to his face.

"Oh, I'm afraid Maggie has gone now. I only dressed like a woman to mess with your head and hide from the police. Why are you looking at me like that? Is it my new face? I thought I'd make myself look more like Jack Anderson, seeing as you find *him* so irresistible and attractive. Do you like it? Doctors can do almost anything nowadays. Just give them a picture from a magazine, along with a big fat check, and away you go. I was hoping for a nice Jack-shaped six-pack, too, but life made other plans. I'm afraid it's just you and me again now. Does that make you sad, Baby Girl?"

"Stop calling me that."

"You said that's what Maggie called you. I thought you liked it. I thought that's why you left me and never came back. I made you some breakfast." He lifts a blue bowl and spoon to my lips.

I keep my mouth closed and turn away.

"Come on now, don't be like that. It's porridge in your favorite bowl. Do you remember what I told you when it got chipped? Things that are a little bit broken can still be beautiful."

"Please untie me."

"I want to. I really do, but I'm scared you'll run away again. Do you even remember that day? I never ate chicken again after he made me kill that bird."

"Why have you dressed me like this?"

"Don't you like it? If you're upset about the red shoes, I'm afraid they don't fit anymore. You could say you got a little too big for your boots." He laughs at his own joke, then waits, as though expecting me to do the same. When I don't, his smile vanishes and his whole face seems to twist and darken. "If you don't like the clothes I got you, I can always take them off." He roughly pulls up my skirt and starts to roll down the white tights.

"No, don't! Please!"

"What's the matter? Once upon a time you used to like it when I took your clothes off. You kept saying you wanted to have a baby together, despite me telling you that wasn't a good idea. You understand now, right? Besides, it isn't like I haven't seen it all before." He pulls the tights down to my thighs and puts his hand there, moving it slowly up. "It isn't like I haven't seen every single part of you, tasted you, been inside you. There is nobody on this earth who knows you better than I do. *I know who you are.* Who you *really* are. And I still love you."

I turn my face away as his hand moves higher.

"You can pretend like you didn't want it now, if that makes you feel better. But we both know that you did. Having me inside you was about the only thing that seemed to calm those nerves of yours, wasn't it? Before a big interview, or one of your silly *red carpet* events?"

"I didn't know who you were—"

"Didn't you?"

I don't answer.

"Had I really changed that much when we first met as adults? Look at you, with your perfect tits and curls and big pretty eyes. You could have had anyone, but you wanted me. Your own brother."

"What do you want from me?"

"I just want us to be together. That's all I ever wanted, but it was never enough for you, too busy flirting with directors or actors like Jack Anderson. Well, we're going to be together now, till death do us part. We might not have very long. I'm sick."

He climbs on top of the bed and arranges his body around mine. His fingers entwine with my own, and his head rests on my chest, so that I can smell his hair and see the pink skin beneath the beginnings of a bald patch. The weight of his body crushes me, but I don't say anything. I keep perfectly still and silent until he falls asleep.

As he starts to gently snore, I hear only one voice inside my head, and it is Maggie's, not my own.

So long as you never forget who you really are, acting will save you.

I silently repeat those words as I lie wide awake. I cradle the idea in my tired mind, rocking it gently, trying not to wake it or him, trying to keep the thought as quiet as possible, scared that someone else might hear it and snuff it out. Right now, it's all I have left to hold on to. My fear thaws into hate, just enough to allow me to dare to think of a way out of this, to imagine an ending that isn't my own. I start to re-hearse my lines and play out the next scene in my imagination. Life is like a game of chess; you just have to play it backwards and work out all the moves you need to make in advance, to get where you need to be.

The wind starts to pick up, a mournful howl singing through the old house. Outside the window I can see the tree I used to climb when I was a little girl. It looks dead. Its branches sway in the breeze, creak-ing with effort, and its fingers of twigs tap on the glass like blackened bones.

Tap. Tap. Tap.

It gets dark inside the room before it does outside the window, and when it is almost completely black, I know exactly what I need to say and do.

Seventy-four

I kiss the top of his head.

Gentle, tender, loving kisses.

He stirs on top of me, then looks up.

"Kiss me," I whisper. "Please." He kisses my mouth, still half-asleep. The taste of him makes me want to retch, but I kiss him back. His eyes are open the whole time, filled with confusion, examining my own. As soon as our lips part, I let the words out.

"I always knew that it was you."

He stares at me for a long time, a frown folding itself onto his brow. "You knew?"

"I pretended not to, but of course I knew who you really were. I remember everything, you know that about me, so how could I forget my own brother?" I can see that he wants to believe me, but that he doesn't. I need to try harder. "I've missed you since you left me. I know what that feels like now, and I don't want us to be apart again."

"You want us to be together?" He raises an eyebrow.

"Yes." I nod.

"Together how?"

"In every way. Now that we've come back home, nobody needs to know who we are or what we do. We can start again. We can both have what we wanted."

He frowns. "You still want to have a child, even though you know who I am?"

"Yes. That's what I always wished for—a child. It would be a second chance. For both of us."

I Know Who You Are | 283

He sits up a little. "I'm sorry about the Fincher movie."

This catches me off guard and I struggle to keep my face neutral. "How do you know about that?"

"Because I know all your passwords, and I read all your emails, and I told Alicia White where he would be. It would have been too much for you. You would have been away too long again."

I swallow the hate down. "You're right. You've always known what was best for me."

He seems surprised by my answer, concentration scratching itself onto his face.

"I did have a passport made for you, in your real name, just in case there were any complications with the van on the ferry. We could change the way you look a little, and you could have a life here. A real life. You hate all the attention acting brings anyway—"

I seize on this. The most believable lies always contain fragments of truth.

"Yes! I *do* hate it, you know I do. I get so scared all the time. A new life, a simpler life here with you, that's all I want now. Kiss me how you used to. Please."

He does, still watching me, as though this is a test he is expecting me to fail. He undoes the white blouse slowly, one button at a time, examining my face for any sign of betrayal. Then he reaches up to untie my hands, but I already know he has no intention of doing so. I know him just as well as he knows me.

"No, don't, leave them tied. I want you to know you can trust me. I'm never going to run away again. I need you. I fall apart without you and I've been so lonely since you left."

He looks confused, then he kisses my breasts, still checking for a reaction. I arch my back and feel him harden against me. He never needs a blue pill when I play my part. His head moves lower and I moan the way I know he wants to hear. He unties the rope around my feet, removes my white tights, and I smile while he unfastens his belt.

When it is over, he unties just one of my hands and holds it, then lays his head on my chest. When I think enough time has passed, I ease my fingers out of his, and when he starts to snore, I reach for the Jesus statue, stretching my arm as far as I can without moving the rest of my body. My fingers make contact with the cold metal. I grip it with all of the strength I have left, then smash it hard against his skull. He whimpers like a wounded animal, blood running down his face and over his eyes, as they stare at me in disbelief. I hit him again.

I know I don't have any time to waste. I untie my other hand and crawl out from underneath him, fleeing from the room, wearing nothing except the white blouse. I run through the house, trying to remember the layout in the darkness, bumping into things I don't remember, trying to find the nearest way out. I can already hear him coming after me before I reach the back door. The flaking wood has swollen over time, and I have to yank it hard to force it open.

It's freezing outside and the howling wind takes my breath away. The tarmac driveway bites my bare feet, and I wrap the open blouse around myself, not that anyone lives close enough to see me in the darkness. Or hear me, if I were brave enough to scream. In my terror I can't remember the geography of the place, and as I stumble towards what I think is the main road, I realize too late that I am running towards the back of the property and the sea. I hear the door slam behind me.

"Where you going, Baby Girl? I thought you wanted to be *together*. I thought you weren't going to run away anymore?" He sounds like the version of himself that attacked me in our bedroom the night before he disappeared; the version of him that I believed might kill me.

I trip and fall, knowing he isn't far behind.

I'm lost in the darkness. I've turned in the wrong direction again, and this time it will mean the end of me, not the beginning.

I hear the whiny sound of wood fighting elderly hinges, and make out the shadowy shape of a shed door banging in the wind. I run for it, choosing to hide from whatever comes next. I can't see what I'm walking over in the shed, it feels like straw. The metal hooks that my daddy used to hang the chickens on are swinging up above me, disturbed by the storm. Screeching and scraping against one another to produce an animal-like warning. When I look up, I see their silver smiles lit by moonlight.

"Big brother will always find you." I hear him close the shed door, trapping me inside with him. The gale outside is picking up, and the door doesn't want to stay shut. It continues to bang against its hinges, as though wanting to set me free. I fall to the floor and crawl away from the sound of my brother's voice. Knowing there is nowhere left for me to run away to now, nowhere left to hide.

That's when my fingers find it.

I don't know what it is at first. My hand slides along the length of the wood until it meets the cold metal end, still sharp enough to cut my finger.

I pick it up and turn around, crouching and facing the sound of his footsteps coming closer and closer. The shed door flies open, and the moonlight illuminates the face of my brother right above me. He's distracted by the sound of the door, and I swing the ax with every last bit of strength that I have. It lodges itself in the side of his neck, blood spurting out of him as he falls to the floor.

I don't move.

I can't.

Nothing moves, except for the steady stream of blood.

I bend down, drawn to the sight of his broken body. With his eyes closed, and all the changes he has made to his face, he looks like a complete stranger to me now. A monster I never knew I'd met. His eyes open, and the hate I see in them makes me grab the handle of the ax once more. I yank it from his partially severed throat, lift it high above my head, and swing it down.

His eyes are still open, as if they are looking at me, as his head rolls across the shed floor.

Six Months
Later . . .

I do not like movie junkets, they are always so melodramatic and distasteful.

One interview after another after another. The same questions, the same answers over and over. The eyes of journalists and their cameras all pointing in my direction, studying me, trying to catch me out, trying to see what lies lurk beneath my surface.

"Last one," says Tony, before getting up to answer the knock on the door.

The production company has hired a hotel suite for the interviews today. There's something quite surreal about working on a movie for months, then having almost nothing to do with it until sometimes a year later, when you're in the middle of a completely different project. It's as if I have become a time traveler, talking about different characters, in different stories, in different countries all over the world. I know that Jack is in the room next door, and I'm glad he's not too far away. I'm also glad my agent is here; I don't think I can do this on my own today. Just the thought makes me furious with myself; I've never needed anyone, and I don't like the idea of needing someone now.

Nobody knows what really happened last year, and I plan to keep it that way.

Jennifer Jones sashays into the room, her cameraman desperately trying to keep up behind her while carrying all the gear himself. I can't believe I agreed to do this.

"Aimee, darling, you're looking so well!" She kisses the air on either side of my face, making sound effects with her lips. They are hot pink today and match her figure-hugging dress. "So, I know we don't have very long, your agent has made that *very* clear." She gives him a little wave. "No personal questions, *I promise*." I look at Tony, a tiny shard of panic piercing my armor, but he nods reassuringly and I try not to fiddle with the hem of my dress.

"Rolling," says the cameraman.

Jennifer Jones hones in on me, sharpening her tongue. "So, *Sometimes I Kill* is a *great* movie." Her level of insincerity is genuinely impressive.

"Thank you." I smile.

"And congratulations, how long do you have left to go?" She stares down at my bump.

"Three months."

"Wow! And how is the father-to-be?"

He lost his head.

I look at Tony before answering. So much for no personal questions. "Jack is fine."

"It's just like a fairy tale, it really is. The two of you meeting on set last year, falling in love, getting married . . . I noticed that you've kept your name . . . again."

"Yes, I have."

"And now a little mini Aimee or Jack on the way, how delightful!"

"I'm very lucky." I move my hand to my belly, as though wanting to protect my unborn child from Jennifer Jones's potentially poisonous comments.

"So lucky that you've also just finished filming another project, this time with Fincher directing no less! I mean, wow, lady! How do you have the time?"

"Because of my growing bump, we filmed all my scenes in just a few months. It was full-on, but such a great experience, I loved every minute."

And I finally have everything that I wanted.

"He'd originally cast someone else in that role, is that right?"

I hold her stare and try not to shift in my seat. "Yes, he did."

"It must have been hard for you. Stepping into Alicia White's shoes after she vanished without a trace."

"I feel so sorry for Alicia and her family. She hid it very well, but she was obviously a very troubled individual."

"It's almost six months since she disappeared, and *still* no sightings or any explanation. What do *you* think happened to her?"

"Can we stick to questions about the film please," Tony interrupts, sensing my unease.

"Of course," says Jennifer Jones. "I'm not going to lie, your character in this film is really scary. And an actress playing an actress, that must have been fun. We've been getting the other actors to do a little something to camera for a promo, would you mind doing one? You just say the name of your character, a little something about who they are, then the name of the film."

"Sure."

"Great stuff. Just look straight down the barrel of the camera when you're ready . . ."

I turn to face the camera and oblige her for this one, final request.

"My name is Aimee Sinclair. I was that girl you thought you knew, but you couldn't remember where from. I think you'll remember me now. Sometimes I kill."

I sit back in my chair, confused by the expressions on everyone's faces. Jennifer Jones smashes the silence with her cackle of a laugh, tilting her head back so that I can see her impressive collection of fillings. "You are *so* funny," she says, but I'm still oblivious as to why. "You're supposed to say your *character's* name, not *your* name. We don't want the audience to think Aimee Sinclair is going around killing people!"

"I'm so sorry." I feel my cheeks blush. "It's been a very long day and I'm afraid my pregnancy brain is getting the better of me." I turn to face the camera. "Let me try that again. I never make the same mistake twice."

Acknowledgments

Second novels are an interesting journey, one that can be tricky to navigate, and I might not have found my way without the following amazing people.

Thank you to Jonny Geller for believing in me, even when I don't. I still don't know how I managed to get the best agent in town, but I'm very grateful, and this book wouldn't exist without you. Thanks also to the wonderful team at Curtis Brown.

Thank you to Kari Stuart, for being the perfect blend of kind and clever. Thank you for your patience and compassion, and for all the miracles you perform.

Thank you to Amy Einhorn, editor extraordinaire with secret powers in her pen, and to the brilliant team at Flatiron. Authors just write stories, publishers make books, and Flatiron is without doubt the A-Team.

Thank you to my family, for telling me I could.

Thank you to my friends, for still being my friends, even when I disappear inside a book.

Thank you to Daniel, for not divorcing me while I was writing this one.

Most of all, thank you to the people who are kind enough to read my books. Writers are nothing without readers, and you have changed my life in ways I didn't dare dream. I hope you continue to enjoy my stories, and I'm forever grateful.

I Know Who You Are

by Alice Feeney

PLEASE NOTE: In order to provide reading groups with the most informed and thought-provoking questions possible, it is necessary to reveal important aspects of the plot of this novel—as well as the ending. If you have not finished reading *I Know Who You Are*, we respectfully suggest that you may want to wait before reviewing this guide.

1. "Not everybody wants to be somebody. Some people just want to be somebody else." Aimee confesses to being shy. So why has she chosen to live a life in the spotlight?

2. Did you enjoy the style of writing? Have you got any favorite quotes from the book?

3. Do you believe that Aimee didn't know what had happened to her husband at the start of the novel, when Ben's things were missing from the house?

4. "I do what Maggie tells me to do, because I've learned that bad things happen to me when I don't." Aimee loves Maggie by the end of the childhood chapters, despite the bad things. Why do you think that is? Do you think she is happy living with Maggie and John?

5. Which parts of the novel shocked you the most? The childhood chapters or Aimee's story in the present? Did you enjoy the different timelines?

6. What was your favorite twist in the novel?

7. If you were one of the characters in this book, with whom would you most relate and why?

8. "'Spell promises,' it says, and then it reads out each letter as I type them onto the screen.

'L I E S.'
'That is incorrect. Spell promises.' "

There were several '80s references in the childhood chapters: Rainbow Brite, She-Ra, *Story Teller* magazine, Fisher-Price toys, Speak & Spell, *The NeverEnding Story*, *Cagney & Lacey*, penny sweets. Did you spot any others, and did they bring back any memories of your own?

9. Who is the real villain of this story? Maggie? John? Ben? Jack? Alicia? Jennifer Jones? Or Aimee herself?

10. The person behind it all had been calling herself Maggie and dressing up as Aimee for a very long time. Why were they so angry, and what did they really want?

11. We learn that Aimee had a very difficult childhood. Does it make you understand her and forgive the behavior of the woman she has become?

12. Many of the characters in the novel were pretending to be someone or something they were not. Can you remember them all? Isn't that something we are all guilty of from time to time? What other themes did you spot while reading?

13. How does this novel compare to others you have read in the genre? Have you read Alice Feeney's previous novel, *Sometimes I Lie*? If so, which of her books did you enjoy most and why?

14. Do you think that Aimee really did know the true identity of her husband all along?

15. Let's talk about that ending!

You can find out about Alice's latest books
and news on Twitter and Instagram at @alicewriterland,
and at facebook.com/AliceFeeneyAuthor

Or on her website: www.alicefeeney.com

Turn the page for a sneak preview
of Alice Feeney's next novel

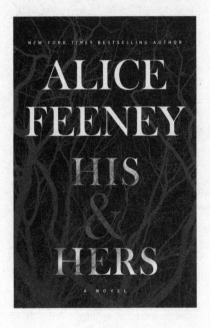

Available July 2020 from Flatiron Books

It wasn't love at first sight.

I can admit that now. But by the end, I loved her more than I thought it was possible to love another human being. I cared about her far more than I ever cared about myself. That's why I did it. Why I had to. I think it's important that people know that, when they find out what I've done. If they do. Perhaps then they might understand that I did it for her.

There is a difference between being and feeling alone, and it is possible to miss someone and be with them at the same time. There have been plenty of people in my life: family, friends, colleagues, lovers. A full cast of the usual suspects that make a person's social circle, but mine has always felt a little bent out of shape. None of the relationships I have ever formed with another human being feel real to me. More like a series of missed connections.

People might recognize my face, they may even know my name, but they'll never know the real me. Nobody does. I've always been selfish with the true thoughts and feelings inside my head; I don't share them with anyone. Because I can't. There is a version of me I can only ever be with myself. I sometimes think the secret to success is the ability to adapt. Life rarely stays the same, and I've frequently had to reinvent myself in order to keep up. I learned how to change my looks, my life . . . even my voice.

I also learned how to fit in, but constantly trying to do so is more than just uncomfortable now, it hurts. Because I don't. Fit. I fold my jagged edges inside myself, and smooth over the most obvious differ-ences between us, but I am not the same as you. There are over seven billion people on the planet, and yet I have somehow managed to spend a lifetime feeling alone.

I'm losing my mind and not for the first time, but sanity can often be lost and found. People will say that I snapped, lost it, came unhinged. But when the time came, it was—without doubt—the right thing to do. I felt good about myself afterward. I wanted to do it again.

There are at least two sides to every story:

Yours and mine.

Ours and theirs.

His and hers.

Which means someone is always lying.

Lies told often enough can start to sound true, and we all sometimes hear a voice inside our heads, saying something so shocking, we pretend it is not our own. I know exactly what I heard that night, while I waited at the station for her to come home for the last time. At first, the train sounded just like any other in the distance. I closed my eyes and it was like listening to music, the rhythmic song of the cars on the tracks getting louder and louder:

Clickety-click. Clickety-click. Clickety-click.

But then the sound started to change, translating into words inside my head, repeating themselves over and over, until it was impossible not to hear:

Kill them all. Kill them all. Kill them all.

Her

Anna Andrews
Monday 06:00

Mondays have always been my favorite day.

The chance to start again.

A clean enough slate with just the dust of your own past mistakes still visible—almost, but not quite wiped away.

I realize it's an unpopular opinion—to be fond of the first day of the week—but I'm full of those. My view of the world tends to be a little tilted. When you grow up sitting in life's cheap seats, it's too easy to see behind the puppets dancing on its stage. Once you've seen the strings, and who pulls them, it can be hard to enjoy the rest of the show. I can afford to sit where I want now, choose any view I like, but those fancy-looking theater boxes are only good for looking down on other people. I'll never do that. Just because I don't like to look back doesn't mean I don't remember where I came from. I've worked hard for my ticket and the cheap seats still suit me fine.

I don't spend a lot of time getting ready in the mornings—there is no point putting on makeup, just for someone else to take it off and start again when I get to work—and I don't eat breakfast. I don't eat much at all, but I do enjoy cooking for others. Apparently, I'm a feeder.

I stop briefly in the kitchen to pick up my Tupperware carrier, filled with homemade cupcakes for the team. I barely remember making them. It was late, definitely after my third glass of something dry and white. I prefer red but it leaves a telltale stain on my lips, so I save it for weekends only. I open the fridge and notice that I didn't finish last night's wine, so I drink what is left straight from the bottle, before taking it with me as I leave the house. Monday is also when my trash gets collected. The recycling bin is surprisingly full for someone who lives alone. Mostly glass.

I like to walk to work. The streets are pretty empty at this time of day, and I find it calming. I cross Waterloo Bridge and weave my way through Soho toward Oxford Circus, while listening to the *Today* program. I'd prefer to listen to music, a little Ludovico perhaps or Taylor Swift depending on my mood—there are two very different sides to my personality—but instead I endure the dulcet tones of middle-class Britain, telling me what they think I should know. Their voices still feel foreign to my ears, despite sounding like my own. But then I didn't always speak this way. I've been presenting the *BBC One O'Clock News* bulletin for almost two years, and I still feel like a fraud.

I stop by the flattened cardboard box that has been bothering me the most recently. I can see a strand of blond hair poking out the top, so I know she's still there. I don't know who she is, only that I might have been her had life unfolded differently. I left home when I was sixteen because it felt like I had to. I don't do what I'm about to do now out of kindness; I do it because of a misplaced moral compass. Just like the soup kitchen I volunteered at last Christmas. We rarely deserve the lives we lead. We pay for them however we can, be it with money, guilt, or regret.

I open the plastic carry case and put one of my carefully constructed cupcakes down on the pavement, between her cardboard box and the wall, so that she'll see it when she wakes. Then, worried she might not like or appreciate my chocolate frosting—for all I know she could be diabetic—I take a twenty-pound note from my purse and slide it underneath. I don't mind if she spends my money on alcohol; I do.

Radio 4 continues to irritate me, so I switch off the latest politician lying in my ears. Their over-rehearsed dishonesty doesn't fit with this image of real people with real problems. Not that I'd ever say that out loud or on-air during an interview. I'm paid to be impartial regardless of how I feel.

Maybe I'm a liar too. I chose this career because I wanted to tell the truth. I wanted to tell the stories that mattered most, the ones that I thought people needed to hear. Stories that I hoped might change the world and make it a better place. But I was naïve. People working in the media today have more power than politicians, but what good is trying to tell the truth about the world when I can't bear to be honest about my own story: who I am, where I came from, what I've done.

I bury the thoughts like I always do. Lock them in a secure secret box inside my head, push them to the darkest corner right at the back, and hope they won't escape again any time soon.

I walk the final few streets to Broadcasting House, then search inside my handbag for my ever-elusive security pass. My fingers find one of my little tins of mints instead. It rattles in protest as I flip it open and pop a tiny white triangle inside my mouth, as though it were a pill. Wine on my breath before the morning meeting is best avoided. I locate my pass and step inside the glass revolving doors, feeling several sets of eyes turn my way. That's okay. I'm pretty good at being the version of myself I think people want me to be. At least on the outside.

I know everyone by name, including the cleaners still sweeping the floor. It costs almost nothing to be kind and I have a very efficient memory, despite the drink. Once past security—a little more thorough than it used to be, thanks to the state of the world we have curated for ourselves—I stare down at the newsroom and it feels like home. Cocooned inside the basement of the BBC building, but visible from every floor, the newsroom resembles a brightly lit red-and-white open-plan warren. Almost every available space is filled with screens and tightly packed desks, with an eclectic collection of journalists sitting behind each one.

These people aren't just my colleagues, they're like a dysfunctional surrogate family. I'm almost forty years old, but I don't have anyone else. No children. No husband. Not anymore. I've worked here for almost twenty years but, unlike those with friends or family connections, I started right at the bottom. I took a few detours along the way, and the stepping-stones to success were sometimes a little slippery, but I got where I wanted to be, eventually.

Patience is the answer to so many of life's questions.

Serendipity smiled at me when the previous news anchor left. She went into labor a month early, and five minutes before the lunchtime bulletin. Her water broke and I got my lucky break. I'd just come back from maternity leave myself—earlier than planned—and was the only correspondent in the newsroom with any presenting experience. All of which was overtime and overnight—the shifts nobody else wanted—I was that desperate for any opportunity that might help my career. Presenting a network bulletin was something I had been dreaming of my whole life.

There was no time for a trip to hair and makeup that day. They rushed me on set and did what they could, powdering my face at the same time as they miked me up. I practiced reading the headlines on the teleprompter, and the director was calm and kind in my earpiece. His voice steadied me. I remember very little about that first half-hour program, but I do recall the congratulations afterward. From newsroom nobody to network news anchor in less than an hour.

My boss is called the Thin Controller behind his slightly hunched back. He's a small man trapped inside a tall man's body. He also has a speech impediment. It prevents him from pronouncing his Rs, and the rest of the newsroom from taking him seriously. He has never been good at filling gaps on rosters so, after my successful debut, he decided to let me fill in until the end of that week. Then the next. A three-month contract as a news anchor—instead of my staff position as a correspondent—swelled into six; after that it was extended to the end of the year, accompanied by a nice little pay raise. Viewing numbers went up when I started presenting the program, so I was allowed to stay. My predecessor never returned; she got pregnant again while on maternity leave and hasn't been seen since. Almost two years later, I'm still here and expect my latest contract to be renewed any day.

I take my seat between the editor and the lead producer, then clean my desk and keyboard with an antibacterial wipe. There is no telling who might have been sitting here overnight. The newsroom never sleeps, and sadly not everyone in it adheres to my preferred level of hygiene. I open up the running order and smile; it still gives me a little thrill to see my name at the top:

News Anchor: Anna Andrews.

I start writing the intros for each story. Despite popular opinion, we don't just *read* the news, we write it. Or at least *I* do. News anchors, like normal human beings, come in all shapes and sizes. There are several who have crawled so far up their own asses I'm amazed they can still sit down, let alone read a teleprompter. The nation would be appalled if they knew how some of their so-called national treasures behaved behind the scenes. But I won't tell. Journalism is a game with more chutes than ladders. Getting to the top takes a long time, and one wrong move can land you right back down at the bottom. Nobody is bigger than the machine.

The morning breezes by just like any other: a constantly evolving running order, conversations with correspondents in the field, discussions with the director about graphics and screens. There is an almost permanent line of reporters and producers waiting to talk to the editor beside me. More often than not, to request a longer duration for their package or two-way.

Everyone always wants just a little more time.

I don't miss those days at all: begging to get on-air, constantly fretting when I didn't. There simply isn't time to tell every story.

The rest of the team are unusually quiet. I take a quick look to my left, and notice that the producer has the latest roster up on her screen. She closes it down as soon as she sees me looking. Rosters are second only to breaking news when it comes to influencing stress levels in the newsroom. They come out late and rarely go down well, with the distribution of the most unpopular shifts—lates, weekends, overnights—always cause for contention. I work Monday to Friday now, and haven't requested any leave for over six months, so, unlike my poor colleagues, there is nothing roster-shaped for me to worry about.

An hour before the program, I visit makeup. It's a nice place to escape to—relatively peaceful and quiet compared with the constant noise of the newsroom. My hair is blow-dried into an obedient chestnut bob, and my face is covered with HD-grade foundation. I wear more makeup for work than I did for my wedding. The thought forces me to retreat inside myself for a moment, and I feel the ridge of indentation on my finger, where my ring used to be.

The program goes mostly according to plan, despite a few last-minute changes while we are on-air: some breaking news, a delayed TV package, a camera with a mind of its own in the studio, and a dodgy feed from Washington. I'm forced to wrap up an overenthusiastic political correspondent in Downing Street, one who regularly takes up more than their allotted time. Some people like the sound of their own voices a little too much.

The debrief begins while I'm still on set, waiting to say good-bye to viewers after the weather segment. Nobody wants to hang around any longer than absolutely necessary after the program, so they always start without me. It's a gathering of correspondents and producers who worked on the show, but is also attended by representatives of other departments: home news, foreign news, editing, graphics, as well as the Thin Controller.

I swing by my desk to collect my Tupperware carrier before joining everyone, eager to share my latest culinary creations with the team. I haven't told anyone that it's my birthday today yet, but I might.

I make my way across the newsroom toward them, and stop briefly when I see a woman I don't recognize. She has her back to me, with two small children dressed in matching outfits by her side. I notice the cute cupcakes my colleagues are already eating. Not homemade—like mine—but shop-bought and expensive-looking. Then I return my attention to the woman handing them out. I stare at her bright red hair, framing her pretty face with a bob so sharp it could have been cut with a laser. When she turns and smiles in my direction it feels like a slap.

Someone passes me a glass of warm prosecco, and I see the drinks trolley that management always orders from catering whenever a member of staff leaves. It happens a lot in this business. The Thin

Controller taps his glass with an overgrown fingernail, then he starts
to speak, strange-sounding words tumbling out of his crumb-covered
lips.

"We can't wait to welcome you back . . ."

It's the only sentence my ears manage to translate. I stare at Cat
Jones, the woman who presented the program before I did, standing
there with her trademark red hair, and two beautiful little girls. I feel
physically sick.

". . . and our thanks to Anna of course, for taking the helm while
you were away."

Eyes are turned and glasses are raised in my direction. My hands
start to tremble and I hope my face is doing a better job of hiding my
feelings.

"It was on the roster, I'm so sorry, we all thought you knew."

The producer standing next to me whispers the words but I'm unable to form a reply.

The Thin Controller apologizes too, afterward. He sits in his
office, while I stand, and stares at his hands while he speaks, as though
the words he is struggling to find might be written on his sweaty fingers. He thanks me, and tells me that I've done a great job filling in for
the last . . .

"Two years," I say, when he doesn't appear to know or understand how long it has been.

He shrugs as though it were nothing.

"It is *her* job, I'm afraid. She has a contract. We can't sack people
for having a baby, not even when they have two!"

He laughs.

I don't.

"When does she come back?" I ask.

A frown folds itself onto the vast space that is his forehead.

"She comes back tomorrow. It's all on the . . ." I watch as he tries
and fails to find a substitute for the word "roster," like anything
beginning with the letter *R*. ". . . it's all on the woster, has been for some
time. You're back on the correspondent desk, but don't worry, you can
still fill in for her, and present the program during school holidays,

Christmas and Easter, that sort of thing. We all think you did a terrific job. Here's your new contract."

I stare down at the crisp white sheets of A4 paper, covered in carefully constructed words from a faceless HR employee. My eyes only seem able to focus on one line:

News Correspondent: Anna Andrews.

As I step out of his office, I see her again: my replacement. Although I suppose the truth is that I was only ever hers. It's a terrible thing to admit, even to myself, but as I look at Cat Jones with her perfect hair and perfect children, standing there chatting and laughing with *my* team, I wish she was dead.

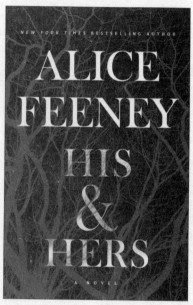